A SECRET GARDENER?

(or Death among the Delphiniums)

by

Judy Ford

The 13th Bernie Fazakerley Mystery

Bernie Fazakerley

Publications

A SECRET GARDENER?

Published by Bernie Fazakerley
Publications

Copyright © 2019 Judy Ford.

ISBN13: 978-1-911083-63-4
ISBN10: 1-91-108363-5

DEDICATION

Dedicated to

The Medaille Trust

"Refuge and Freedom from Modern Slavery"

CONTENTS

GLOSSARY OF OXFORD UNIVERSITY JARGON

This glossary is by no means exhaustive. A fuller list of Oxford terminology may be found on the University website here: www.ox.ac.uk/about/organisation/history/oxford-glossary?

Bursar – The member of staff responsible for the finances of a college.

Buttery – A college shop where members can purchase provisions.

Dean – Except at Christchurch,

where the Principal is known as the Dean, the Dean of a college is a senior fellow responsible for student discipline.

Don – A member of the academic staff.

DPhil – Doctor of Philosophy, the postgraduate research degree that is known as a PhD at almost all other universities.

Fellow – A member of staff holding a Fellowship at one of the colleges. Fellowships may be Tutorial (i.e. teaching) or Research.

Gown – Members of the university are entitled to wear gowns that indicate their level of scholarship. The term may also be used to refer to the university community as a whole, as in "Town and Gown" which expresses the, sometimes uneasy, relationship between the residents of Oxford and the members of the university,

Hall – the dining hall of a college. This term may also be used to denote the evening meal ('dinner') served there. 'Formal Hall' means that staff and students are required to dress formally in gowns when attending.

High Table – The table in a college dining hall, often on a dais, at which the Head of House and Fellows dine.

Hilary Term – The second term of the university year, which starts in

January.

JCR – Junior Common Room. This may either refer to a room for undergraduate students belonging to a college to meet or to the undergraduate student body of a college collectively.

Long Vacation – The period in the summer between the end of *Trinity Term* and the start of *Michaelmas Term* each year.

Master – The principal of a college. Each Oxford college is headed by a senior Fellow. Each college uses its own terminology for this. These include: Master, Principal, President, Rector, Dean, Warden, Provost.

Michaelmas Term – The first term of the university year, which starts in October.

Pigeon Post – Nickname for the University Messenger Service, the internal mail system.

Research Fellow – A member of staff holding a Research Fellowship at one of the colleges

Scout – A college servant responsible for cleaning. Each scout is usually assigned to a specific part of the college. A student may refer to "my scout" meaning the scout responsible for cleaning his or her room.

SCR – Senior Common Room. This may either refer to a room for the academic staff (Fellows) belonging to a college to meet or to the academic staff of a college collectively.

Senior Member – Anyone who has achieved an Oxford MA automatically becomes a Senior Member of the University. The Senior Members of a college are its fellows.

Staircase – The older Oxford colleges are designed on a 'staircase' system, in which a group of rooms is accessed by a staircase that opens on to one of the quadrangles around which the college is built. Typically, rooms are identified by a combination of the name of the quad, the number of the staircase and the room number within the staircase group.

Subfusc – Formal attire worn by students and academics on formal occasions, including matriculation, examinations and graduation.

Trinity Term – The third term of the university year, which starts in April.

Tutor – A member of staff (or a postgraduate student) who gives tutorials to undergraduate students.

Tutorial – A session in which one or two (or occasionally more) students are taught by a Tutorial Fellow or some other person appointed by their college. Typically, this involves students preparing work in advance and talking about it during the tutorial.

Tutorial Fellow – A member of staff holding a Tutorial Fellowship at one of the colleges.

GLOSSARY OF UK POLICE RANKS

Uniformed police

Chief Constable (CC) – Has overall charge of a regional police force, such as Thames Valley Police, which covers Oxford and a large surrounding area.

Deputy Chief Constable (DCC) – The senior discipline authority for each force. 2nd in command to the CC.

Assistant Chief Constable (ACC) – 4 in the Thames Valley Police Service, each responsible for a policy area.

Chief Superintendent ('Chief Super') – Head of a policing area or department.

Police Superintendent – Responsible for a local area within a police force.

Chief Inspector (CI) – Responsible for overseeing a team in a local area.

Police Inspector – Senior operational officer overseeing officers on duty 24/7.

Police Sergeant – Supervises a team of officers.

Police Constable (PC) – 'Bobby on the beat'. Likely to be the first to arrive in response to an emergency call.

Police Community Support Officer (PCSO) – A uniformed civilian member of the police service.

Crime Investigation Department (CID) – Plain clothes officers

Detective Superintendent (DS) – Responsible for crime investigation in a local area.

Detective Chief Inspector (DCI) – Responsible for overseeing a crime investigation team in a local area. May be the Senior Investigating Officer heading up a criminal investigation.

Detective Inspector (DI) – Oversees crime investigation 24/7. May be the Senior Investigating Officer heading up a criminal investigation.

Detective Sergeant (DS) – Supervises a team of CID officers.

Detective Constable (DC) – One of a team of officers investigating crimes.

These descriptions are based on information from the following sources:

[1] Mental Health Cop blog, by Inspector Michael Brown, Mental Health co-ordinator, College of Policing. https://mentalhealthcop.wordpress.com/, accessed 31st March 2017.

[2] Thames Valley Police website, www.thamesvalley.police.uk, accessed 22nd May 2019.

BERNIE'S "FAMILY"

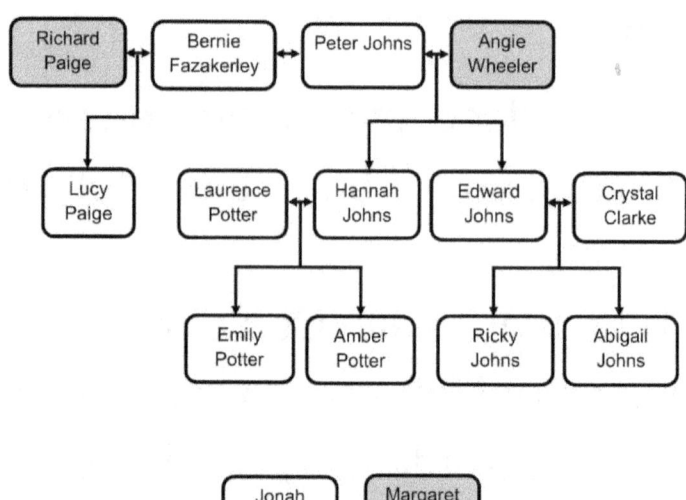

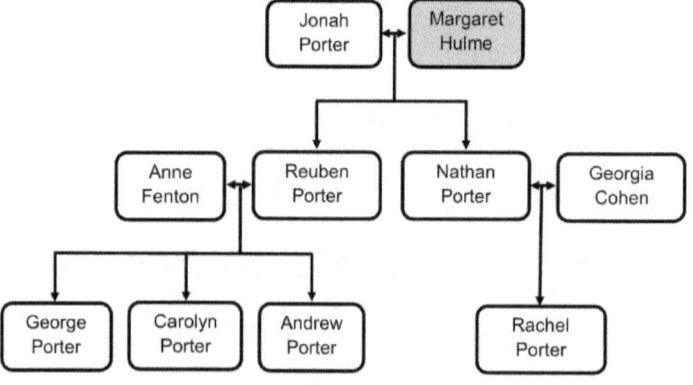

1. HABEAS CORPUS

'That's odd! Someone's left the door to the Fellows' Garden open!'

Dr Martin Riess, Fellow in Geology at Lichfield College, pointed towards a wide wooden door set into the high stone wall that ran alongside the road. His friend and colleague, Professor Paula Wellesley, Fellow in Physical Science and holder of the Robert Boyle Chair of Physics, turned her head to look.

'One of the gardeners, up early?' she suggested.

'It's a bit too "crack of dawn" even for them,' Martin murmured, looking at his watch. 'Still – we might as well get the benefit, even if we had better report it as a security breach afterwards.'

He gently pushed the door, expecting it to swing wide, but his fingers met with resistance. He grasped the wood more firmly and applied more pressure. Still the door refused to move. There was something behind it, something soft but resilient. Martin squeezed his slender frame through the gap between the edge of the door and the honey-coloured Cotswold stone and peered down to see what the obstacle could be.

THE SECRET GARDENER

'What is it?' Paula called through the crack, hearing Martin's sharp intake of breath as he recognised the object that lay at his feet. 'What've you found?'

'It's ... You're not going to believe this,' Martin replied in a strange, shocked voice. 'It's a body – one of the gardeners, I think, judging by what he's wearing.'

'Dead?' queried Paula. 'Or has he just fainted, d'you think? Or a fit or a stroke, maybe?'

'No; he's dead alright,' Martin answered decisively. 'There's too much blood about ... and ...,' he bent down and gingerly touched the man's face, 'he's quite cold. I think he's probably been here all night.'

'Let me see,' Paula said, pushing her way through the narrow aperture. Martin moved a little further into the garden to make room for her to stand next to him, staring down at the mysterious corpse.

It was a man. Martin guessed that he must be over sixty – maybe more like seventy or eighty, but perhaps he looked older because he was dead. Martin's experience of dead bodies was limited – non-existent, in fact. He was wearing grey overalls with the distinctive red and black Lichfield College crest on the front pocket – just like all the college outdoor staff. He lay on one side with his head in the herbaceous border that ran along the right-hand side of the path leading from the external door across the garden to the glass doors of the Senior Common Room. His legs and most of his body were on the path obstructing the door. A pool of blood had oozed out from under his chest and congealed on the gravel path.

'Has he been stabbed?' asked Paula. 'Or could it have been an accident of some sort?'

'I don't know.' Martin took out his phone. 'I'm going to call the police. Don't touch anything. At least …,' he hesitated. 'Better close the door. We don't want anyone else wandering in.'

Paula pulled her sleeve down over her hand to avoid leaving any fingerprints and pushed the door closed. The catch snapped shut making it impossible for anyone to enter from the road without a key. Then she prowled silently round the body, taking care not to disturb it, peering as close as she dared, trying to work out what could have happened.

'I think I've seen him around,' she told Martin when he finished his call. 'I'm almost certain I've seen him working in the garden. He must be one of the gardeners.'

'Not one I recognise.' Martin bent down to look more closely at the man's face. 'But then, you're around college more than I am. I'd better ring the Master and let him know about this,' he added, turning to his phone again, 'and the porters, or they'll have a fit when the police turn up.'

'We might as well go through to the Porters' Lodge and tell them in person,' Paula pointed out as Martin concluded his call to the college principal. 'We can wait there for the police and then show them through to the garden.'

'OK. Good idea,' Martin agreed. 'There's just one more phone call I want to make first.'

'Martin! What's up at this time in the morning?' Bernie switched her phone to loudspeaker and put it down on the bedside cabinet so that she could listen to her friend while continuing to work on pulling up and fastening Jonah's trousers. Although she was very fond of the little don, Martin's call was an unwelcome interruption to their daily routine. Washing, toileting and dressing a severely disabled man took plenty of time every morning, without any disruptive telephone calls.

'I've found a body in the Fellows' Garden,' Martin told her bluntly.

'A body?' Bernie left the zip undone and snatched up the phone. 'Are you having me on?'

'No. We were just coming back from the canal along Goose Lane and we saw the door into the Fellows' Garden was open. And then, when I looked behind it, there was this dead man lying there!'

'A dead man!' echoed Jonah excitedly, twisting his head towards Bernie, his eyes shining with anticipation. 'Who is it? How did he die? Have you called the police?'

'Paula reckons he's one of the gardeners,' Martin told them, 'although I don't recognise him myself. He's wearing a boiler suit with a Lichfield College logo on it, so I suppose she must be right. I don't know what killed him, but there's a lot of blood about on the path where he's lying. And yes – the first thing I did was call the police. I don't know quite why I'm ringing you, except that I'd quite like someone who's used to this sort of thing on my side.'

'We'll be over right away,' Jonah said at once.

'Just as soon as we've had breakfast,' Bernie added, giving Jonah a look that told him that *she* understood the importance to his digestive system and general well-being of sticking to regular mealtimes, even if he did not.

'Don't let anyone near the body until the police say so,' Jonah added urgently. 'And whatever you do, don't touch anything!'

'It's OK.' There was a tinge of amusement in Martin's voice. 'We've locked the door into Goose Lane and we're on our way over to the Porters' Lodge to get reinforcements to stop anyone going into the garden from the SCR or the main quad. That only leaves the private door from the Master's lodgings, so – Oh! Here he comes now! I'd better go. See you later.'

'Right! Now hurry up and get me ready,' Jonah ordered impatiently. 'I want to get down there before Uniform go trampling all over the evidence!'

'Aren't you forgetting something?' Bernie smiled, hurrying to finish dressing him. 'You're retired. It isn't your call. There'll be a perfectly competent officer from CID in charge and they most likely won't take kindly to having you putting your oar in.'

'Breakfast's ready!' Bernie's husband, Peter, put his head round the door. 'And what's all that about Jonah putting his oar in?'

'Martin Riess has found a body and he's invited us over to have a look at it,' Bernie told him with a smile. 'Naturally, Our Jonah is relishing the chance of interfering in a police investigation and no doubt thinks that he will solve the case when everyone else fails!'

'Well, you'll have to count me out,' Peter told them. 'I've got the grandkids today. They'll be here any minute, which is why I was hoping you'd be ready for breakfast by now.'

THE SECRET GARDENER

'We're nearly done. Help me get his nibs into the chair and then I'll put his shirt on while you deal with his shoes.'

In less than a minute, they had their friend transferred from the bed into his hi-tech electric wheel chair. A few minutes later, he was fully dressed and on his way to the kitchen for breakfast. Bernie smiled as she watched him manoeuvring the chair expertly round a tight corner in the hall. The prospect of a murder enquiry certainly put a spring in his step, so to speak!

Arriving in the kitchen they found Bernie's daughter, Lucy, already sitting at the long wooden table shovelling down breakfast cereal at a great pace. She looked up and smiled towards Jonah.

'I'm sorry I can't stop to feed you today,' she apologised, through a mouthful of bran flakes. 'I promised I'd be in early today. Don't worry; I'll be back in time to help you with your tea.'

Lucy, home from university where she had just finished the first year of a medical degree, was volunteering in a local hospice two days a week. It was good work experience as well as breaking the monotony of the vacation reading list that she had been given in preparation for the resumption of her course next term. She got up and carried her empty bowl over to the sink.

'I'll get off now,' she said over her shoulder as she headed for the kitchen door. 'I should think I'll be back about-'

She broke off as the door burst open and a small, dark-skinned boy with curly black hair hurtled across the room. It was Peter's three-year-old grandson, Ricky. Like most children of his age, he had unbounded energy and only one speed setting: full throttle. Peter, fearing that he was about to collide with the table, stepped forward and swept him up in his arms.

'You're early today,' he declared. 'We haven't finished breakfast yet. Would you like to help me make the toast?'

'Yes!' Ricky nodded vigorously as his grandfather carried him over to the side of the room and stood him on a chair so that he could reach the work surface. Peter handed him two slices of bread and watched carefully as he put them into the toaster and pushed the knob down to set it going.

Lucy made her escape, first standing back to allow Peter's son, Eddie, to come in with Ricky's younger sister, Abigail in his arms. To anyone who did not know the family, Abigail was always a surprise. Unlike her parents and brother, she had white skin, green eyes and a shock of ginger hair.

THE SECRET GARDENER

Through the wonders of genetics, she had somehow inherited her colouration from her paternal grandfather – and presumably also from some long-forgotten ancestor on her mother's side – and turned out unique and different from all her closest relatives.

'Here you are, Dad,' Eddie said fastening his daughter into the high chair that stood at the end of the table. 'I'm afraid I've got to fly now; the traffic's been worse than ever on the A34 this week. Crystal will be over to pick them up about four.'

Bernie helped Jonah to cereal and fruit juice while Peter poured boiling water into a large brown teapot and set it down in the middle of the table. Ricky called out to tell him that the toast had popped up, and was rewarded for his watchfulness with half a slice for himself.

'Now take the other half and give it to Abbie,' Peter instructed, lifting him off the chair and setting him down on the floor. Ricky obediently toddled over and put the toast on the tray in front of his sister's high chair, before clambering up next to her and sitting with his elbows on the table staring round expectantly.

Meanwhile, Peter put on more toast and poured the tea: bone china mugs for him and Bernie, and plastic beakers with a lid for Jonah, Ricky and Abigail.

THE SECRET GARDENER

'Don't worry about the washing up,' he said to Bernie as they munched their toast a few minutes later. 'I know you both want to get off down to Lichfield to view that body of Martin's. Ricky and I can do it together, can't we, Rick?' He turned to look at his grandson, who grinned and waved a buttery hand in acknowledgement. 'Ricky's a dab-hand at drying up. I don't know what I'd do without him!'

'That's the door Martin was telling us about,' Bernie said, pointing along Goose Lane towards the entrance to the Fellows' Garden, now crisscrossed with blue-and-white police tape and with a uniformed officer standing in front of it. 'And that's Stella Gilbert guarding it!'

They hurried along the narrow street, Jonah's wheelchair rumbling noisily over the cobbles.

'Hi Stella!' Bernie greeted the young trainee police constable. 'I see you've secured the crime scene.'

'Hello Bernie – DCI Porter,' Stella responded, smiling round at them nervously. 'You've heard about it then?'

'Martin Riess – he's the one who found the body – rang us,' Bernie explained. 'He's a friend of ours.'

'Have CID arrived yet?' Jonah

demanded. 'Who are they putting in charge?'

'No – at least I don't think so, sir.' Stella still sounded nervous. She had only recently joined Thames Valley Police and was very much in awe of Jonah, whom she regarded as a legendary police hero. 'PC Hughes is round the other side. He'd be able to tell you more. I expect when they come it'll be that way.'

'Then we'd better go round the other side,' Jonah declared, immediately turning his wheelchair and setting off towards the junction of Goose Lane with Lichfield Street.

'See you later! I'd better go after him before he gets himself into trouble.' Bernie gave Stella a shrug and a grin before running to catch up with her friend. Stella smiled back nervously and then stood up straight with her hands behind her back and eyes forward, on guard. She took her duties very seriously.

A police car and a Crime Scene Investigation van were blocking the street outside the main entrance on Lichfield Street. Jonah had to wait while staff in protective clothing unloaded equipment from the van and disappeared through the archway that led to the college's main quadrangle. When he attempted to follow them through, he was immediately stopped by one of the porters.

'I'm sorry sir,' the man said firmly.

THE SECRET GARDENER

'The college is closed to visitors.'

'We have an appointment with Dr Martin Riess,' Bernie explained. Shall I ring him to ask him to come and escort us?'

'It's alright!' At the sound of a familiar brogue, Bernie turned to see another old friend. Forensic pathologist Mike Carson had arrived. He held up his identification card. 'I can vouch for these two. They're here with the Scenes of Crime team: DCI Jonah Porter and his PA Dr Bernie Fazakerley.'

They followed Mike through the dark tunnel, past the Porters' Lodge and out into the bright sunshine of the quadrangle. Ahead of them lay a square of neatly cut grass with a stone sculpture in the centre of it.

'That's the sundial that they put up in memory of the bursar who was killed[1],' Bernie whispered, pointing. 'You remember! He left money to the college in his will, provided that they used part of it to put one up.'

'It's a bit over-elaborate for a sundial,' Jonah muttered, briefly glancing across at the gothic-style masterpiece. 'Hadn't he heard of digital watches? Now, where's this other door?'

'Over there.' Bernie pointed to the right.

---

[1] You can read about the bursar's untimely demise in *Awayday* © 2015, ISBN 978-1-911083-06-1

THE SECRET GARDENER

Looking across the grass, Jonah saw another high Cotswold stone wall, with another door set into it, and another uniformed police officer standing in front of a cordon of police tape. This door, however, was open and Scenes of Crime Officers were lifting the tape to pass under it and into the garden beyond. He hurried along the paved path to join them.

'Hello sir!' PC Gavin Hughes greeted him. 'What brings you here? Have you got bored with retirement already?'

'Hi Gavin,' Jonah responded warmly. Gavin was an old friend and a trusted colleague. He would never win any prizes for his intellect, but he was a good solid officer and someone who could be relied upon in a tight spot. 'We're looking for Dr Riess. Is he through there?'

'No, sir. Only the SOCOs are allowed in. Dr Riess and the other witnesses are all in the Senior Common Room. It's just over there.' He pointed along the path to where a flight of worn stone steps led up into the building on the far side of the quad from the street entrance. Jonah noted with relief that there was also a concrete ramp for wheelchair users.

'Thanks. We'll go and find him.' He turned to go, then hesitated briefly and turned back to Gavin. 'And say a few kind words to Stella Gilbert when you see her. She's doing a fine job and I think she's rather nervous of the responsibility. I imagine this will be her first murder scene.'

'I'll do that, sir. Can I tell her you said so? She thinks the world of you. She's very keen. She'll make a good officer, given time.'

However, Jonah was already speeding away towards the ramp, intent on hearing all about the mysterious corpse from the man who had found it. Bernie hurried after him, mounting the steps in order to reach the door in time to open it for him. Being paralysed apart from three fingers meant that Jonah could control his wheelchair, but he could not reach out to press the large button provided for wheelchair users to gain access to the building.

The SCR was a large airy room furnished with easy chairs and small tables. Two of the walls were panelled in oak from floor to ceiling. The other two had large windows looking out on to the Fellows' Garden on one side and the main quadrangle on the other. The glass double doors, which led to the garden, were closed and a garland of police tape hung across them.

Bernie looked around, trying to spot her friend among the clusters of people chatting together in low voices in different parts of the room. She recognised the chaplain, Simon

Sutcliffe, who was over by the glass doors, deep in conversation with a middle-aged man dressed in grey overalls and work boots – giving pastoral care to one of the victim's colleagues, she supposed.

Ah! There he was – over by the large fireplace on the far side of the room. Martin and Paula were standing together trying to look attentive while the Master, Dr Featherstone Grainger, seemed to be speaking to them at great length. Bernie caught Martin's eye and, with a look of gratitude on his face, he excused himself and came over to meet her.

'Thank you for coming,' he said in tones of relief, 'although I'm not sure what I'm expecting you to do.'

'Thank you for calling us,' Jonah responded, looking up at him with a lop-sided smile. 'I'm looking forward to this. Tell us all about it.'

'Good morning Inspector!' The Master came up behind Martin and greeted them in an authoritative voice. He remembered Jonah from the investigation into the late bursar's untimely death and assumed that he was in charge of the current police operation. 'As you probably remember, I'm Dr Featherstone Grainger, the Master of Lichfield, and this is Dr Martin Riess, who found the body. I see that you have a team of people here already. Is there anything else you need us to do for you?'

'We're not the police investigators,' Bernie put in hastily. 'We're just here to see Martin.'

A puzzled frown crossed the Master's brow and he looked enquiringly towards Jonah.

'Alas, I'm only acting in a personal capacity,' Jonah told him ruefully. 'I retired from the police service last year. Dr Riess is an old friend of ours and-'

'I rang Bernie because she knows more about this sort of thing than we do,' Martin added quickly. 'I thought it would be useful to have someone around who had experience of – of murders and stuff – to advise us, just in case …'

'The press will be on to this just as soon as they manage to roll out of bed,' Jonah picked up, as Martin's voice trailed away. 'Before you know it, they'll be all sorts of speculation about what happened. And, despite what they say, not all publicity is good publicity.'

'And are you offering-?' the Master broke off as a tall man in grey overalls emblazoned with the Lichfield College crest approached him. Bernie had seen him come in through a door on the opposite side of the room from where she and Jonah had entered. She recognised his uniform and guessed that he must be another of the gardeners who tended the outdoor areas of the college.

'Milton!' the Master called to him. 'Thank you for coming right away. I assume you've been told about what's happened?'

'Well, yes Master,' Head Gardener Russell Milton answered, looking round the room self-consciously and stuffing his grimy hands into the pockets of his overalls. 'But I can't quite make it out. They said one of the gardeners has been found dead, but that can't be right. There's only me and Brian and Kev and young Connor, who's on work experience, and I've seen them all this morning. They're all fine.'

'But I'm sure I've seen him

working in the Fellows' Garden,' Paula broke in. 'I've been thinking about it, since we found him, and I'm quite sure he was pruning the roses in the bed by the gate into the main quad when I went out that way on Friday night last week. I remember thinking it was strange that he was working so late.'

'And he's wearing Lichfield overalls,' Martin added, 'like the ones you've got on now.'

'That's as maybe,' Milton argued, sounding more confident now, 'but he can't be one of us, because we're all accounted for. Can I have a look at him?'

'That will be for the police to decide,' the Master answered, looking towards Jonah.

'We'd better wait until CID get here,' Jonah told them. He would have liked to go straight out to view the body himself, but he knew that he would have been overstepping the mark, now that he was a mere civilian and no longer a senior officer with an unrivalled service record and a legendary reputation. 'They'll want someone to identify the body, but we mustn't risk contaminating the crime scene by barging in uninvited.'

2. POSITIVE IDENTIFICATION

The door from the main quad opened and a woman wearing a clean white apron over a floral print dress came in. Bernie recognised her as Amanda Bridgefield, the Head of Housekeeping, (or, in Bernie's mind, "Chief Scout"). She held the door open for two plain-clothes police officers to enter: DCI Anna Davenport and DS Andrew Lepage. Bernie smiled as she recognised two old friends. At least Anna could be relied upon not to take offence at Jonah's presence or to consider his advice to be unwarranted interference, and Andy had been his most trusted lieutenant during the days immediately prior to his retirement.

Anna stood for a moment surveying the room and its occupants. Then she walked briskly across to the group near the fireplace.

'Good morning,' she hailed them. 'I'm DCI Davenport and this is my assistant DS Lepage.'

'Featherstone Grainger – Master of Lichfield,' the Master responded at once, stepping towards her and holding out his hand. 'I take it you are in charge of the police investigation?'

'That's right,' Anna confirmed. 'We'll be taking care of interviewing witnesses and taking statements. You may already have met the Crime Scene Manager, Ruby Mann. She's in charge of the forensics team. We need to keep people out of the Fellows' Garden altogether until they've finished. She'll let you know when that is. Now, perhaps I could start by speaking to the couple who found the body?'

'That's Dr Riess and Professor Wellesley,' the Master told her, nodding towards each of them in turn.

'Good.' Anna turned to Martin and Paula. 'Perhaps you could both sit down and we can go through what you saw?'

'But first,' Jonah put in quietly but forcefully, 'you need to know that there's some confusion about who our victim actually is.'

'Oh?' Andy looked at him in surprise. 'Ruby told us he'd been identified as one of the gardeners.'

'He's wearing Lichfield College overalls, like the gardeners do,' Martin confirmed, 'but apparently all the gardeners are present and correct, so ...'

'It seems that he is an imposter,' Jonah concluded cheerfully. 'Have the SOCOs found any ID on him at all?'

'I don't know. Mike Carson's looking at the body at the moment,'

Anna told him. 'I'll ask them about that after he's finished. Meanwhile, I'd like to get on with interviewing Dr Riess and Professor Wellesley.' She gestured towards four chairs grouped together facing the windows that overlooked the garden. Paula and Martin sat down in two of them.

'Can I go now?' asked Milton, who was feeling more and more uncomfortable in the rarefied atmosphere of the Senior Common Room.

The Master looked towards Anna for an answer. 'This is Russell Milton, our Head Gardener,' he told her.

'In that case, please could you

wait here until the pathologist has finished with the body?' Anna said, looking Milton up and down. 'Even if the victim isn't one of your staff, you may know who he is – or at least be able to confirm that he isn't who he appears to be.'

'Come and sit down over here and I'll get you some coffee.' Bernie looked round at the sound of a new voice and saw a youngish man in a clerical collar. It was Simon Sutcliffe, the chaplain. He had evidently been watching them and, noticing Russell's unease, had stepped in to help. 'I don't suppose we'll have long to wait.' They moved away together to another corner of the room.

'Do you mind waiting here as

well?' Anna asked the Master. 'I'll need to ask you some questions too, but I'd like to talk to Dr Riess and Professor Wellesley first, if that's alright?'

'Very well. Let me know when you're ready for me.' The Master turned to Amanda. 'Don't go, Mrs Bridgefield. I think you'd better arrange for some breakfast to be brought to the SCR – and perhaps have a trolley of tea and coffee brought out to the main quad for the police team. And then, I'd like to discuss what arrangements we need to make for the conference delegates who are going to start arriving before noon. Can we direct them in through the back entrance, to avoid them seeing all this police activity?'

Martin and Paula sat down. Jonah positioned his wheelchair next to Paula, and Bernie perched on the arm of Martin's chair, leaving the other two armchairs for Anna and Andy. Anna looked at them for a few seconds, trying to assess exactly what the relationships were between the four people in front of her. Why had Dr Reiss called Bernie in time for her to arrive on the scene before the CID team? Were he and Professor Wellesley merely colleagues or was there something more between them? Was Jonah here simply for the thrill of the chase, or did he also have a personal interest?

'Dr Riess,' she began at last. 'Please tell me exactly what happened this morning.'

'We were coming down Goose Lane when we noticed the door was open – the one through the wall into the Fellows' Garden. It's supposed to be kept locked. So we-'

'Just a minute,' Anna interrupted. 'What time was this – approximately?'

'About half past seven, I should think.'

'It had just turned twenty-five past when we came round the corner into Goose Lane,' Paula added. 'I remember looking at my watch.'

THE SECRET GARDENER

'I see,' Anna said thoughtfully. 'That's quite early to be on your way to work.'

'We'd just got back from a few days on the canal,' Martin told her. 'I've got a narrow boat moored down behind Worcester[2]. We arrived back there late last night – too late for me to go home – so we stayed on the boat, and then the plan was to come to breakfast in Hall.'

'I see,' Anna repeated. 'Or at least ... why was it too late to go home? Where's home?'

'Headington.'

'Martin and his mum live just

---

[2] Worcester College is one of the colleges of the University of Oxford.

round the corner from us,' Bernie volunteered.

'When I say it was too late, I mean I didn't want to disturb my mother.' Martin explained. 'She finds it hard to get back to sleep if she's woken in the night.'

Andy held out a notebook towards Martin. 'If you wouldn't mind writing your address and telephone number down there, please sir.'

Anna turned her attention to Paula. 'And what about you, Professor Wellesley? Where do you live?'

'Here in college,' Paula answered promptly 'I have rooms at the top of Main Quad six. So my address is just "Lichfield College", but I'll write down my mobile number for you if you like.' She took the notebook from Martin, added her number below his and handed the book back to Andy.

'OK. Thanks.' Anna looked towards Martin again. 'Now, to get back to this morning: you saw the door was open and then what?'

'As I said, it's supposed to be kept locked,' Martin continued, 'so I went to close it. But then, I thought we might as well take advantage of it being unlocked, and cut across the Fellows' Garden instead of going all the way round to the main gate. So I tried to push the door open.'

'I thought you said it *was* open?' Andy objected.

'Only an inch or two,' Martin explained. 'I had to push it to make enough room to get through, but it wouldn't open because there was something behind it. I squeezed through and looked to see what it was – and it was a man's body. He was lying on his side with his head in the flowerbed and his legs on the path. I thought he must be one of the gardeners because he was wearing one of their overalls with the college crest on it. I thought at first he might have fainted, so I bent down and touched his face, but it was stone cold and sort of stiff. Then I noticed there was a big stain on the gravel at the back of him and a tear in the back of his overalls caked in what I assume was blood. It looked like a suspicious death, so then I called 999.'

'Did you recognise him at all?' Anna asked. 'Had you ever seen him before?'

'Not that I remember, but Paula thinks she has.'

'I'm sure of it,' Paula insisted emphatically. 'I think I've seen him around a few times, doing odd jobs in the gardens, and I'm absolutely certain he was there last Friday night. He was cutting dead flower heads off the roses in the bed by the gate from Main Quad and dropping them in a bucket. I said something to him about it being a lovely night and he nodded and said something about how it looked as if maybe summer had come at last.'

There was a tapping sound outside and Anna looked up to see Ruby Mann, the Crime Scene Manager, outside the glass doors. Andy got up and opened them.

'There's a lot of ground to cover out here,' Ruby announced. 'It'll take us the rest of the day at the very least. Meanwhile, I thought you might be interested in this.' She held up a slim imitation leather wallet in her gloved hand. 'You can take it – we've finished with it.' She dropped it into Andy's outstretched palm. 'Oh! And Mike says he's finished with the body for now, so I've arranged for it to be taken to the mortuary. The PM will most likely be tomorrow, but he'll email you to confirm.'

'Could you hold off from taking it away just for a few minutes?' Anna asked. 'I'd like a few people from the college to have a look at him in case they know who he is.'

'OK. I'll have him bagged up and bring him over.' Ruby paused for a moment. 'Or you might like to try using the photo on his driving licence. It's not a bad likeness.'

At this, Anna snatched the wallet from Andy and looked inside it. There were three ten pound notes and two fives, a debit card in the name of Mr R G Hillier and a driving licence bearing a photograph of the deceased and an address in

Headington.

'Robin Hillier,' she read out, looking towards Martin and Paula. 'Does that name mean anything to either of you?'

'No.' They both shook their heads.

'About the body?' Ruby asked Anna again. 'Is it OK to take it away?'

'Yes, go ahead,' Anna murmured absently.

She stood up and turned round, scanning the room with her eyes until she located Russell Milton, sitting on the edge of an easy chair in a corner of the room looking rather out of place in his overalls and gardening boots. She strode across and held out the wallet towards him with the driving licence clearly visible.

'Do you know this man?' she asked. 'His name's Robin Hillier.'

Russell stared down at the photograph for a few moments and then looked up at Anna.

'No. I've never seen him as far as I remember, and I don't know that name either.'

'Can I have a look?' asked Simon, the chaplain, from the next chair. 'That name sounds slightly familiar, but I can't place it.'

Anna handed him the wallet. He studied the photograph carefully before handing it back with a shake of his head. 'No. It doesn't ring any bells, I'm afraid. Is this the dead man?'

'Yes,' Anna confirmed, 'and since he was wearing Lichfield College overalls when he died, it seems likely that someone here must know him.'

She went round the room showing the driving licence to everyone present. By now, several more dons had congregated there, all keen to be on hand to hear the latest news. However, none of them remembered having seen the man in the photograph.

'You ought to try Bernard,' Martin suggested when she arrived back from her fruitless errand. 'He's the Head Porter. He's been here for donkey's years and knows everyone.'

'Andy!' Anna handed the wallet over to her assistant. 'Take care of this, and as soon as we've finished here take it round all the college staff and see if any of them recognise him.'

Andy nodded, pocketing the wallet. Anna returned to her seat and turned to address Martin and Paula again.

'OK,' she said. 'Let's get back to what you did this morning. You found the body and rang 999. What then?'

'I rang the Master to let him know what was going on,' Martin told her. 'And … and then I rang Bernie,' he added, looking a little shamefaced. 'I hope you don't mind. It's just … we've know each other for a long time and she's … I mean, with her being married into the police and …'

'It's alright,' Anna assured him with a smile. 'Jonah and I go back a long way too, and I don't have a problem with him being here. Now go on – what did you do after you'd finished your phone calls? Did you stay with the body?'

'No,' Paula answered. 'We closed the door into the street and then went to the Porters' Lodge to warn them and to be there to meet the police when they arrived.'

'You closed the door?' queried Anna. 'Just closed it? Or closed it and locked it?'

'It's got a Yale-style lock,' Paula explained. 'It locks automatically if you just push it to. Anyone can open it from the inside of the garden, but you can only get in from the outside if you have a key.'

'And how many people have keys?' Anna asked.

'You'd have to ask Bernard,' Martin told her. 'He's in charge of all the college keys.'

'I think the gardeners have one,' Paula added. 'I've certainly seen them using that door to bring their wheel barrows through. It's wider than the one from the main quad.'

'Do either of *you* have a key?'

'No,' Martin answered for both of

them. 'They try to keep the number of keys to external doors down to a minimum for security reasons. All members of college – fellows and undergraduates – are issued with a key to the wicket gate in the main entrance, so they can come and go after the main doors are locked. We all have keys to our own rooms and tutorial fellows have a key to the Pendleton Seminar Room, which is used for teaching. The other internal doors have combination locks.'

'OK. I think I'd better speak to this Head Porter of yours,' Anna murmured. 'Where will I find him?'

'He'll be in the lodge, I should think,' Martin answered.

'Or in the main quad, keeping an

eye on your people coming and going,' Paula suggested. 'I could ring him on his mobile if you like.'

'Yes. Please do that,' Anna said gratefully. 'Ask him to come in here so I can ask him a few questions.'

Bernard Malpas, the Head Porter, was an elderly-looking man with a bald head and pale blue eyes behind half-moon glasses. Paula met him at the door of the SCR and led him across the room to where Anna was waiting for him. At a gesture from her, he sat down in the chair vacated by Paula, who pulled up another for herself.

'What can I do for you, then?' he asked, looking Anna directly in the eye.

'First of all, do you know this man at all?' Andy asked, leaning forwards and showing him the driving licence. 'His name's Robin Hillier and he's wearing Lichfield College overalls.'

'Robin?' Bernard exclaimed, hardly glancing at the licence. 'Of course I know Robin! At least, I *did* when he worked here, but that's a good few years back now – in Brian Bingley's time.'

'Brian Bingley?' Anna queried.

'The last Head Gardener – before Russell Milton took over. That must've been … let me think now … two thousand and … fifteen, it must've been. Robin left a few months before he did – a great pity that. He was all lined up to take over from Brian, but he threw in the towel and took early retirement.'

'Oh?' said Jonah with interest. 'And what prompted him to do that?'

He ...,' Bernard paused as if unsure whether to go on. Then he sighed and looked round at each of the group in turn. 'I suppose someone'll tell you even if I don't. I'm not one to speak ill of the dead – especially not a senior member of the college but ... well, the thing is ...'

'Yes?' prompted Jonah.

'See that address there?' Bernard pointed at the driving

licence. 'That's not Robin's house, where his wife and kids live. That belongs – belonged – to one of the fellows. Dr Augusta Peckforton was Modern Languages Fellow for more than twenty-five years. She was already here before I started as a junior porter under my predecessor, Frank Jessop. She died last year. There's a bench in the Fellows' Garden with a plaque on it with her name on.'

'So you're saying that this Robin Hillier was living with a Lichfield Fellow?' exclaimed Bernie. 'How very Lady Chatterley's lover!'

'How long had that arrangement been going on?' asked Jonah.

'I couldn't say precisely,' Bernard

answered. 'They didn't make an official announcement about it, but it must've been the late eighties I reckon – a good long time ago anyway. There'd been rumours about her before, but nothing was ever proved.'

'What sort of rumours?' demanded Anna sharply.

'Something about an affair with a young research fellow, I think it was. As I said, nothing came of it and after he left the rumours died down.'

'You were telling us about why Robin Hillier took early retirement,' Jonah reminded him. 'I gather he was one of the college gardeners?'

'That's right,' Bernard nodded. 'He left so's he could look after Dr

Peckforton full-time. She was a lot older than him, you see, and not in the best of health.'

'I see,' Jonah said thoughtfully, pursing his lips in concentration. 'And you said he had a wife and children? Do you have their address, by any chance?'

'No, I'm afraid not.' Bernard shook his head. 'I rather fancy they had a house out Cowley way, but I may be wrong about that. They could easily have moved since then, anyhow.'

'You don't happen to know his wife's name, do you?' asked Anna hopefully.

'No, but I daresay his HR records may have it – assuming they've still got them. We all have to give details of our next-of-kin because of the death-in-service benefits. The Master would be able to tell you how to find them. He'd know more about Dr Peckforton too.'

'Thank you. I'll ask him about it.' Anna looked up from the notebook that she had been using to record the information that Bernard had imparted. 'Now, I think we can let you go.' She handed him a business card. 'If you think of anything else that might help us to work out what Robin Hillier was doing in the Fellows' Garden or who might have killed him, please ring this number.'

'Right you are!' Bernard took the card, glanced down at it briefly and then put it in his jacket pocket before getting up and heading for the door. Anna looked round the room in search of the Master. She caught his eye and he came hurrying over to join them.

'Your Head porter has identified our victim,' Anna told him. 'He says it's a Robin Hillier, who used to work as a gardener here. Do you remember him at all?'

'I'm sorry,' the Master shook his head, 'I can't say I do. When did he leave? If he wasn't employed here anymore, what was he doing in the garden?'

'According to Mr Malpas, about five years ago,' Anna answered. 'Apparently Hillier was living with a retired don called Augusta Peckforton, who died recently. What can you tell me about her?'

'August-? Oh! Now I remember!' The Master looked round at them all with a mixture of amusement and disapproval on his face. 'Augusta was a bit of a character. She had a very strong personality and liked to get her own way. Yes, I do remember one of the gardeners moving in with her. I'd just forgotten the name. She left a substantial sum to the college in her will.'

'She was well-off then?' Anna queried.

'I suppose so. I gather the house she had in Headington was worth a good bit. Oxford property prices are well above average as I'm sure you are aware. If you really want to know, the person you need to speak to is the bursar. She dealt with the executor. She may even still have a copy of the will. Would you like me to take you to her office?'

'Yes please.' Anna got up, closing her notebook as she did so and putting it into the pocket of her jacket. 'I'd be very interested to know whether she left anything to Robin Hillier, and also what relatives she had who might have expected to have inherited from her.'

The Master walked across the room, heading for the door into the main quadrangle. Anna started to follow him. Then she turned back to address her sergeant. 'Andy! I'd like you to talk to the Head Gardener again and get him to introduce you to the rest of his staff. Find out what they know about Robin Hillier.'

Jonah watched as Andy had a short conversation with Russell Milton, after which the two men left through a door on the opposite side of the room from the one through which Jonah and his friends had entered. He caught a brief glimpse of stone pillars with sunlight slanting between them across a paved floor before the door swung closed behind them.

He swivelled his chair back round to face the others. Martin and Paula were sitting in adjacent chairs, talking together in low voices. Bernie was standing by the glass doors gazing out at the team of SOCOs as they systematically worked their way across the garden painstakingly hunting for evidence that might explain what had happened to Robin Hillier.

'Where does that door lead?' she asked sharply, turning to Martin. 'The one in the wall on the right.'

Jonah, Martin and Paula all came over and looked out through the door or window at the Fellows' Garden. Bernie pointed to where two of the crime scene investigation team were examining a doorway in the wall of a tall building that ran along the right-hand side of the garden.

'I'm not sure,' Martin confessed. I'd never really noticed it before. That's the chapel you can see there, but ...,' he paused to think. 'The chapel's at a higher level. You go up steps to get to it from the quad, and that door looks as if it's down a couple of steps from the garden.' He turned to Paula. 'What d'you reckon? Is there a room under the chapel?'

'A sort of crypt, do you mean?' asked Jonah excitedly.

'I'm not sure.' Paula shook her head. 'I can't say I'd noticed it before either. But I agree with Martin. I think it must go under the chapel.'

They all watched as the two

SOCOs continued their examination of the door and doorframe. After a few minutes, evidently satisfied that they had collected any evidence that these had to offer, they disappeared through the opening into the darkness beyond.

Jonah turned to Martin and Paula. 'Did either of you know Augusta Peckforton?'

'I'd never heard of her until she died,' Paula said at once. 'She must've retired well before I arrived.'

'I remember her,' Martin answered, 'but I wouldn't say I really knew her. She retired a few years after I came back from America and then, like a lot of academics, she came back for a while to deliver a few lectures each year and to supervise her remaining DPhil students.'

'What was she like?'

'Old,' Martin shrugged. 'Rather intimidating. Thought very highly of herself. I believe that she was brought in when the college decided to go co-ed back in the seventies. They wanted a few female dons to help temper the all-male environment, which they were afraid might frighten off women from applying.'

'She was single, presumably,' suggested Jonah. 'Or was that why she didn't marry this Robin Hillier who seems to have been so devoted to her?'

'As far as I know,' Martin shrugged. 'As I say, I didn't really know the woman. We just bumped into each other occasionally in here or when the Master required us to dine on High Table. I never heard the rumours about her shacking up with one of the gardeners. Obviously I'm not as well-informed as the domestic staff!'

Anna meanwhile was having an interesting time in the bursar's office. Fatima Mubarak, a small olive-skinned woman wearing a pale grey hijab over a darker grey tunic and trousers, was immediately able to locate a copy of Augusta Peckforton's will in one of the tall filing cabinets that lined her room.

'She left a very generous legacy to the college,' she told Anna, pointing to the relevant clauses in the will. 'A small amount was dedicated to putting a new bench in the Fellows' Garden and the rest was to endow a travel bursary for Modern Languages students.'

'Was there any particular reason why she wanted the bench put there?' asked Anna. 'Did she have any special connection with the garden?'

'The will says something about "fond memories",' Fatima answered, pointing down at the document.

'Make of that what you will!' She smiled, catching Anna's eye for a moment. 'I suppose you know about her liaison with one of the gardeners?'

'Yes. That's why we're interested in her. In particular, I'd like to know if he's mentioned in the will at all.'

'Nope!' Fatima pursed her lips and shook her head. 'There's just this legacy to the college and then the residual legatee and executor is her sister.'

'She had a sister?' Anna asked eagerly. 'You don't happen to have an address for her, by any chance?'

'Yes, I do. We had quite a bit of correspondence. In fact, it's here in the will, on the front page where she appoints her as executor.'

'And that address is still current?'

'It was last time we communicated, which was only a couple of months ago.'

'Good. That's very useful. Can you let me have a copy of this?'

'Yes, of course.' Fatima spun her chair round and handed the document to her secretary, a red-faced young man with a sparse ginger beard and acne, who was sitting at a desk positioned against the wall behind her. 'Here Ben! Take this and make a photocopy for the inspector.'

The lad got up slowly and walked in a leisurely manner across the room to the photocopying machine.

Fatima turned back to Anna.

'Was there anything else?'

'Yes. Do you know if the college still has a record of Robin Hillier's home address – or his wife's name? He's the gardener who went to live with Dr Peckforton and has now been found dead in the Fellows' Garden. I've been told he retired from his job early about five years ago.'

'I should think we'll still have those details on file.' Fatima started pulling up records on her computer screen as she spoke. 'We usually keep that sort of thing for former members of staff in case there are any queries about their pension. Often widows aren't sure what to do about it when their husband dies and we have to guide them through the process. Ah! Here we are!'

She leaned back to allow Anna to look at the screen. His wife's name is Jill and when this record was last updated they had two dependent children – but they must be grown up by now, it looks as if nothing's been changed since the nineteen eighties.'

'So that address may be out-of-date,' Anna murmured. 'Never mind! It's better than nothing. At least it gives us somewhere to start.'

'Shall I print that off for you?' Fatima asked, clicking on the "print" icon without waiting for a response.

'Yes please. And now, to get

back to Dr Peckforton's sister – can you tell me anything more about her? Is she younger or older than Augusta was? Does she have a family at all?'

'As far as I know, she's a younger sister, unmarried and no children or partner. She's an archaeologist. I gather she was quite eminent in her time, so you can probably look her up on Wikipedia.'

'Thanks.' Anna collected the printout and the copy of Augusta's will and prepared to leave. She handed Fatima one of her cards. 'If you think of anything else that might help our investigation, please give me a ring on this number.'

3. POST MORTEM

'Mrs Jill Hillier?' Anna looked towards the grey-haired woman in dressing gown and slippers, who peered out from behind the front door of the terraced house in Temple Cowley, and held up her warrant card. 'I'm Detective Chief Inspector Anna Davenport and this is Detective Sergeant Lepage. May we come in?'

'Detectives?' the woman looked puzzled. 'What's all this about?'

'Could you answer my question first please?' Anna asked gently but firmly. 'Are you Mrs Jill Hillier, and is Mr Robin Hillier your husband?'

'I'm Jill Hillier, yes,' the woman looked if anything more puzzled. 'And I suppose you could say Robin's my husband, but I haven't seen him for years, so if it's him you want …'

'I'm afraid we have some bad news for you,' Anna told her. 'It would really be better if we could come in.'

'What's happened? Has there been an accident? Is it the girls?' Jill Hillier's eyes widened and she looked round at them anxiously.

'It's your husband, Mrs Hillier,' Anna said. 'If we could just come in for a few minutes?'

'Yes, yes of course.' She held the door open while Anna and Andy both came through, and then closed it behind them. 'Come in here and sit down. Please excuse the mess. I was working late last night and I've only just got up.'

Anna and Andy followed her into the small front room and sat down on the sagging sofa that stood along one wall. Mrs Hillier collapsed into a matching chair opposite them. She picked up a packet of cigarettes from a low coffee table and waved it towards Anna.

'Do you mind if I?'

'No, no – go ahead.' Anna watched as the woman fumblingly took out a cigarette and lit it. Then, taking a deep breath, she began again. 'Mrs Hillier, I'm sorry to have to inform you that your husband, Robin Hillier, was found dead yesterday morning.'

Jill looked at them without speaking. When the silence became uncomfortable Anna went on, 'He seems to have been attacked, but we don't know by whom or why. That's why we need to ask you some questions.'

'But I told you – I haven't seen Robin for years!' Jill protested. 'If you want to know about him, you'd better ask that old bat he's been living with the last goodness know how long – Dr Augusta Snootyface or whatever she calls herself!'

THE SECRET GARDENER

'I'm afraid she's dead too,' Anna told her calmly. 'She died of pneumonia nearly a year ago, following several years suffering from chronic obstructive pulmonary disease.'

'I suppose that's not surprising,' Jill murmured. 'She must've been in her eighties I should think.'

'She was seventy-six,' Anna informed her. 'Not very old at all by today's standards, but she'd been ill for some time. Your husband retired early to look after her.'

'He would!' Jill muttered angrily. 'He always had time to do whatever *she* wanted! The grasping old bag! I never understood what he saw in her.'

'We were wondering if you could tell us anything about what he's been doing since she died,' Andy said. 'Has he been in touch at all?'

'No. Like I said – I haven't seen hide nor hair of him for donkey's years.'

'So, when was the last time you heard from your husband, Mrs Hillier?' asked Anna. 'He still *is* your husband, is he? We couldn't trace a divorce.'

'Yes, we're still married. He never asked me for a divorce and I never met anyone else, so we didn't bother. To be fair to Rob, he never asked me for anything much, just to see the girls every so often. And he kept up the mortgage payments, 'til it was paid off in 2005.'

'So did he still own the house jointly with you?' Anna asked sharply. She was separated from her own husband and acutely aware that there could be trouble if he were ever to need his share in the equity in the family home.

'Yes, I suppose he must've. We never did anything to change it.' Jill looked round anxiously and dragged nervously on her cigarette. 'Now he's dead, it'll all come to me, won't it? I mean, he couldn't leave his half to someone else, could he?'

'I don't think so, not with it being your home,' Anna tried to be reassuring, 'but it depends on some legal technicalities. Do you know if he made a will at all?'

'We both made wills when Imogen was born,' Jill told her. 'My dad advised us we ought to – just in case anything happened to either of us before she was old enough to … They're with our solicitor. Would you like the name and address?'

'Yes please.' Andy held out his notebook. 'Could you write it down there for us?'

'I'll have to look it up.' Jill stubbed her cigarette out in an ashtray that lay next to the cigarette packet and got to her feet. 'I think I've got a letter from them somewhere, if you could just wait a minute.'

She left the room. Andy and Anna looked at one another.

'Not exactly grief-stricken, is she?' Andy whispered.

'If she hasn't set eyes on him for more than a decade, I suppose it'd be surprising if she was,' Anna replied.

The door opened again and Jill came back in carrying a piece of paper, which she held out towards Andy. He took it, noted down the address of a local firm of solicitors and handed it back.

'And these wills that you had drawn up?' he asked. 'When exactly was that?'

'1980,' Jill replied promptly. 'Imogen was born in the February and we got them done a couple of months after.'

'And you haven't updated them since?' Anna asked. 'Not even after your husband left?'

'No. I never thought about it. I mean, he was always very good about the girls – buying their school uniform and that – and there wasn't anyone else. So, I suppose I thought, if anything did happen to me, he'd have to be the one who looked after them.'

'And, as far as you know, he never made a new will either?' Anna pressed her.

'No. You don't think …?' Jill looked round anxiously again. 'He wouldn't have … I mean, I'm sure he'd always have wanted the girls to be provided for.'

THE SECRET GARDENER

'Don't worry, Mrs Hillier,' Anna said soothingly. 'I'm sure you're right. We'll get in touch with the solicitors and they'll be able to tell us if he contacted them to make a new will. Assuming he didn't then the old will will still be valid. He left everything to you, I assume?'

'That's right,' Jill nodded. 'We each left everything to each other or, if we both died, to a trust for the girls until they were eighteen. Of course, that's all gone by the board now, seeing as they're both coming up to forty now. Where do all the years go! It seems like only yesterday Rob brought me home from the hospital with Imogen in her carry cot, in the new second hand car he'd bought for us now we were a proper family!'

Her lip quivered and she reached for a tissue from a box on the coffee table. She dabbed her eyes and blew her nose, before looking up at Anna again.

'Is that all?' she asked with a slight tremor in her voice. 'I think I'd like you to go now.'

'Not quite,' Anna replied apologetically. 'Just a couple of other things. Firstly, we'll need to speak to your daughters – can you write down their names and addresses for me?'

Andy handed Jill his notebook and a pencil. They waited while she carefully wrote down two names.

'We need to speak to them as

soon as possible,' Anna told her. 'Would you like us to break the news to them or would you rather we gave you time to tell them yourself?'

'Oh, you tell them please, if you don't mind,' Jill said quickly, handing the notebook back to Andy. 'They may have questions that I wouldn't be able to answer and ... I don't know – it'd seem strange me telling them anything about their dad after all this time. I mean, I'm sure they saw a lot more of him than I ever did.'

'OK, that's fine,' Anna assured her. 'We'll deal with that. Now, the other thing I wanted to ask you ...,' she hesitated, unsure how to phrase her next request. 'We need someone who knew him well, preferably a family member, to formally identify him. Would you …?'

'You want me to look at his body?' Jill asked.

'If you think you could,' Anna answered gently. 'It would be a big help. It's just a formality really, but it has to be done.'

'Right away, now?'

'As soon as possible. If you don't mind, we could give you an hour or so to get ready and then we'll send someone to drive you over there.'

'OK. I'll do it. Can you make sure it's over by eleven? I've got to be in work before lunchtime.'

'No problem,' Anna assured her. 'Where is it you work? We could get them to drop you off there afterwards, if you like.'

'Holy Cross College. I work in the kitchens. I had to stay late last night to clear up after dinner. That's why I'm up late today.'

'Were you working late on Wednesday night too?' Andy asked, trying to sound casual.

'Yes – why?'

'No particular reason,' Andy answered lightly. 'Holy Cross backs on to Goose Lane, doesn't it?'

'Yes. That's how they deliver supplies to the kitchen.'

'Right, well, we'd better be going,' Anna said firmly, getting up and making for the door. 'I'll send a car round to pick you up at about half past nine. Is that OK or would you like a bit longer to get ready?'

'No. Half nine will be fine. I'll show you out.'

'She could've met him in Goose Lane after work,' Andy said as they drove back towards the centre of Oxford. 'Maybe they argued and she stabbed him with a knife from the college kitchen.'

'But in that case, how did he end up *inside* the Fellows' Garden, behind a door that was always kept locked?' countered Anna.

'Perhaps he let her in, opening the door from the inside,' Andy suggested. 'Remember what

THE SECRET GARDENER

Professor Wellesley said about him working in the garden. He must've had some way of getting in there. Say they arranged to meet there to discuss selling the house and splitting the proceeds – if he needed the money now his fancy woman wasn't keeping him any longer – and she brought a knife with her and killed him, so that she wouldn't have to move out.'

'She seemed genuinely surprised to hear about his death, Anna said sceptically, 'and you'd think she'd have tried to appear more upset about it if she'd killed him. However, I agree that we can't rule her out as a suspect. You'd better go and see that solicitor later and check out Hillier's will, and then after that,' she added, 'you can go and break the news to Imogen Hillier. She lives in Blackbird Leys and works at a dementia care home in Littlemore. You ought to be able to find her at one or the other.'

'What about the other daughter?' asked Andy. 'We ought to tell her too.'

'I'll get Monica Philipson on to that.' Anna told him. 'Celia Hillier is an air steward based at Luton. I'm going to ring Monica now and get her to take Alice with her and try to track her down. It'll be just our luck if she's in mid-Atlantic.'

'I don't think you can fly transatlantic from Luton,' Andy

smiled. 'So I guess the worst case will be waiting for her to get back from Prague or Cyprus.'

'Well, anyway, we can't be sure how long it will take them to track her down, which is why I don't want to wait until one of us is free.'

They parked the car in a small yard off Lichfield Street, which served as the college car park, blocking in both the Master and the bursar. Andy scribbled apologetic notes on pages from his notebook and put them under the windscreen wipers of each car. Then they walked the short distance to the main entrance where Ruby was waiting to show them round the crime scene. Her staff were busy packing equipment back into the van, now that their examination of the area was complete.

'We've found a number of things that you ought to know about,' Ruby told them, walking briskly across the quadrangle and through the narrow wooden door that led to the garden. She stopped and pointed to the right. 'See that door there? It leads to a sort of store room under the chapel. We think the deceased was probably sleeping there at night. We found a sleeping bag and a rucksack full of spare clothes, and some bags of compost had been laid out on the floor to make a sort of mattress.'

'That's interesting,' commented Andy. 'Can we have a look?'

THE SECRET GARDENER

Ruby led the way down three steps and pushed open the heavy oak door that led to the store room.

'We found a clump of long black hairs caught in this doorway,' Ruby told them, 'as if someone had had the door slammed on them as they were coming through and their hair got trapped between the door and the frame. Some of them were pulled out by the roots, so we should be able to get DNA from them.'

'So the door was closed when you examined it?' asked Anna.

'That's right – closed but not locked. The key was in the lock – on the outside. You'll have to check with the college authorities whether that's how it was usually left. Oh! And the light was on.' She felt around on the wall next to the door and pressed a switch. A fluorescent tube on the ceiling buzzed and flickered into action.

'That means that the person with the long black hair must've been the last person to come through the door,' Andy pointed out. 'Judging by your description, those hairs definitely don't belong to the victim, so if he was sleeping in here, whoever they do belong to must've been here sometime on the day he died.'

'How long is long, and how black is black?' asked Anna.

'Forty or fifty centimetres and Mediterranean or South Asian black,' Ruby answered. 'Probably not straight enough to be Chinese.'

'That rules out Mrs Hillier then,' Anna murmured. 'Her hair's not that long and it's going grey. OK, show us where you found the sleeping bag and rucksack.'

'The sleeping bag was laid out on these bags of compost,' Ruby told her, pointing at a row of plastic sacks labelled "All Purpose Compost". The rucksack was at the end, as if it was being used as a pillow. We've taken both of them away for examination.'

'Good.' Anna stood gazing round at the interior of the store room. Along one side were ranged gardening tools of all kinds: spades, forks, hoes, edging shears, a power lawn mower and a wheelbarrow. Fixed to the wall opposite these were wide shelves. The lowest shelf held more bags of compost. Higher up there were stacks of empty flowerpots and seed trays and bottles of plant food, insecticide and slug pellets. Also on that wall was a low door. 'What's through there?' she asked sharply.

'More storage space,' Ruby answered. 'If you want to have a look, you'll need this,' she added, handing Anna a torch.

Anna took the torch and opened the door. Peering through it, she saw a large, dark space. It was more like a room than a cupboard, but with a very low ceiling – only about five feet from the floor. As she flashed the torch around, Anna caught glimpses of dusty gardening implements and old wooden crates and cardboard boxes.

'The chapel above this is built at two levels,' Ruby explained. The main part is lower than the bit at the end where the altar is.'

'I see.' Anna withdrew and closed the door again. 'OK. What's next?'

'Hang on a minute! Look at those.' As they all turned to go, Andy pointed towards the back wall of the store room, opposite the door through which they had come in.

Anna looked and saw a row of five hooks. On four of them hung grey boiler suits bearing the Lichfield College crest, similar to the one that Robin Hillier had been wearing when he died.

'It looks as if that's probably where he got his overalls from,' she observed. 'But it doesn't explain *why* he wanted to masquerade as one of the gardeners.'

'The other interesting part of the crime scene is the area around where the body was found,' Ruby told them, leading the way back out into the sunshine. 'In addition to the pool of blood under the victim, we found blood spatter on the grass and smears of blood on the door leading to the street. We've taken samples, just in case any of it came from his assailant rather than from the victim himself.'

'Are you suggesting that someone touched the door with bloody hands?' asked Anna. 'Did you get any fingermarks?'

'That's the most likely explanation for the smears on the door, but they were just that – smears, not discernible prints. We have collected quite a lot of prints, though. There were plenty of them on that door and on the door to the store room. We've also taken prints from the other entrances to the garden. That's: the door we came in through, the double doors from the SCR and the Master's personal door. I doubt if they'll tell us much though, because there must be lots of people going in and out of them all the time.'

'OK. Let's go and have a look.' Anna led the way along the gravel path to the door that led to Goose Lane.

'The body was lying there,' Ruby told her, indicating a darker area of gravel a short distance from the door. 'And its head and shoulders were in that bed there.' She pointed at several herbaceous perennials that had been crushed by the impact of some heavy object. 'There's a footwear print in the bed quite close to where the body fell.'

Anna followed Ruby's pointing finger and saw a quite distinct imprint of a man's shoe at the edge of the flowerbed.

'It looks as if he was heading for the street and just stepped off the path into the bed,' she murmured thoughtfully. 'Presumably it doesn't match the victim's feet?'

'No,' Ruby confirmed. 'It's nothing like. It's a size smaller and a very different type of footwear. The victim was wearing work boots. This looks more like some sort of fashion shoe. We're checking its make and model on the database.'

That afternoon, while Andy talked to Robin Hillier's solicitor, Anna watched Mike Carson performing the post mortem on his body. As she had expected, this confirmed that he had died from a single stab wound to the chest, which had pierced his heart and lungs. There were also cuts on his arms and the backs of his hands, suggesting that he had attempted to defend himself from his adversary.

Unexpectedly, there was blood on the hair at the back of his head, but no corresponding wound there to explain its presence. Indeed, the blood was all on the surface of the hair and did not penetrate to the skin.

'Could he have transferred it there from the bleeding on his hands?' Anna asked.

'Unlikely,' Mike shook his head. 'Try it yourself. If you put your hand up to the back of your head, it's easy enough to wipe your palms against your hair, but you'd need to be a contortionist to do it with the backs.'

Anna experimented and had to agree that accidental transference of blood from the wounds on the backs of Hillier's hands to his hair was unlikely.

'Maybe the attacker got blood on his hands and transferred it to the body,' she suggested.

'Maybe,' Mike agreed. 'We'll take a sample and check its DNA, just to be sure that it is from the victim. Now what else do I need to show you ...?

Ah, yes!'

He held up Hillier's left arm and pointed at the wrist.

'See there? It looks like he usually wore a watch – often enough to have produced a pale mark in his tan – but there was none on him when we found him.'

'We know he was sleeping in a store room in the garden where he was found,' Anna told him, 'which presumably means that he was homeless and down on his luck. If the watch was valuable, he probably sold it. I'll get someone to check all the pawn shops and second hand shops.'

'There's something else that I found when I undressed him,' Mike went on. He went over to a counter at the side of the room and picked up a plastic evidence bag. He held it up so that Anna could see the contents.

'Two long black hairs,' she murmured. 'The SOCOs found some like this caught in the door of that store room I was telling you about. They're hopeful of getting DNA from them. If the blood on his head isn't his, you'd better check it against anything they come up with from those.'

'Will do,' Mike nodded. 'Now what else do I need to tell you?'

'Time of death would be nice,' Anna prompted.

'Well, as usual it's impossible to be precise about that,' Mike hedged, as always reluctant to commit himself. 'And in this case, there's the added complication that he could have survived for some time after the fatal wound was inflicted.'

'Even with a hole in his heart?' Anna asked in surprise.

'It was a thin knife,' Mike explained, 'which is probably how it managed to slip between two of his ribs into the chest cavity. When the knife was withdrawn, the wound to the heart could have sealed itself again sufficiently for the heart to continue pumping for quite some time. The injury to his lungs may well have been more significant in causing death as they filled up with blood and prevented him taking in oxygen. Anyway, to get back to your question: I'd say he almost certainly died after midnight, but he could've been stabbed any time from, say, nine-thirty in the evening.'

'The solicitor confirms that Robin left everything to his wife,' Andy reported when Anna and he met up later that afternoon to review what they knew so far. 'And they owned the family home as *joint tenants*, which he went to great trouble to explain to me means that, whatever Robin may have put in any later will, the house goes to Jill Hillier regardless.'

'Hmmm,' Anna mused. 'Supposing he was putting pressure on her to sell the house so that he could use his half of the equity to buy somewhere to live. That would certainly give her a motive to want him out of the way – provided she wasn't as ignorant about the law as she made out when we spoke to her. What about the daughter? Was she aware of any recent contact between her parents? Or did she back up her mother's assertion that they hadn't communicated for years?'

'She seemed to back up her mother,' Andy replied cautiously, 'but I don't know. I got the impression she may have been holding something back. According to her, none of them have seen much of Robin since he retired from the college. Her take on it is that Augusta kept him a virtual prisoner in her house after that.'

'Oh?'

'While he was still working, he used to make flying visits to his grandkids during the day,' Andy explained, 'never in the evenings or at weekends. After he stopped working, he stopped coming altogether. The only contact they've had from him since then has been presents through the post for birthdays and Christmas. Imogen's take on it is that Augusta didn't like him having any interests apart from her and only ever let him out to go to work.'

'Coercive control you mean?'

'That's how she made it sound,' Andy nodded, 'but you've got to bear in mind that she's talking about the woman who stole her father and broke her mother's marriage. She may be exaggerating. She's also a single mother with two kids and looks to be struggling a bit financially. If her own partner also left her for another woman, she may well be biased.'

'Did she know that Hillier was homeless?'

'She says not. She claims not to even have known that Augusta had died. She -,' Andy hesitated before continuing, 'she seemed very angry when I told her that she didn't leave Hillier anything in her will. She ranted on a bit. I got the impression that she'd been expecting to get something out of it – as if her dad had promised her something.'

'You mean he was expecting to inherit from Augusta and had indicated to his daughter that he'd pass some of it on to her?' asked Anna.

'Something like that – at least …' Andy hesitated again. 'Maybe I'm reading too much into it. She didn't actually *say* any of that. It was just an impression I got. See seemed to think that Augusta was very rich and her dad was expecting to inherit. I'm trying to remember how Imogen put it … I know! She said that Hillier had told her that Augusta would "see that he was provided for." Those were the words she used, I'm sure.'

'And yet, in her will – a will that she made long after Hillier left his family to live with her – she made no mention of him at all,' Anna mused. 'I can certainly see why his daughter might be angry. I would have thought he might have been pretty angry about it too.'

There was a knock at the door and DS Monica Philipson entered, followed closely by DC Alice Ray. Andy jumped up to get seats for them from a pile of plastic stacking chairs in a corner of the room.

'There's coffee in the jug,' Anna

told them, indicating a glass jug keeping warm on a hotplate on top of one of the filing cabinets that lined her office. 'Help yourselves and then tell us how you got on in Luton.'

'Celia was having a rest day,' Monica reported, 'so we spoke to her at home. 'She didn't pretend to be very upset to hear that her father was dead. She said she hardly knew him. He'd left home when she was only a baby, and she says she hasn't seen him for years. She thinks her older sister, Imogen, saw more of him.'

'Not according to her,' put in Andy.

'How old was Imogen when her father left?' asked Anna. 'Was she more resentful of Augusta because she remembers what it was like before she came on the scene and took her dad away?'

Andy shuffled through his notes. 'She must've been about six,' he said at last. 'So yes, it probably was worse for her than for her sister.'

'Did Celia tell you what she thought of Augusta Peckforton?' Anna asked, turning back to Monica.

'She said she only remembers meeting her once,' Monica answered, 'and that was when she was quite a small child.'

'She said she was scary,' Alice added. 'They were with their dad in the college gardens and "this old woman" as she described her came up and started asking them questions.'

'I've just remembered something that could be important,' Andy broke in. 'Imogen has long dark hair.'

'Like the hair the SOCOs found at the crime scene, you mean?' asked Anna at once.

'That's right,' Andy nodded.

Anna turned to Monica and Alice. 'What about Celia? What's her hair like?'

'It's dark,' Alice replied at once, 'but I'm not sure how long it is.'

'How long does it need to be?' asked Monica.

'Ruby said forty or fifty centimetres,' answered Andy promptly. He had checked in his notes after getting back from Imogen Hillier's house. 'I'm not sure how that would look when it was still on someone's head.'

'Try one of mine,' volunteered Alice, pulling the elastic off her own ponytail and plucking out a hair at random from the back of her head.

Monica took it and held it out straight on Anna's desk. Anna picked up a ruler and measured it.

'That's thirty-five centimetres,' she reported, straightening up and looking round at the others. 'So we're looking for someone with hair longer than Alice's.'

'I think Imogen's would probably fit the bill,' Andy said, 'although it's hard to compare because she had her hair loose. It might look longer like that, mightn't it?'

Alice shook her hair out over her shoulders and turned to face him. 'How about that? Do you still think hers was longer than mine?'

'Ye-es,' Andy answered cautiously. 'I think so.'

'And now, what about Celia?' Anna turned to Monica and Alice again. 'Can you try to remember how long hers was?'

'It's difficult,' Monica hedged. 'She had it all done up at the back of her head.'

'Like this,' added Alice, gathering her hair together at the nape of her neck and then winding it round into a tight coil.

'OK then. How did it compare with that?' persisted Anna.

'I don't know,' answered Monica slowly. 'I think it must've been about the same, but won't it all depend how thick the hair was as well as how long it is?'

'OK. Never mind.' Anna sighed. 'We'd better put them both down as suspects for the time being. Either of them could have motives for killing their father. We can't take what they told us about their relationship with him at face value.'

She looked at her watch. It was getting late. She was just about to announce that they could all go home when a knock on the door heralded the arrival of PC Gavin

Hughes.

'I'm sorry to interrupt,' he apologised as he eased his bulk into the already crowded office, 'but the custody sergeant said you'd want to know about the guy I've just brought in for suspected theft.'

'Oh?' Anna looked at him enquiringly.

'His name's Doug Finney,' Gavin continued. 'He's one of the rough sleepers. He's got a spot off Goose Lane where he dosses down most nights. It's a sort of cubbyhole in the wall. I think there used to be a horse trough there years ago.'

'Are you suggesting he might be a witness to the killing at Lichfield College?' asked Monica excitedly.

'I don't know about that,' Gavin replied, still addressing Anna. 'The sarge just said you'd want to know that I'd arrested him on suspicion of stealing a fancy gold watch and trying to use it to buy a drink with it.'

'Thanks Gavin,' Anna said kindly. PC Hughes was not the brightest button in the box, but he was a good solid police officer and very dedicated to his job. She glanced down at her watch again and sighed. 'I'd better go and talk to him. Will you come with me? I know he'll trust you. The rest of you might as well get off home.'

'We'll need to get the watch over to forensics,' Anna told Gavin as they walked together down the long corridor to the custody suite. 'I want it checked for fingerprints and DNA.'

'Right you are, ma'am.' Gavin hesitated before going on, 'but, I can't see they're going to find anything. I mean, we know who stole it – assuming it is stolen – and so many other people have handled it. I have for a start.'

'I know, but the thing is: it may have come from a man who was killed the night before last. His watch was missing. If we can establish that the watch that this rough sleeper of yours was trying to sell is his, then …'

'If you're trying to say Doug killed him, you've got it all wrong!' Gavin retorted with unexpected vehemence. He had made it his life's work to build up a good relationship with the homeless community and saw many of them as friends. 'He's not violent. He just ... when the craving for drink gets the better of him, he isn't above taking whatever he can find. I've no doubt he stole that watch, but he'd never have killed someone for it.'

'OK Gav,' Anna sighed. It had been a long day. 'I accept that you may be right. It would be far too simple for this to turn out just to be a robbery gone wrong. But if he didn't kill him, maybe he can tell us who did. We won't tell him about the murder – or at least, not initially.

THE SECRET GARDENER

We'll just ask him about the watch, and see what story he comes up with.'

Douglas Finney was not an attractive sight. His brown hair flopped greasily across his bloodshot eyes. His beard was dirty and ragged. He wore a grimy tee-shirt and faded blue denim jeans, ripped at the knee, beneath a grey-and-black bomber jacket. His feet were clad in dirty trainers with one sole flapping loose at the front.

'Hi Doug!' Gavin opened the conversation. 'This is DCI Davenport. She wants to ask you a few questions about that watch you were trying to sell.'

'I told you!' Finney protested. 'It was my old dad's.'

'Come on, Doug,' Gavin admonished him gently. 'You can't expect us to believe that. I must've known you for upwards of five years and I've never seen you with a posh watch like that one. Just tell us where you got it and the chances are we'll be able to let you go.'

'I *have* told you,' Finney insisted doggedly.

'OK. Let's put that to one side for now. Have a look at this and tell me if you've ever seen this man.' Anna held up her phone, displaying the small photograph of Robin Hillier, which one of the administrators at the college had found in an archived folder of HR records.

Finney looked briefly at the image and then shook his head vigorously. 'No. Never seen him in my life.'

'Are you sure?' Anna persisted. She turned the phone round to face her colleague. 'PC Hughes?'

Gavin took a long look and then also shook his head.

'His name's Robin Hillier,' Anna told them. 'We believe that he's been sleeping rough in the Goose Lane area. That's where you doss down, isn't that right, Mr Finney?'

'So what if it is?' growled Finney. 'I told you: I've never clapped eyes on him, OK?'

'He was found dead yesterday

morning,' Anna went on relentlessly. 'His body was lying just inside the open door between Goose Lane and the garden of Lichfield College … and his watch was missing,' she added menacingly. 'Did you find him there, Mr Finney? Did you take his watch?'

'No! I keep telling you: I never-'

'It'd be understandable if you did,' Anna cut in. 'He was dead. He didn't need his watch any more, did he? Is that what happened? Did you find him lying there and take his watch, thinking it was just a cheap one that you could swap for a drink?'

'No! I told you-'

'It belonged to your dad,' Anna finished for him. 'Yes, I heard you the first time. The trouble is I don't believe you. Look at you! You've got nothing! If you've had that watch for so long, where've you been keeping it?'

'On my arm, where d'you think?'

Anna put out her hand and pushed back the sleeves of Finney's jacket to reveal his wrists. She shook her head and pursed her lips as she turned them over comparing the colour of the skin on the inside and outside of his arms.

'I'm sorry, Mr Finney, that won't wash,' she said, fixing him with her eye. 'Where's the mark to show you ever wore a watch? You've been out in the sun, haven't you? If you'd been wearing a watch, there'd be a white mark where it had been – just like the one that we found on Robin Hillier's body!'

There was silence for several seconds. Then Gavin had a go. 'We're not that bothered about the watch, Doug,' he said. 'What DCI Davenport wants to know is what happened to this guy who died.'

'And I keep telling you,' Finney insisted. 'I don't know anything about it. I've never seen him – dead *or* alive!'

'OK Doug, I hear you,' Gavin said calmly. 'That's fine, but I'm afraid I don't buy your story about you having that watch for years. I know you: you never keep hold of anything for long – it all goes for the price of a drink sooner or later, doesn't it? So now, tell me, if you didn't take it from this dead man, where did you get it?'

No answer.

'Look Doug,' Gavin persisted. 'I know for a fact that you didn't have that watch on you three weeks ago when you were taken in for "drunk and disorderly".'

'Would you like me to ask the custody sergeant to check the list of your personal effects?' asked Anna, becoming suddenly more impressed with her colleague, whom she had previously viewed as rather slow-witted. 'I'm sure her records will go back that far.'

Finney looked from Gavin to Anna and back again. He appeared to be thinking.

'OK,' he muttered at last. 'I admit it wasn't mine – but I didn't steal it from any dead man!' he added hastily. 'I found it in the road – just lying there. I thought it was an old one that nobody wanted, but I thought it might be worth enough for a drink or two. That's all!' He snapped his mouth shut and sat back, staring straight ahead defiantly.

'Whereabouts?' demanded Anna. 'Which road?'

'Goose Lane.'

'Where in Goose Lane?'

'Don't remember.'

'And when was this?' Anna persisted wearily, raising her eyes to the clock on the wall. She should have been home by now. Was there any point prolonging this interview?

'Yesterday morning.'

'Are you sure?' Anna was alert again. Was this her opportunity to trip up her slippery suspect? 'What time in the morning?'

'Dunno – I don't have a watch, do I?' Finney grinned at his own wit and then switched suddenly back to an expression of sulky defiance.

Before or after eight a.m.?' Anna demanded.

'Probably.'

'Which?' snapped Anna in exasperation.

'I told you. I don't know!'

'By eight, we had a police cordon

across the gate into the garden and police officers in Goose Lane,' Anna told him. 'Does that jog your memory at all?'

'I suppose it must've been before that,' Finney conceded, looking rather flustered. 'Hang on! There was a smell of bacon frying in the college kitchen. It must've been about when they start cooking breakfast.'

'Alright,' Anna sighed. 'We'll leave it at that for now. You can spend the night in the cells and we'll take you over to Goose Lane tomorrow and you can show us exactly where you found that watch.'

4. TWO SISTERS

Bernie asked Martin to tea the next day and told him that Paula was welcome to come too. At Jonah's insistence, the invitation was extended to include Mike Carson and Andy Lepage. He would have liked Anna to be there too, but Peter put his foot down, saying that she saw little enough of her own family as it was without being summoned to irregular case conferences by retired officers who didn't know how to keep their noses out of things that didn't concern them.

Saturday high tea was something of an occasion in Bernie's house. There were usually guests – friends from church or ex-colleagues from the university or the police force – and the evening was often rounded off with a sing-song around the piano. On this occasion, as they sat round the enormous wooden table in the farmhouse-style kitchen tucking into fresh bread, the conversation was all about the dead body in the Fellows' Garden.

'So the only person who stands to benefit from his death, as far as I can see, is Hillier's wife,' Andy said, concluding his summary of the case so far. 'She now owns their house outright and she'll inherit anything else that he had – not that it looks as if that's likely to amount to much.'

'If you ask me,' Mike responded, 'his injuries didn't look like the work of someone killing for gain. I'd say it was more like a fight in which the other person pulled out a knife.'

'A couple of homeless people falling out?' suggested Paula.

'Yes,' agreed Martin. 'Didn't you say that other guy was in the habit of sleeping somewhere in Goose Lane? Maybe he thought Hillier was encroaching on his patch.'

'What does Gav Hughes think?' asked Peter. 'He knows all the rough sleepers. Does he think this Doug Finney could've done it?'

'I don't know,' Andy confessed.

'It was getting late when he brought him in and Anna sent the rest of us off home.'

'Surely no one would have been so stupid as to try to sell a watch belonging to someone they'd just killed,' argued Lucy.

'Or one they'd taken from the body of someone that had been killed by somebody else,' Jonah said drily. 'I don't know, Lucy: if that watch was the one that was missing from Hillier's wrist, this Finney fellow must have been daft to try to fence it so soon, whether he killed him himself or not.'

'I reckon there must be more to it than a couple of rough sleepers falling out,' Andy broke in, suddenly remembering another piece of evidence from the crime scene. 'There'd been someone else in that funny room under the chapel that he was sleeping in. The SOCOs found a clump of long hair stuck in the door. It looked like he was sharing with a woman.'

'He had some hairs that sound much the same as those on his clothes too,' Mike added.

'So where is she now?' demanded Jonah through a mouthful of bread, which Lucy had just fed to him. In his excitement, he inhaled while the bread was still in his mouth and it became lodged in his windpipe. He tried to cough it up, but was unable to get enough air into his lungs to dislodge it. He looked round in alarm, fighting for breath.

Immediately, Peter, Bernie and Lucy were on their feet, quickly followed by Mike, who hurried round the table to provide assistance.

'Get him away from the table!' he commanded, 'and someone ring for an ambulance.'

Grateful to be able to do something to help, Martin pulled out his mobile phone and dialled 999. Fighting down rising panic, Jonah moved his chair back from the table to make more room. Peter and Bernie leapt towards him, but Lucy, who had been seated next to him, was first. She swiftly applied the brakes and then took hold of him by the shoulder, leaning him forward in his wheelchair.

'That's right!' Mike called. 'Hold him there while I try to dislodge it.'

While Bernie and Lucy supported Jonah by the shoulders, Mike gave him five hard slaps on the back with the heel of his hand.

'Any sign of the blockage coming loose?' he asked, as he pulled Jonah firmly back so that he was once more supported by the chair's backrest.

Lucy held his mouth open and peered in. 'No.'

Jonah continued to strain for breath, trying vainly to cough. Bernie felt her heart pounding in her chest as she saw his lips starting to take on a bluish tinge.

'Try to stay calm,' Mike ordered. 'I'm going to try some abdominal thrusts to force air out of the lungs. Do the arms of this chair come off?'

'They fold down,' Lucy told him eagerly, reaching for the knob to release the one on her side.

Bernie quickly did the same on hers. With the arm rests out of the way, Mike's strong arms were able to reach round the back of the chair to enable him to apply pressure with his fist beneath Jonah's rib cage, jerking his body upwards – once … twice … his face continued to turn more blue … three, four, five times.

'Any good?' Mike demanded, straightening up, his own breathing a little faster than usual.

'Try this,' Peter handed Lucy a small torch, which he had fetched while Mike had been applying the Heimlich manoeuvre. She opened Jonah's mouth again and shone the light inside.

'No,' she shook her head. 'I can see the bread there, but it's still stuck.'

'OK. Let's have another go,' Mike said calmly. 'Don't worry. We'll soon have this sorted.'

'The ambulance is on its way,' Martin added from across the table.

Mike repeated the routine of five slaps on the back followed by five abdominal thrusts twice more. The others watched anxiously as

Jonah's colour continued to become more unnatural and his eyes, usually so calm, widened in alarm while he continued to struggle for breath.

'Right! Let's get him out of the chair on to the floor,' Mike ordered.

Peter and Bernie took hold on either side of Jonah and lifted him, while Lucy released the brake and moved the chair out of the way. The moment they had him on the floor, Mike was down on his knees, tipping Jonah's head backwards to straighten the airway.

'Let's have that torch again!' he called to Lucy, who immediately dropped to her own knees and held it above Jonah's face with the beam directed inside his mouth.

THE SECRET GARDENER

Mike peered inside. Then he thrust in two fingers, straining to reach the fragment of bread. He took them out again and sat back on his heels.

'You have a go, Lucy,' he said, after a moment's thought. 'Your hands are smaller than mine. See if you can hook it out. Just take care you don't push it further in.'

Dropping the torch, Lucy leaned forward eagerly and slipped her hand into Jonah's mouth. She could feel the bread with the tips of her fingers, but could not grip it to pull it out. She twisted her hand in the hope of finding a position in which it would slide further in, but it was no good.

Bernie continued to stare anxiously at Jonah's face. The look of terror had gone now. He had slipped into unconsciousness. Thoughts raced unbidden through her mind. Was this the end? What a ridiculous way for a police hero to go – choking on a piece of bread! How would they manage? After ten years in which Jonah's needs had dominated their lives, it was hard to imagine life without him. But she must stop thinking that way. She must concentrate on making sure it did not come to that. She dragged herself back to the present reality.

'We'd better start basic life support,' Mike was saying as he leaned forward and took hold of

Jonah's jaw and forehead in hairy, muscular hands.

Bernie watched as the doctor alternately blew air into Jonah's lungs (thank goodness she could see his chest rising confirming that it was managing to get past the obstruction in his throat) and then compressed his chest with quick thrusts of his hands. It seemed to go on forever. Peter offered to take over and Mike gratefully moved over to make room for him. Nobody spoke. It felt as if they were all holding their breath.

In the distance, a siren heralded the approaching ambulance. Bernie hesitated, torn between staying with her friend and going outside to make sure that it found the house. Martin, seeing her looking round, jumped to his feet.

'I'll wait for them in the road,' he announced. 'In case they're not sure of the address.'

Bernie nodded towards him gratefully and then turned her attention back to Jonah. Was she imagining it, or was his colour a tiny bit better? His eyelids flickered. He was conscious again. Mike had also noticed the difference. He grabbed the torch and shone it into Jonah's open mouth. Then he dropped it again and, reaching inside with one finger, he hooked out a fragment of bread.

'Got you, you little bastard!' he

shouted triumphantly holding it up for them all to see. The he turned back to Jonah. 'Now let's get you into the recovery position. Just try to relax and breathe normally for a bit.'

'This way.' Bernie heard Martin's voice from behind her. She turned to see him holding open the door for two green-suited paramedics to enter the kitchen. They quickly sized up the situation and strode across the room to where Jonah was lying, completely helpless now that he was out of his chair.

'We finally managed to shift the obstruction,' Mike told them. 'I think we can stand you down now.'

'Thank you for getting here so fast,' Peter added gratefully, not wanting them to think that it had been a wasted journey. 'It was very touch and go for a while.'

'It was lucky we had a doctor in the house!' Bernie added trying to make light of the incident.

'Maybe we ought to take you to A and E,' suggested the first paramedic, kneeling down to address Jonah. 'It might be a good idea to get you checked over, just in case.'

'No. I'm fine now,' Jonah insisted hoarsely. 'And, as Bernie says, we've got Mike here to keep an eye on me. Thanks, but no thanks.'

'Well, if you're sure …?' the paramedic glanced towards Mike who nodded his approval; then she got to her feet and turned to her colleague. 'OK Dale, let's make tracks.'

'I'll show you out.' Peter led the way back through the hall to the front door.

The others all stood in silence, looking at one another. After the drama of the last few minutes, there was a feeling of anti-climax and nobody knew quite what to say. Jonah broke the silence.

'Don't just stand there gawping,' he growled irascibly. 'Get me back in my chair, can't you?'

Bernie and Lucy immediately sprang into action. Lucy brought back the chair and adjusted it to its lowest position. Then she and

Bernie rolled Jonah on to his back before lifting him between them and depositing him gently back into it. Once he was seated, they put the armrests back up and Bernie settled his left hand on the control panel and strapped it in place. He immediately pressed buttons to raise it to the correct height and move it back into its place at the table.

'Let that be a lesson to you not to talk with your mouth full!' Bernie berated him severely. 'Didn't your mother teach you any manners?'

They heard the front door closing and Peter's returning footsteps in the hall. Soon everyone was once again seated round the table. Peter and Bernie handed round the bread again and invited everyone to take more cheese, cooked meat and salad.

Jonah shook his head, as Lucy reached across to cut some of his favourite creamy Lancashire cheese. 'I think I'll just have a drink,' he said. 'My throat's sore from having Mike's great hairy fist down it.'

'There's summer pudding to follow,' Peter told him. 'Why not move straight on to that?'

That's a good idea,' Lucy agreed. 'You can't miss out on one of Peter's summer puddings, and it's so soft, even you won't be able to choke on that!'

Peter got up and fetched the

dessert from the fridge.

'That looks good!' Paula declared, looking at the red dome topped with ripe strawberries. 'If you don't mind, I think I might go straight on to that too.'

Bernie fetched bowls from a cupboard and a jug of cream from the fridge. Then Peter served out a slice of the pudding to everyone, to eat when each was ready. Once everyone was settled and eating again, Jonah resumed the conversation.

'I'd like to know more about Dr Augusta Peckforton. What was she like? Why did she have an affair with one of the gardeners? And, having kept him on a string for all those years, why didn't she make any provision for him in her will?'

'Maybe she just forgot to update it,' suggested Mike.

'No. That's no good,' Andy told him. 'I saw the date on the will. It was a new one, made not long before she died.'

'Martin?' Bernie looked across at her friend. 'You said you remembered her. What was she like?'

'Like I said, she frightened me rather,' Martin answered sheepishly. 'I kept out of her way as much as possible. She didn't suffer fools gladly and tended to assume that everyone but her *was* a fool.'

'So why on earth would she want

to hitch up with a gardener?' demanded Bernie.

'Who knows?' Martin shrugged. 'Perhaps she was hoping to get him to implement some grand plan she had for re-designing the gardens. She always seemed to know how to do other people's jobs better than they did.'

'Was she particularly interested in the gardens?' asked Jonah.

'Not that I know of,' Martin answered. 'But you can be sure she thought they weren't being looked after properly. That's just what she was like.' He paused, as if wondering whether to go on. After a few seconds, he resumed. 'She taught German. She got very excited when she discovered I was born in Wittenberg. She was all for getting me to give conversation classes to her students – until she actually heard me speaking German. Then she declared that my accent was "barbaric" and my grammar "a disgrace" and she forbade me saying a word to them except in English! I have to say it was a great relief to me. She was also extremely disappointed that I'd never read Goethe. My education has been sadly lacking in all sorts of ways, I gather!'

'Did she know you left Germany when you were only eight?' asked Bernie. 'She could hardly have expected you to be studying Goethe at that age.'

'I don't think she bothered to think about that,' Martin grimaced. 'She just seemed to enjoy putting people down.'

'It strikes me,' said Peter, 'that the surprising thing is not so much that *she* took up with the gardener as that *he* left his wife and family for *her.*'

'You're right, Peter,' Jonah agreed, with just the smallest tincture of surprise in his voice that his friend should have come up with something so astute. It passed over the heads of Martin and Paul, but Peter and Bernie both noticed, and Bernie opened her mouth to protest, but then changed her mind as Jonah continued. 'That's a very good point. The affair doesn't seem to have meant anything to her, but he gave up everything for it. What was there in it for him?'

Nobody had an answer to this. For a minute or two, they all ate in silence.

'I've been doing some research on Augusta's sister,' Bernie announced at last. 'The one who inherited the residue of her estate. Mariella Peckforton is also an academic – or she was; she's retired now. Judging by her list of publications and her h-index, she's even more eminent than big-sis Augusta.'

'H-index?' queried Jonah.

'It's a measure of how important a person's publications are,' Martin explained. 'A seminal work will be cited by lots of other scholars in your field. A high h-index means that you've written lots of papers that have been cited lots of times.'

'Is she married? Does she have a family?' asked Andy.

'Not that I could see,' Bernie answered. 'But, of course, the places I was looking wouldn't say. Why?'

'I was just wondering if that was why her sister left everything to her,' Andy explained. 'If she had kids, Augusta might have thought they needed the money more than Hillier.'

'Especially if they had any sort of

special needs,' agreed Jonah, nodding. 'It'd be worth following up on that idea.'

'Another thing that would be worth following up on,' Bernie announced dramatically, 'is her movements this last week!'

Everyone turned to look at her, as she paused for effect.

'And why's that?' asked Jonah at last, unable to contain his curiosity.

'She was here in Oxford on Wednesday night,' Bernie declared. 'Although technically she's retired, she's still active in her research. She was giving a lecture to academic staff and postgraduate students that afternoon; then she dined on High Table at her old college, and stayed there overnight. I know the maths tutors at Holy Cross and one of them told me she arrived on Tuesday evening and didn't leave until after breakfast on Thursday.'

'Holy Cross?' asked Andy excitedly. 'That's where Hillier's wife works!'

'*And* it's only just across the lane from that entrance to the Fellows' Garden at Lichfield, where Hillier was killed, isn't it?' exclaimed Jonah. He turned to Andy. 'What does Hillier's wife do at the college?'

'She works in the kitchens,' he answered promptly. 'I'm not sure exactly what she does, but I do know she was there until after dinner was cleared away that night.'

'She could have met Mariella Peckforton,' Bernie said thoughtfully. 'She might have been serving on High Table and recognised her; or she might have been involved in setting out the places and recognised the name.'

'Could she have told Mariella where to find Robin Hillier?' asked Paula. 'I mean, in her place, I might have been interested in meeting him – either with a view to giving him a handout or-'

'Or to make sure he wasn't planning to contest the will or cause trouble in any other way,' Jonah finished for her.

'Are you suggesting that *she* killed Hillier?' asked Peter dubiously.

'It doesn't sound very likely to me. She ought to be grateful to him for looking after her sister all those years. And the idea of him contesting the will is nonsense. He's got no legal case, and anyway, it's too late: the assets have already been distributed – there's a bench in the Fellows' Garden to prove it!'

'Peter's right,' Bernie agreed.

'But what if he hadn't really been looking after her so well?' Lucy cut in. She had recently done a safeguarding course and was well versed in the various types of abuse that can be committed against vulnerable people by their carers. 'What if he was really neglecting her? Or stealing from her? Maybe her sister blames him for her death.'

'I suppose you may be right,' Peter agreed reluctantly. 'But I still can't really see an elderly woman stabbing a powerful man in the heart like that. Where did she get the knife, for a start?'

'Certainly Lucy could be right!' Jonah declared. 'Mariella definitely deserves some attention. How old is she, anyway?'

'She's sixty-eight,' Bernie answered, 'the same as Peter. That's not old these days.'

'But Peter's right,' Andy backed up his old boss, feeling that Jonah was not giving him the credit that he deserved. 'It's unlikely that she would have had the physical strength to kill Hillier. He looked like a pretty powerful guy.'

'I know some of the archaeologists,' Martin volunteered. 'I could ask if they were at the lecture and find out what she was like. I mean, they'd be able to tell me if she was a seven-stone weakling or a strapping amazon! If she's anything like her sister,' he added wryly, 'she'll be a match for any man. I certainly always had to look up to her!'

'But then you have to look up to me,' Paula pointed out. 'So that doesn't say much.'

'You said she was in Oxford to give a lecture,' Jonah resumed, determined to get back to the main issues. 'That means she doesn't live here. How far did she have to come?'

'The address on the will was Northumberland,' Andy replied, 'and the bursar told us it was still current.'

'So she couldn't have had a lot of contact with her sister,' Jonah mused. 'It'd be a long way to come for visits; but presumably they were close or she wouldn't have left all her money to her.'

'According to her will,' Andy explained, 'the house, which probably formed the bulk of the estate, was the family home, which Augusta inherited from her parents. So she may have felt obliged to leave it to her sister.'

'You'd still have thought she could've left something to Hillier though.' Peter said with feeling. 'That is, assuming he *was* looking after her for all those years. It must have been galling for him to know he was less important to her than a garden bench!'

'Of course!' Jonah exclaimed. 'Why didn't I think of that before? She'd have been bound to want to visit Lichfield, while she was down in Oxford, and have a look at the bench with her sister's name on it. You ought to talk to that Head Porter again, Andy, and see if she asked to be let into the Fellows' Garden at all.'

'OK,' Andy agreed. 'I'll suggest it to Anna on Monday.'

THE SECRET GARDENER

A beeping noise interrupted their conversation. It was the alarm attached to a sensor hidden in Jonah's trousers, alerting him that his urine bag was full. Bernie got to her feet.

'Excuse us. We won't be long. Why don't you all go through to the lounge for coffee?'

She and Jonah left the room. Peter stood up and started clearing away the crockery and stacking it next to the sink. Paula and Martin busied themselves helping him while Lucy took charge of returning uneaten food to the fridge and store cupboards.

'Let us help you with the washing up,' insisted Paula, looking at the pile of plates and dishes. 'We can't leave you to do all that on your own.'

Jonah led the way down the hall and into the small suite of rooms, which had once been the dining and breakfast room, and now formed his own ground-floor apartment. Doors opened automatically at a command from Jonah delivered wirelessly from the controls on his wheelchair, allowing him to pass through the small living room or study into his bedroom with its private bathroom.

'You certainly had us going earlier!' Bernie told Jonah as she rolled up his trouser leg and felt for the urine bag. 'For a moment I was afraid we'd lost you.'

She detached the bag and slid it out from his trousers. Straightening up and turning to carry it through to the bathroom to empty it, she added, 'I hope you're not going to make a habit of it. My nerves won't stand many more scares like that one!'

'*Your* nerves!' exclaimed Jonah, trying to make light of the incident. 'What about mine? I won't deny I was pretty scared myself. I'm not afraid to meet my maker when the time comes, but I'd like a few more years of this life before I move on to the next!'

'In that case, you'd better start taking better care of yourself,' Bernie retorted from behind the bathroom door. 'Slow down a bit and stop trying to do other people's jobs for them.'

'I'm not!' her friend protested. 'I'm just taking a friendly interest in the case – and Martin *did* ask us to help.'

'Tell it your own way,' Bernie smiled as she kneeled down to re-attach the bag. 'Now let's get your plumbing connected again and you can go back and wow them with a song or two to show that there's more to you than just a detective brain.'

'I'm not sure about singing,' Jonah said doubtfully. 'I wasn't joking when I said my throat was sore. Maybe I'll just stay quiet and listen.'

'That'll be the day!' Bernie joked. 'I didn't think you knew how. OK. All done! You can go back to the party now.'

Jonah glided towards the door. Then he stopped, blocking the way. Bernie waited patiently for him to go on.

'Bernie?' he said in an unusually subdued tone, after a long pause. 'I really did think – when I passed out back there – that I wasn't going to wake up again.'

Bernie came up behind him and put her arms around his shoulders, holding him to her and resting her cheek on the top of his head. She knew that he found it as difficult as she did to admit to any form of weakness. 'Yes,' she murmured. 'I was afraid of that too.'

'And it seemed such a ridiculous way to go,' Jonah continued.

'I know!' Bernie agreed. 'That very same thought crossed my mind. I could just see the headlines in the tabloids: "Police hero chokes to death at dinner party!", "Sandwich kills the wheelchair cop!", "The cheese butty of doom!" And then I thought how ludicrous it was to be worrying about that when what mattered was trying to keep you alive.'

She leaned round and kissed him on the cheek. 'Don't worry! We're not ready to let you go yet either. We'll do whatever it takes to keep you with us for a while more yet.'

'Don't you ever regret taking me on? Wouldn't you like a bit of privacy now and then – and time to yourself, and your family?'

'I've told you enough times, it's about time you remembered: you *are* family now,' Bernie protested.

'But seriously …?'

'Seriously, if we get fed up with having you around, you'll be the first to know,' Bernie promised.

Meanwhile, the others finished washing the dishes and made their way to the living room. Lucy and Martin immediately gravitated to the piano and started sorting through piles of sheet music and songbooks. Jonah positioned himself next to Mike, intent on asking him for full details of the post mortem on Hillier's body, but then he caught Bernie's eye and abruptly changed his mind. Perhaps she was right and it was time to take a break from the investigation and turn to other things.

'Have you got "English Country Garden" in your repertoire?' he called out to the pianists.

'I'm not sure,' Martin grinned back, 'but if you hum it, I'll see if I can pick it up!'

5. MISSING PERSONS

'I'm sorry Anna, I'm going to have to transfer some of your officers to DCI Khan's team,' Chief Superintendent Alison Brown said, looking across her desk with an apologetic frown on her face. 'It'll only be temporary. It's just that this teenager who went missing on Friday still hasn't turned up and he needs to work quickly in case she's in danger. That has to be our top priority at the moment.'

'Higher priority than a murder investigation?' asked Anna, knowing in her heart what the answer would be.

'I'm afraid so. *Your* victim is already dead. Nothing worse can happen to him, whereas, with the girl …'

'OK. Who do you want?'

'Khan has asked for DS Philipson and DCs Ray and Pitchfork. He would've liked Lepage as well, but I told him he had to leave you with someone reliable.'

'I was planning to send Monica up to Northumberland to interview the sister of the victim's late partner.'

'Is that really necessary? What do you expect to learn from that?'

'I'm not sure,' Anna admitted. 'It's just that Andy Lepage has found out that she – the sister – was in Oxford the night the victim died. It makes her a potential suspect.'

'A bit tenuous,' the Chief Superintendent observed sceptically. 'Do you have any forensic evidence to link her to the crime scene?'

'Not yet,' Anna admitted. 'We're waiting on the lab results to identify some hair and blood that we think may have come from the murderer.'

'Well, carry on waiting, and if, when they come back, the results suggest that this sister in Northumberland was there, you can send someone to interview her then – or get Northumberland Police to arrest her and do it by video conferencing. We've got to start working smarter. We can't afford to be wasting officer time travelling to the other end of the country on a hunch.'

'Yes Ma'am.'

'So tell them all to report to DCI Khan right away.' The Chief Super looked down as if intending to resume the study of some papers on her desk.

'They're all out at the moment interviewing witnesses. We've got a briefing scheduled for …,' Anna looked down at her watch, '… twenty minutes time. Could this wait until after they've had a chance to report back?'

'Very well,' Brown looked up for one final time. 'I'll let Khan know to expect them at two p.m. Will that do for you?'

'Yes Ma'am. Thank you.'

Anna hastened to the briefing room and was pleased to see that a large proportion of her team was already assembled there ahead of time. Gavin Hughes was also present, looking rather out of place in his uniform, and rather uncomfortable among so many CID officers.

'Who're we waiting for?' she demanded, looking towards Andy.

'Just Monica,' he answered promptly. 'A call came through a few minutes ago in answer to your appeal for people to come forward if they'd seen Hillier in the last few days before he died. Someone said they thought they'd seen him hanging round the railway station on Wednesday morning. She went off to interview them.'

'It's OK!' Alice called out from her habitual seat near the back of the room. 'I've got notes of all the interviews we did this morning. We don't need to wait for Mon.'

'It's not OK if she doesn't get back here before two,' Anna told them grimly. 'Where's she gone to talk to this witness?'

'Iffley,' Alice answered promptly. 'She won't be long – but what's so special about two o'clock?'

'That's when you, Monica and Josh are being transferred to Arshad

Khan's team to help with the investigation of the disappearance last Friday of Pandora Birch,' Anna told her. 'Apparently he needs more hands on deck and you've been chosen as the lucky ones. You're to report to him at 2p.m.'

She waited for a few seconds for this news to sink in before clapping her hands for silence and raising her voice to address the room.

'OK. We'd better start with Alice, seeing as she'll be leaving us shortly. Listen up while she tells us what they found out from interviewing the college domestic staff.'

Alice stood up and came forward holding a notebook open in her hand.

'We've interviewed everyone from the cleaners to the Master of the college himself,' she announced. 'Only a few of them remembered Hillier from when he was employed there. One of the gardeners seemed to have known him quite well, but even he lost touch when he retired.'

'Did he have any idea how Hillier's liaison with Augusta Peckforton started?' asked Andy.

'No – except that he did seem to think that it was Dr Peckforton who initiated it, rather than Hillier.'

'That figures,' Anna commented. 'She was a don and he was just a gardener. But go on: did you find out anything else interesting?'

THE SECRET GARDENER

'Not really,' Alice admitted. 'Lots of people thought they'd seen Hillier working in the gardens more recently than 2014, but that may be just their memories playing tricks on them. On the other hand, the Head Gardener admits that he'd noticed jobs being done without him having set any of his staff to do them – especially in the Fellows' Garden. The grass never seemed to need mowing, for example, in spite of the unusually wet weather this summer.'

'Professor Wellesley was sure she'd seen him the week before last,' Andy pointed out. 'She was very definite about the day and the time.'

'Yes,' agreed Alice, 'and she just

assumed that he was still on the staff. That's what everyone else thought too. It looks as if, by simply wearing college overalls and doing the sorts of things that gardeners do, he was able to wander round the college grounds more or less at will.'

'So, are you suggesting that he had some sort of agenda?' asked Anna. 'He wasn't just using the store room as a convenient shelter?'

'Maybe; I don't know,' Alice shrugged. 'It just occurred to us that it was strange that he allowed himself to be seen so much. It was as if he needed to be mixing with the members of the college in order to do whatever it was he was there for. We wondered if maybe he was spying on someone.'

'Hanging around the Fellows' Garden hoping that one of them would say something incriminating, for instance?' queried Anna.

'Something like that. We hadn't really thought it through in detail.'

'Well, it's an interesting theory.' Anna was unconvinced but avoided dismissing her colleague's hypothesis out of hand. Young detectives should be encouraged to think outside the box and postulate ideas that could be tested against future evidence. 'Anything else?'

'No.' Alice shook her head regretfully. 'I'll leave our notes here for you to read, but most of the interviews were rather repetitive, I'm afraid.'

'OK.' Anna turned to look at Lepage. 'Tell everyone what you found out by talking to Augusta Peckforton's neighbours, Andy.'

Andy stood up and turned to face his colleagues.

'I interviewed the next-door neighbours on both sides of the house in Headington where Hillier lived with Professor Peckforton,' he told them. 'They confirmed that he moved in sometime in the 1980s – definitely before 1988, which was when the left-hand neighbours moved into the road themselves and found him already established there. The right-hand neighbours had been there longer. They remembered him coming just for days and weekends to work in the garden. Apparently the house has large grounds that had got rather out of hand over the years and Augusta brought him in to sort them out.'

'Oh! So is that how it all started?' Anna exclaimed. 'She asked him to help her with her garden and then … things ... developed.'

'That's how Mr Roberts from number twenty-six sees it,' Andy agreed. '*Mrs* Roberts reckoned the garden was probably just a ploy. She says that Hillier was a good-looking young man and Augusta was an unmarried woman of a *certain age* as they say.' He grinned. 'She's convinced that Augusta was determined to "get her hooks into him" as she described it, and he didn't stand a chance of saying *no*.'

'What sort of relationship did Hillier have with Augusta?' asked Anna. 'I mean, were they a happy couple? Did the neighbours hear them fighting at all?'

'Not fighting, no, but Mrs Roberts reckons Augusta definitely wore the trousers in that relationship and kept Hillier under her thumb. After he stopped working, he hardly left the house, according to her.'

'But that could've been because she couldn't be left on her own,' Anna pointed out. 'It doesn't necessarily mean she was *preventing* him from leaving.'

'Yes,' agreed Andy. 'The Johnsons from number twenty-two saw it a bit differently. They thought Hillier was wonderful the way he took so much care of Augusta. They originally assumed that he was her son – what with the age difference and him being so devoted to her – and only discovered that he was her partner a couple of years after they moved in there. They confirmed that he didn't go out much after he retired. They even got all their groceries delivered to the house so he didn't need to go shopping.'

'Weren't the neighbours surprised that Hillier didn't inherit the house when Augusta died?' asked Alice. 'If they all thought he was so dedicated to her, you'd think they'd have been expecting her to leave everything to him.'

'Yes,' confirmed Andy. 'Mrs Johnson in particular did think that it was rather unfair that he had to move out. She said that Augusta's sister allowed him to stay until the house was sold, and apparently he didn't complain at all, but I could see she didn't think Augusta had done the right thing by him.'

'So Robin Hillier did meet Mariella Peckforton then,' mused Anna, 'and he had every right to be angry that she got his home and the remainder of Augusta's money, while he got nothing.'

'Could *he* have attacked

Mariella?' suggested Alice, 'and she turned the knife against him.'

'Mr Roberts suggested that I spoke to Gordon Sillitoe, who's an elderly widower living across the road at number twenty-seven,' Andy continued. 'He grew up there and knew the Peckfortons when Augusta and Mariella were still children. He told me that their parents were killed in a skiing accident when Mariella was only in her early teens – an avalanche in Austria he thought it was. He said that Augusta brought Mariella up after that.'

'So, are you telling me that the house was their family home?' asked Anna. 'It belonged to their parents?'

'That's right,' Andy nodded.

'So maybe Augusta wasn't at liberty to leave it to anyone other than her sister,' Anna said thoughtfully. 'You'd better get on to the solicitor that drew up her will and find out. It could be that she only had a life interest in it or that Mariella owned half or …'

'OK. I'll get on to it.' Andy looked down at his notes. 'I think that's all. The new people who've moved into Augusta's house told me that Hillier showed them round it before they bought it and they said he was pleasant enough, but they thought he was just a caretaker brought in to look after the house while it was empty. They hadn't realised that he'd lived there for years.'

'Thanks Andy.' Anna turned and looked towards Gavin. 'And now PC Hughes has some interesting information from talking to some of the rough sleepers. Come up to the front Gavin and tell us all about it.'

Gavin got to his feet and lumbered his way to the front of the room, looking very self-conscious. He was a large man and moved slowly. Public speaking always made him nervous and, aware of his own intellectual shortcomings, he found all these bright young CID officers a rather intimidating audience.

'Like DCI Davenport said,' he began, 'I've been having a word with some of the homeless people I know. I asked them abou-'

He broke off at the sound of Anna's mobile phone. She snatched it up from the desk in front of her and studied the screen.

'It's Mike Carson,' she announced. 'I'd better take it.' she answered the call, switching the phone to loudspeaker so that her colleagues could also hear what the pathologist had to tell them.

'The lab reports are back on the hair and blood that we found on your victim's body,' Mike said cheerfully, 'and they're rather interesting.'

'Oh?'

'As I thought, the blood isn't the victim's. It's from a woman – but not the same woman as those two hairs that I found on his collar.'

'So, you're saying our victim had close contact with two separate women shortly before he died?' demanded Anna in surprise.

'That's right – close, but not intimate. Did I mention at the post-mortem that there was no sign of recent sexual activity?'

'And do you have any idea who these women were?' Anna asked. 'Could either of them have been one of his daughters, for example?'

'Not if his daughters really are his daughters,' Mike replied. Anna could picture his eyes twinkling as he said this. 'There's no familial match. But, of course, people's fathers aren't always who they think they are.'

'Hmm,' Anna considered the matter. 'We'd better ask his wife and daughters to give us samples. Meanwhile, can you ask the lab to check against any and every DNA profile they can think of – known criminals, missing persons, the lot. If neither of those women is our killer, they must surely be able to tell us more about what Hillier was doing in the lead-up to his death.'

'OK. Will do.'

'Oh! And Mike? Was the hair you found on the body from the same woman as the hair the SOCOs found caught in the door of the store room?'

'Dunno – I'll ask them to check.'

'Thanks.' Anna ended the call and turned to address her team. 'Did you all hear that? There were probably two women present with Hillier at the scene shortly before he died – and one of them suffered an injury that caused her to bleed. My guess is that he attacked one or both of them and they killed him in self-defence.'

'Or it could be that they attacked him and he injured one of them defending himself,' Andy pointed out. 'So far, nobody who knew him has suggested that Robin Hillier was a violent type.'

'True,' Anna admitted. 'We'd better keep an open mind on that, which brings us back to Gavin here,' she added, turning to PC Hughes. 'Gavin is on good terms with most of the homeless community in Oxford and he's been using his contacts to try to find out more about Hillier and about Douglas Finney, whom we suspect of stealing Hillier's watch from his wrist after he was dead. Go on Gavin – tell us what you've found out.'

'Like DCI Davenport says,' Gavin began again, 'I asked them about Robin Hillier and Doug Finney. They all agree that Doug wouldn't have the guts to kill anyone, and I think they're right. I reckon Doug found the body and took the watch, thinking dead men don't need to tell the time. Of course, he's afraid to admit it in case we try to pin the murder on him, but I'm sure he didn't do it.'

'What about Hillier?' asked Anna, trying to divert him away from defending his friend. 'What did they have to say about him?'

'Most of them didn't know who I was talking about. A few of them remembered seeing him around, but they said he always kept himself to himself and didn't mix with the others. There was one thing though – one of them said he had a black girlfriend.'

'That's interesting,' Anna agreed. 'Did he give you a description?'

'No.' Gavin shook his head. 'He just said she was dark-skinned with long black hair.'

Suddenly the room fell silent. Officers who had been surreptitiously checking their phones or whispering to their neighbours sat up and paid full attention. They had not expected anything useful to come from this middle-aged bear of a man who had been a constable for over thirty years, apparently content to continue to his retirement in the same role. This dramatic news from such an unexpected quarter caught them all off guard.

'When they said "girlfriend", what exactly did they mean?' asked Andy. 'Was it a long-term relationship? Or …?'

'To be honest, I think all he

meant was he'd seen them together. It may've only be once. He was a bit vague, to be honest, when I tried to pin him down to when and where, but he said she had him by the arm and they went off somewhere together.'

'OK, thank you Gav. You can sit down now.'

Gavin returned to his seat with evident relief that his ordeal was over. Anna stood up and addressed the room again.

'As you've heard, Douglas Finney was picked up trying to sell an expensive-looking gold watch in exchange for a drink. We suspected that the watch was Hillier's and we now have proof of that. There was a partial fingerprint belonging to Hillier on the watch glass and some of his DNA on the wristband. Finney's still in the cells. We've got-'

She broke off as the door opened and DS Monica Philipson slipped inside the room and sat down next to Alice at the back.

'We've got a few more hours to question him before we let him go,' Anna resumed. 'I'm hoping to convince him that he's got no choice but to admit that he took it from the body. I agree with Gavin that it's unlikely he's our killer, so we need him to tell us what time it was that he stole the watch in order to narrow down the time of death. Now, Monica – what did your witness tell you about Hillier's movements before he died?'

'Not a lot, I'm afraid,' Monica admitted. 'In fact, I'm not certain that he wasn't making it all up because it made him feel important. He was one of those fussy little men who always have to give their opinion on everything whether they know anything about the subject or not.'

'But he must've said something,' Anna insisted. 'What did he think he saw?'

'He and a friend of his were collecting for charity outside the station all Wednesday afternoon,' Monica told her. 'He claims he saw Hillier arrive there soon after they started.' She paused and looked round the room before continuing, 'which was twelve forty-three: he had it all written down, so he could work out how much money they collected per hour. He and his mate accosted Hillier as he entered and he dropped some small change into their collecting bucket. Then he hung around the station building for the rest of the afternoon.'

'Doing what?'

'Nothing much,' Monica shrugged. 'According to our witness he watched the arrivals board and got up whenever a train came in from the north. Our man reckons he was waiting for someone, but whoever it was never came – or not until after the next shift of charity-collectors clocked on at five twenty-seven.'

'Could he have been waiting for Mariella Peckforton?' suggested Alice. 'She was coming down from Northumberland to do her lecture that day.'

'If it really was Hillier at all,' Monica said sceptically. 'It's just as likely that it was someone completely different and our guy just imagined it was him after he saw his photograph on the news.'

'Still, we can't afford to ignore this,' Anna decided. 'Someone had better find out what train Professor Peckforton arrived on – assuming she did come by train. And we'd better talk to the station staff and see if any of them noticed Hillier hanging around that afternoon. Unfortunately, you, Alice and Josh have all been taken off this enquiry as of ...,' she looked down at her watch and then up at Monica again, 'two minutes ago. You'd better all report to DCI Khan right away. You're to join his team working on finding that teenage girl who's gone missing.'

After the three officers had left, Anna looked round the room at her depleted team. The civilian staff could take care of any more calls that came through in response to her public appeal for information about Hillier's movements in the days leading up to his death. They could also harass the labs for news on the various forensic tests that were underway, and enter data into the computer system. But she needed police officers to go out looking for witnesses and questioning them when they found them, and the only experienced officer that she was left with was Andy Lepage.

'OK Andy,' she snapped, 'you'd better follow up on this station sighting. Talk to the staff there. See if they noticed anything unusual last Wednesday afternoon. Then after that, get on to whoever at the university invited Professor Peckforton to give a lecture. They may well have booked her train ticket or arranged for her to be met at the station. I'd better interview Finney again and try to get him to give us a straight story about how he came by that watch – and speaking of the watch,' she added, remembering something else that had been in the forensics report, 'they found some words scratched on the back of it: *To R from A.*'

'To Robin from Augusta?' suggested Andy.

'It seems likely,' Anna agreed, 'but we mustn't make assumptions. After I've dealt with Finney, I'm going to talk to Mrs Hillier again and see if she can identify the watch as belonging to her husband. He may have had it since before he left home, and she may know someone else whose name begins with *A*. OK, let's get going!'

'Peter! Jonah!' Bernie called across the sunny garden as she came out of the house to find them a few days later. 'That was Sally Pearson on the phone. She's going to bring Charles Jayakody to tea on Saturday.'

'Charles who?' asked Peter in bewilderment. 'Am I supposed to know about this?'

'Don't you remember? Sally told us she'd been approached by a Sri Lankan minister whose daughter went missing after finishing her degree last year. Well. He's finally got his visa to come over and look for her and he's arriving tomorrow.'

'I'm sorry,' Peter's face was still blank. 'I don't remember any of this.'

'I do,' Jonah broke in. 'The girl's name's Amanda, isn't it? And wasn't she at Lichfield College?'

'That's right,' Bernie agreed. 'She studied Maths. Tom Carrington was her tutor. After Sally mentioned it, I asked him about her, but he hadn't heard anything from her since she graduated.'

'Come on Peter!' Jonah admonished. 'You must remember! The family were in the intercessions for weeks.'

'Peter doesn't always come to church with us,' Bernie reminded him. 'Perhaps he wasn't there – oh! I know! It must've been last August. Don't you remember? Father Damien got him going to the eleven o'clock mass because he wanted him to be there for the holiday discussion group he'd organised for young people. You said Peter was being shown off as "Exhibit A – a rare adult convert"!'

A year earlier, Peter, for most of his adult life an agnostic, had been formally admitted into the Roman Catholic Church following a compelling – and, to Jonah, baffling – encounter with the Virgin Mary. Sundays were now frequently complicated affairs with loyalties divided between St Cyprian's

Church, which was a short walk from the family home in Headington, and the Methodist church in East Oxford, where Bernie and Jonah were members and where Sally Pearson was currently the minister.

'OK,' Jonah conceded. 'I suppose that must've been when it was. I'm still surprised he di-'

'Never mind all that,' Peter interrupted. 'Tell me about it now – and especially who this Charles Jaya- ... Jaya- ...'

'Jayakody,' Bernie finished for him. 'As I said, he's a Methodist minister in Sri Lanka. His daughter, Amanda, studied at Oxford and then, a few weeks after graduating, she just disappeared.'

THE SECRET GARDENER

'And why's Sally bringing him here?' asked Peter, still feeling that he had not been told the whole story.

'She thinks it would be good for him to talk to you and Jonah before his official meeting with the police on Monday,' Bernie explained. 'She's afraid he isn't being taken seriously.'

'Who's in charge of the case?' Peter wanted to know. 'What've they done to try to find the girl?'

'I'm not sure it's even got to the stage of being a *case*,' Jonah answered. 'That's part of the trouble. At first, nobody reported her missing, because nobody over here realised she hadn't just gone back home to Sri Lanka. It was only later, when her parents started to worry that she'd stopped phoning home, that anyone knew there was anything wrong; and even they assumed initially that she was just very busy with starting a new job.'

'They contacted the Methodist church in Oxford,' Bernie added, taking up the story. 'And Sally asked Jonah to help. So, between them, they made an official *missing person* report.'

'And I looked into the company that she was supposed to be working for and found out that it doesn't exist,' Jonah continued. 'I don't understand – surely you must remember about it now?'

'Ye-es,' Peter said slowly. 'Yes, it does start to sound familiar. I'd forgotten the girl came from Sri Lanka, but I do remember you getting on to Companies House[3] to look up her employer and saying it looked as if she'd been conned.'

'Anyway,' Bernie continued, 'nothing came of it and neither the police nor the Sri Lankan High Commission[4] seems to have done much to try to find her. Her parents couldn't get a visa to come over

---

[3] Companies House is the official registrar of all companies in the UK.

[4] The Sri Lankan High Commission in London, is the equivalent of its Embassy. Commonwealth nations traditionally exchange High Commissioners, rather than Ambassadors.

here, and then her mother was ill and couldn't travel. Sally says she died in March, and since then Charles has been trying to get permission to come here to find his daughter. His visa came through a couple of weeks ago and his church clubbed together to pay his fare and he's arriving tomorrow.'

'That's two missing girls they've got on their hands now,' Peter observed thoughtfully. 'Anna was complaining that she's lost three of her officers because it's all hands on deck looking for that teenager who's gone missing from Summertown.'

'The two cases are hardly likely to be linked,' Jonah replied dismissively. 'They're about a year apart and this Pandora Birch is much younger and still at school.'

'No. I was thinking more that they're going to be rather overstretched trying to cover both of them,' Peter responded. 'I hope this Charles Jaya-whatsit isn't expecting miracles!'

'In my experience-,' began Jonah, but he broke off as the mobile phone attachment on his wheelchair began ringing. With an almost imperceptible movement of one finger, he answered it.

'Hi Jonah!' Anna's voice came through the loudspeaker. 'I need to pick your brains. Is it OK for me to come over?'

'Sure. No problem,' he answered

at once. 'What's it about?'

'Do you remember Mollie Burgess?'

'Of course I do. I was the SIO[5] investigating her disappearance. What about her?'

'That man who was found dead at Lichfield College had a smear of a woman's blood on the back of his head. They've matched it to Mollie Burgess!'

---

[5] Senior Investigating Officer – the police officer in charge of a case.

6. DISAPPEARANCE

'So now we have three separate unsolved missing persons investigations to pursue,' Jonah observed cheerily before Anna even had time to sit down on her arrival at the house in Headington. 'All three involving young women.'

'Three?' queried Anna wearily, wondering how it was that Jonah always seemed so full of energy and enthusiasm when it was as much as she could do simply to keep on top of the essential activities of daily life.

'That's right,' he smiled back.

'This Pandora girl whose face is all over the media at the moment, Mollie Burgess that you're so interested in, and Amanda Jayakody, whose father's over here wanting to know what we're doing to find her now that it's getting on for a year since she vanished.'

'Amanda Jaya-?' Anna began. 'Oh! Do you mean that Sri Lankan student that you reported missing last summer? I thought we decided she'd disappeared deliberately when she was refused a visa to stay on after she graduated. Didn't we pass it on to the Home Office to deal with?'

'That's not how her father sees it,' Jonah told her. 'He hasn't heard anything from her for nearly a year now and he can't understand why the police don't seem to have been doing anything about it. He's made an official complaint and he's got an appointment with the Chief Super on Monday. The Sri Lankan High Commissioner is taking an interest too.'

'But I don't understand,' Anna protested. 'If he was so concerned, why did he leave it so long? As I remember it, the parents stopped asking for updates only a few days after she was reported missing. We assumed they actually knew where she was and didn't want to rock the boat.'

'His wife was dying,' Peter told

her, coming in from the kitchen and putting down a cake tin on the coffee table in front of Anna. 'And he couldn't leave her.'

'And then it took months for him to get a visa to come over here,' Bernie added as she followed behind with a tray of crockery and a pot of tea.

'Well, I'm sorry about all that,' Anna said defensively, 'but we couldn't have known – and in any case, there wasn't anything to go on. She told her friends she'd got a job and the firm was going to arrange a Tier 2 visa[6] for her. She's over

---

[6] The type of visa required for a non-EU national to work in the UK

eighteen and has a right to decide for herself whether or not she keeps in touch with her parents. There was no evidence she'd been abducted or come to any harm. There were other more-'

'It's alright, Anna,' Jonah cut in, 'you don't have to convince us. We all know police resources are stretched to the limit. I was just drawing attention to the way some sort of pattern seems to be emerging of young women disappearing without trace within the Oxford area.'

'Over a long period,' Anna countered. 'You're talking about one this year, one last and Mollie Burgess was even longer ago, wasn't she? That's what I wanted to have a word with you about. As the investigating officer, I was hoping you'd be able to fill me in on her case quicker than I could find out by reading the files.'

'OK,' Jonah replied equably. 'Always happy to help. What did you want to know?'

'Everything!' Anna declared at once. 'Just take me through it from beginning to end.'

'OK.' Jonah thought for a moment. 'It was May 2016.'

'It was a Saturday,' Bernie added. 'Jonah wasn't supposed to work weekends. It was part of the "reasonable adjustments" to take account of his disability: strictly five days on and then two off.'

THE SECRET GARDENER

'But there were a lot of officers off sick with a stomach bug that was making the rounds,' Jonah took up the story again. 'So I was the only senior person available when the call came through. By then she'd been missing for twenty-four hours. I went over to Wheatley to interview her parents.'

'They were well-off business-people with a big house and two flashy cars,' Bernie intervened again, 'and her dad played golf with the Chief Constable or maybe it was the Police and Crime Commissioner – someone in the higher echelons anyway – and he made a point of telling us about it. I had to wonder whether they'd have called Jonah in on his rest day if it'd been a tearaway from a council estate that we were looking for.'

'Anyway,' Jonah continued, 'we rolled up at this big bungalow on the edge of Wheatley on the Saturday evening. Alan Burgess – the father – was there on the drive waiting for us.'

'You took your time!' The voice on the intercom outside the tall wrought iron gates sounded distinctly hostile in response to Bernie's brief explanation of who they were. She climbed back into the driving seat as the gates swung open to allow them to enter. The drive curved round past well-kept beds and a manicured lawn and opened out into a wide expanse of tarmac in front of a large bungalow, which reminded Bernie of a picture in her school history textbook of a Roman villa.

At the foot of three wide steps that led up to the front door there stood a stocky man with grey hair, thinning on top, who looked to be about the same age as Bernie and Jonah. He came up to the car the moment it drew to a halt and accosted Bernie as she stepped out.

'What took you so long?' he demanded. 'My daughter's been kidnapped – or maybe worse – and it's taken three hours for you to send anyone out even to talk to us! What do we pay our taxes for, I'd like to know!'

'Patrols across the area have been put on alert to look out for your daughter,' Bernie told him, walking briskly round to the back of the car to release Jonah from the straps that secured his wheelchair. 'DCI Porter is here now to interview you and your wife and to see your daughter's room. Try not to worry. The majority of teenagers who go missing turn up safe within a few hours.'

'A few hours!' Alan Burgess exploded. 'She's already been gone more than a day. I told your lot on the phone – she never came home last night. Why aren't you taking this seriously? She could be dead in a ditch or- ... what on earth's this?' he demanded, seeing Jonah emerging down the ramp at the back of the car in his wheelchair. 'A bloody cripple? Is this the best you can do? Is this all you think our daughter's worth?'

'Detective Chief Inspector Porter is a highly experienced CID officer,' Bernie told him coldly, emphasising every syllable of Jonah's rank. 'He wasn't on duty today, but the Chief Superintendent called him in because she considers your daughter's disappearance to warrant the attention of a *senior* officer with a proven track record.'

'But ...,' Burgess looked Jonah up and down and then turned back to address Bernie. 'Well, if you're sure he's up to the job, tell him to come in.'

Bernie stared stonily back without replying, which was her way of displaying disapproval at his failure to speak to Jonah directly.

'Is there another way in?' Jonah asked, tilting his head towards the steps. 'We've brought a ramp, but those'll be a bit of a challenge.'

'Oh! Yes, the patio doors will probably be better for you. Follow me.' Burgess led them round the side of the house. The ground sloped gently upwards so that the sliding glass doors that opened from the lounge were only a few inches above the level of the wide paved area that ran along the back of the house. Bernie positioned the ramp to allow Jonah to drive his wheelchair up and into the house.

'What on earth is this?' a woman's voice greeted them as they entered the house. Looking up, Bernie saw an elegant figure in a close fitting blue dress and high heels coming towards them, but looking over their heads to speak to her husband. 'I thought you said the police were here.'

'DCI Jonah Porter,' Jonah informed her briskly, before Burgess could respond. 'And this is my personal assistant Dr Bernadette Fazakerley. We're here to talk to you about your daughter. Won't you both sit down?'

'You're a policeman?' the woman stared in disbelief at Jonah's warrant card, which Bernie was helpfully holding up in front of her. 'I don't understand.' She looked across at her husband again. 'I thought you said they were sending one of their top men?'

'Mrs Burgess,' Jonah said, mustering all his patience, 'if you could just sit down and answer a few questions then we can get on with looking for your daughter.'

'It's Naylor,' the woman snapped back. 'My name's Geraldine Naylor. You've probably heard of me. I'm the CEO and founder of *Naylor's Naturals*.'

THE SECRET GARDENER

'Gerry kept her maiden name when we got married,' Burgess explained. 'It's better for business.' He turned to his wife. 'Let's all sit down like the man says and let him ask his questions.'

He took her arm and guided her to a smart leather sofa. They sat together on the edge of the seat, bolt upright, waiting in silence. Jonah positioned his wheelchair opposite them, where he could watch their faces easily. Bernie found a seat a little behind him and took out a laptop computer from the storage space at the back of his chair, ready to take notes.

'Thank you.' Jonah smiled round at the couple. 'Now perhaps you could tell me a bit about your daughter. Her name's Mollie, is that right?'

'Yes,' Geraldine answered. 'Mollie Isabella. I found you this picture of her.' She got to her feet and snatched up a photograph from the top of a highly-polished antique chest of drawers at the side of the room. 'You'll need it to put out on the TV and in the papers, won't you?' She held it out towards Bernie, who showed it to Jonah. It was a portrait of a girl in school uniform staring towards the camera with a rather bored expression on her face.

'Are these the clothes she was wearing?' Jonah asked, looking towards Geraldine and her husband in turn.

'Alan?' Geraldine prompted.

'No – no I don't think so,' he replied, apparently in some confusion. 'No, I'm sure she must've changed out of her uniform before she went out.'

'It would help if you could remember what she actually was wearing,' Jonah told him. 'People are more likely to recognise her if we can tell them that.'

'I – I'm sorry. I really didn't notice. She just-'

'Oh Alan! *Think*, can't you?' his wife cut in. 'You must've noticed. You told me she came to tell you she was going into Oxford and you offered to take her but she said she'd rather go on the bus. How could you not have seen what she was wearing?'

'Perhaps you'd be able to work that out by having a look in her wardrobe to see what's missing,' Jonah suggested in an attempt to stave off a row between the two parents. 'We can do that in a few minutes when we have a look at her room. If you could just sit down again, please?'

Casting a final look of contempt towards her husband, Geraldine returned to her seat. She clasped her hands tightly together on her lap and fixed her gaze expectantly towards Jonah.

'Let's start at the beginning, shall

we?' he said calmly. 'When was it that you last saw Mollie?'

'Last night,' Alan replied promptly. 'Well, yesterday afternoon, I suppose.'

'Can you remember the time?' prompted Jonah.

'Between five and half past I should think. She'd have been home from school about an hour, I suppose. I come home early on a Friday. I'd just got in and I was in here fixing myself a drink when she put her head round the door and told me she was going out. She said she'd arranged to go to see a film with one of her friends and wouldn't be back until late.'

'Did she say which film?'

'I think she did, but the name didn't mean anything to me,' Alan glanced round apologetically at Geraldine, who had drawn in her breath as if she might be about to round on him again for his forgetfulness. 'I do remember she said they were going to the Odeon in George Street.'

'Good. That's very useful,' Jonah told him encouragingly.

'So I said: would she like a lift? And she said: no she'd rather go on the bus. I think the other girl was going to be joining her on the bus at a later stop.'

'And do you know who this other girl was?'

'Her name's Ella Campbell,'

Geraldine intervened. 'We rang her parents this morning, when we found Mollie was gone. They said Ella was at home all evening.'

'So neither of you waited up for Mollie to come in?' Jonah asked, trying to keep any hint of censure out of his voice.

'*I* didn't get in myself until after three in the morning,' Geraldine replied at once, giving her husband a hard look. 'I was flying back from Singapore. I'd been out in the Far East for ten days negotiating deals on a new range of cotton fabrics. I just assumed she was in bed when I got back – Alan was.'

'I knew I'd have a disturbed night, with Gerry getting in late, so I went to bed early,' Alan explained sheepishly. 'Mollie has her own key and doesn't like us "spying on her" as she puts it.'

'So, the first you knew she hadn't come home was when she didn't come down for breakfast this morning?' Jonah looked at Alan and then at Geraldine.

'Yes,' Alan confirmed. 'We had a bit of a lie-in, with Gerry having only just got back from Singapore, but even so she was up at eight-thirty.'

'I had things to do that couldn't wait,' Gerry cut in. 'I needed to return a call to my agent in Indonesia before he left the office. I gave Mollie until quarter past nine and then went in to wake her. She wasn't there and her bed hadn't been slept in.'

'Can you be sure of that?' Jonah asked. 'I mean, could she have got up and tidied the bed herself? It doesn't take much to straighten a duvet, does it?'

'That's what I keep telling her!' Geraldine complained, 'but I might as well be talking to the cat, for all the notice she takes. No, believe me: if she'd spent the night in that bed, I'd have been able to tell. It was clear it hadn't been touched since Tina – that's our cleaner – did the bedrooms yesterday morning.'

'We rang the Campbells right away,' Alan put in eagerly. 'We thought maybe Mollie had missed the last bus back and they'd put her up for the night. They live in Headington Quarry, so the girls could have walked back there from town.'

'But Mrs Campbell said Ella hadn't been to the pictures last night and Ella said she hadn't even had any plans to go out with Mollie.'

'What about Mollie's other friends?' Jonah suggested. 'Could she have gone with one of them?'

'We rang round everyone we could think of,' Alan told him, 'and they all said the same. None of them had any idea where Mollie could be.'

'OK.' Jonah thought for a moment. Then, addressing Alan, 'I'd like you to write me down a list of all those friends that you contacted and anyone else you can think of who knew Mollie. I want names, addresses and telephone numbers, if you have them. Don't forget your cleaner. You never know if Mollie may have confided in her or if she could have noticed anything when she tidied Mollie's room.'

'Right you are,' Alan nodded. 'Just give me a few minutes to get them all together.'

'And while your husband's doing that,' Jonah continued, turning to Geraldine, 'please could you show us to your daughter's room and have a look in her wardrobe to see which of her clothes are missing?'

'Her best dress is gone,' Geraldine

said a few minutes later, as she perused the fitted wardrobe in her daughter's bedroom, pushing garments along the rail and counting them off in her mind. 'And the red one she wore to my cousin's wedding.'

She turned and looked towards Bernie, who was sitting on the bed with her computer on her lap, taking down notes, while Jonah perambulated round the spacious room in his chair, peering at a scatter of cotton wool balls lying on the dressing table and turning his head on one side to read the spines of a pile of textbooks on the desk. 'I don't understand! She can't have been wearing them both.'

'Could one of them be in the wash?' suggested Bernie.

'I suppose so,' Geraldine still sounded perplexed. 'I'll check the laundry basket if you like.'

She left the room. Jonah spoke softly to Bernie.

'Have a look in these drawers for me, will you? I'd like to know where she kept the makeup that she used those cotton balls to take off.'

Bernie opened and closed each drawer of the dressing table in turn, carefully inspecting the contents of each.

'Nope,' she declared at last, straightening up again. 'Hair bands, bracelets, earrings, a box of tissues and some more cotton wool balls, but no makeup – well, just a few ends of lipstick and some bottles of dried-up nail varnish.'

'No, it's not in the basket,' Geraldine announced, coming back in, 'and Alan says the last load of washing they did was on Wednesday and it wasn't there then. I just don't understand why both dresses would be gone. And – and I can't believe she was wearing either of them when she went out yesterday. They were … special. I'm sure even Alan would've noticed if she'd had them on.'

'Can you tell me where her school bag is?' asked Jonah, apparently ignoring this speech. 'I assume she must have a bag for carrying her books?'

'I don't know,' Geraldine stared vaguely round the room. 'She usually just dumps it on the floor by her desk.

'Ms Naylor,' Jonah said seriously. 'I think you need to realise that it looks rather as if your daughter left home yesterday with the intention of staying away overnight or possibly not intending to come back.'

'She's run away from home you mean? But that's ridiculous! Why would she want to run away?'

'Of course it's ridiculous!' her husband agreed in a loud voice from the doorway. 'I've never heard anything so preposterous in my life.

Here's that list you wanted,' he went on, holding out a sheet of writing paper. Bernie took it, glanced down briefly to check that it contained the information that Jonah had requested and then folded it and put it in her pocket.

'If you could just go over her room and identify anything else that's missing?' Jonah looked calmly towards Geraldine. 'Does she have a makeup bag, for instance? And where does she keep her toothbrush?'

'In the bathroom,' Alan answered. 'I'll go and find it, if you're so bloody interested in it.'

'She had a box for her makeup, not a bag,' Geraldine answered. It was pink with butterflies on it. It's usually there – on the dressing table.'

'We looked in the drawers,' Bernie told her. 'It's not there either.'

'Carry on checking her clothes, please,' Jonah instructed. 'What she took may give us an indication of where she was going. Tell us about anything you notice that isn't here and ought to be and Bernie will put them on her list.'

'Here it is, see!' Alan returned brandishing a yellow toothbrush triumphantly. 'I knew you were talking nonsense. Why would Mollie want to run away from home?'

'Bag it up, please, Bernie,' Jonah commanded at once. 'It may provide us with DNA. And let's have that hair brush too,' he added, pointing towards a long handled brush that lay on the dressing table, 'just in case.'

'In case of what?' demanded Alan. 'What are you implying?'

'Nothing at all,' Jonah replied smoothly. 'Please try not to get agitated. It's all just routine. A DNA profile of your daughter may help us to find her, that's all – and it'll be easier to get one now than if we wait until we know we need one.'

'You think she's dead, don't you?' Alan shouted, his voice rising in alarm.

'No, Mr Burgess, I don't,' Jonah said firmly. 'At the moment it looks as if she went off intending to stay away for a few days – or possibly indefinitely, it's impossible to tell. That means that the chances are we'll find her safe and well quite soon.'

'If she was alive, she'd ring us,' Alan insisted, apparently now convinced that his daughter had come to harm.

'She's got it switched off,' Geraldine added. 'We've tried ringing her, but it just goes straight through to voicemail.'

'Her phone may need re-charging,' Jonah pointed out patiently, 'or she could have lost it or broken it. We'll need details of her account. It may enable us to trace her. Can you get them for me?'

Alan remained staring blankly for a second or two. Then he nodded perfunctorily and left the room. Jonah turned his attention back to Geraldine, who was rummaging through a chest of drawers. Feeling his gaze resting on her, she turned to look at him.

'Her favourite pyjamas are missing,' she reported, 'and a pair of jeans and some tops. Her trainers are gone and so are the shoes she wore to the wedding.'

'Good. I think we're making progress,' Jonah told her. 'Now, to save time, do you think you could answer a few questions while you carry on checking for anything else that's gone?'

'Yes, of course. What did you want to know?'

'Can you think of anywhere that Mollie might have gone to? Any friends who might be willing to put her up for a few nights?'

'Only the school friends that we rang round as soon as we realised she was gone.'

'What about boyfriends?'

'She never talked about any.'

'She's only fifteen,' Alan cut in, returning with another piece of paper, which he handed over to Bernie. 'She's too young for anything serious.'

'I'm afraid she may not agree with you about that,' Jonah observed drily.

'Her riding boots aren't here,' Geraldine murmured as she rummaged through a pile of footwear in the bottom of the wardrobe, 'And I don't remember seeing her jodhpurs either.'

'They were muddy when she came in from her riding lesson on Saturday,' Alan told her. 'The jodhpurs are waiting to be ironed and she left the boots out in the utility room.'

'Could you go and check that they're still there, please Mr Burgess?' Jonah said at once.

'If you like,' Alan muttered, turning to go, 'but this is all just wasting time. Why haven't you got people out there looking for her, instead of standing around here jawing and counting her clothes?'

'We'll need the address of the riding school,' Jonah told Geraldine. 'Did she go there every Saturday?'

'Yes. She loved horses. She kept pestering for a pony of her own, but we told her it was too much of a responsibility, with me being away so much with the business and her needing to work for her exams.'

'Does your husband work for the business too?' Jonah asked casually as if making conversation.

'No. He has his own accountancy firm: Burgess Lipton. Quentin Lipton is an old university chum of his. Why d'you ask?'

'I'm just trying to get an all-round picture of Mollie's background,' Jonah explained. 'It may help us to work out where she could have gone.'

Sensing a shadow in the doorway, he turned to see Alan Burgess standing there looking a little sheepish.

'I can't find the boots or the jodhpurs,' he told them. 'I'm sure they were there yesterday morning. I remember falling over them when I fed the cat.'

'OK,' Jonah said with quiet decision, 'It looks very much as if Mollie has taken herself off voluntarily. That's a good sign. The chances are she'll turn up safe and well in a few days. You need to keep your phones switched on in case she rings and don't leave this house empty at all in case she comes back.'

'But I've got to be in Glasgow for nine in the morning on Monday,' protested Geraldine. 'You'll have to stay at home next week, Alan, if she isn't back.'

'Or you could cancel your trip,' he growled back.

'If she rings,' Jonah continued, deciding not to intervene in this argument, 'keep her talking for as long as you can and try to get her to tell you where she is. Don't let her think you're angry with her.' He looked round the room again. 'We'll need to take her computer with us. Her browsing history and social media activity may give us an idea where she could have gone. Does she have any other devices – apart from her phone?'

'She's got a Kindle Fire tablet,' Alan told him. 'She usually keeps it in the top drawer of her desk.'

Geraldine pulled open the drawer and looked inside. Then she slammed it shut again and opened each of the other drawers in turn. 'That's gone too,' she declared.

'That's probably good,' Jonah told them. 'If she uses it to log in to any of her accounts, it may help us to trace her.'

'We've got it set up so she can't

download anything,' Alan said quickly. 'If she wants a new book or anything, she has to come to me and I'll decide whether to buy it for her on my account. We've got child filters on her computer too. We're not complete idiots. We know all about kids getting into trouble online.'

'It's good to hear you're so responsible,' Jonah replied with the aim of placating the angry parent. 'But however careful you may have been, it's still possible that Mollie has been befriended by someone online and has gone off to meet them. We've got specialist people who can look into her activity and try to identify if that's happened.' He took a final look round the room. 'OK, I think that's all for now. Let me know right away if she calls you or if you think of anywhere else or anyone else that she might have gone to.'

'So there you have it,' Jonah concluded, looking Anna in the eye. 'I was as sure as I could be that Mollie had gone off of her own volition. The question was: why and where and with whom?'

'*Why* seemed pretty obvious to me,' Bernie added. 'Both her parents were too busy with their work to be bothered with her. It wouldn't be hard for a boyfriend to convince her he cared more for her than they did.

Or she could even have run away simply to get them to notice her.'

'Mmm,' Anna murmured, thinking of her own family at home with no parental supervision. 'Jess and Marcus used to complain that I never had time for them because of my job, but at least they had Philip at home with them all day when they were growing up. It'll be more difficult for Donna when she's older.'

Anna's youngest child had arrived unexpectedly when her siblings were already teenagers, and at the same time that her father announced his decision to move down to the West Country to go into partnership with an old friend from his university days. Anna was very conscious of her failure to provide the same levels of security and parental oversight that her older children had enjoyed – or perhaps, judging by their frequent complaints, endured.

'Don't worry,' Peter advised. 'I'm sure she knows you all love her to bits. Only the other day, you were complaining about the way Jessica spoils her. And you never know,' he added hopefully, 'one day, Philip may see sense and come home.'

'He's threatening to do just that,' Anna sighed. 'Part of me thinks that would be the ideal solution to all my childcare problems and I'm being ridiculous turning him down, it's just … I just don't think I could ever trust him properly again.'

She paused in thought for a moment then turned briskly back to Jonah.

'But, getting back to Mollie Burgess, what did you do next?'

'We did the rounds of all the stables within a fifty mile radius of Oxford,' Jonah told her. 'Teenage girls often have an obsession with horses and we thought she might have lied about her age and managed to get a job as a stable lad, or whatever the feminine equivalent of that is.'

'Yes,' Anna murmured, 'you said she took her jodhpurs and riding boots – but two posh frocks too. It seems a strange combination. If she was expecting to spend her days mucking out, you would've thought she'd have taken more jeans and tee-shirts instead of the fancy dresses.'

'We found out later that she had her riding hat with her too,' Bernie commented. 'A bus driver remembered her getting on in Wheatley with a bag on her back and a riding hat over one arm. Wherever she was going, it looks as if she was anticipating that there would be horses there.'

'He confirmed that she got off in the centre of Oxford and that she travelled alone all the way,' Jonah added. 'We found CC-TV footage of her walking along Cornmarket and turning into George Street – still on her own – and that's where we lost her.'

'So she could have been telling the truth when she said she was going to the cinema,' Anna suggested, 'even if she didn't have any intention of coming home again afterwards.'

'None of the staff there remembered seeing her,' Jonah replied, 'but that doesn't mean she wasn't there. My guess is that she'd probably arranged to meet someone there, the question is: who? We had our social media experts go over her online activity, looking for signs of grooming, but everything seemed completely innocent. For a fifteen year old, she seemed to do surprisingly little of that sort of thing, and all her online friends appeared to be people she knew from other places – school and riding lessons and dancing classes and-'

'And the choir and the orchestra and the pony club,' Bernie went on. 'Her social life was a constant whirl of activity.'

It meant that we had an enormous number of her "friends" to interview,' Jonah continued. 'It soon became obvious that none of them – or maybe only one or two – could really be described as friends. She had a "numerous acquaintance" as Jane Austen puts it, but hardly any close friends.'

THE SECRET GARDENER

'The only one that seemed to care about her at all was Ella Campbell, the girl she was supposed to be going to the cinema with,' Bernie put in. 'A lot of the others made a lot of wailing and gnashing of teeth about her disappearance, but I reckon it was all just histrionics. Teenage girls are experts at stirring up imaginary emotions and it made them feel important to think that someone they knew might have been abducted or murdered or even just run away from home.'

'Ella was also the only one who had anything remotely useful to tell us,' Jonah agreed. 'She eventually confided that Mollie had talked about a boyfriend who was older than her and owned a car and a house. Unfortunately that was all she could tell us – no name or address, not even where Mollie had met him.'

'There were television appeals and campaigns on social media calling for anyone who had seen her to come forward,' Bernie continued, 'which produced hundreds of supposed sightings, but they all came to nothing.'

'As did all the man-hours we devoted to house-to-house enquiries and searches of open land near her house,' Jonah added. 'There was a rumour that she'd been seen near the canal, so we sent down divers, but nothing came of it. The case was still open when I retired.'

'And it's still open now,' Anna said grimly, 'but at least now we know that she's still alive – or was last Wednesday night. Thank you for filling me in.'

'Do you think Hillier could've been this older boyfriend that Mollie's friend talked about?' asked Bernie. 'Could that be why she was there with him?'

'Surely not!' exclaimed Peter, who had been doing some mental arithmetic to work out the age difference. 'He must have been more like her grandparents' age. I know teenage girls do sometimes admire older men, but surely that would be going too far?'

'And anyway, where could he have been keeping her all this time?' Jonah asked.

'At Augusta Peckforton's house,' Bernie answered promptly. 'She was ill, remember, and needed looking after. Maybe there were parts of the house that she couldn't get to.'

'Or could he have kidnapped Mollie in order to make her into a sort of nurse or domestic servant for Augusta?' suggested Anna.

'Maybe not even kidnapped exactly,' Bernie speculated. 'Suppose this boyfriend dumped her and Hillier found her wandering the streets and offered her somewhere to stay on condition that she helped out around the house? He may not have realised how young she was. If she told him she was eighteen, he'd probably have believed her.'

'Have you told Mollie's parents yet?' Jonah asked sharply, suddenly remembering that they had been tacitly encouraged to assume that their daughter would never be found.

'No. I was …,' Anna hesitated. 'I was hoping that you might …?'

'Of course! No problem!' Jonah answered eagerly. 'I'll be happy to help. We can go round now, if you like.'

'Oh no you don't!' Bernie intervened, smiling but determined. 'It's far too late. Leave it to the morning. There's no hurry – unless Anna's planning to release the information to the press tonight.'

'No no,' Anna assured them hastily. 'There's no need for that. Tomorrow will be plenty of time. Could you …? Would you be able to come in and brief the team after you've spoken to the Burgesses? I think it would be useful for them to hear about your investigation from the horse's mouth.'

As everybody present knew he would be, Jonah was delighted at the prospect of being back in the thick of things, and he readily agreed to spend the whole of the next day helping Anna. She got up to go, feeling distinctly relieved that her much depleted team was now augmented by a trusted experienced officer with a reputation for solving difficult cases.

Peter escorted her to the door.

'How are the kids doing?' he asked. 'Will Jess be going off to uni next term?'

'Sort of. She's got a place at Oxford Brookes[7]. She insisted that she wanted to stay living at home, so she can carry on helping with Donna.' Anna sighed. 'I'm very grateful to her. I don't know how I'd have managed without her these last two years, but her being at home will make things all the more difficult if

---

[7] Oxford Brookes University is one of several new universities that gained university status in 1992.

Phil does come back.'

'That's really on the cards then, is it?'

'He wants it, and I don't see how I can really refuse at the end of the day. It's just … it's just I can't get over his arrogance, expecting us all to jump to and go with him when he decided to up sticks and go off to Devon. If he'd only talked to us first! And Jess makes no attempt to hide her resentment of him every time he comes to stay. She just can't forgive him for wanting to have Donna aborted.' Anna sighed again. 'But I've bored you with all this before. I'd better be going. Thanks for … well, thanks.'

7. SIGHTINGS

The house in Wheatley did not seem to have changed much during the two years since Jonah's final visit, when he had explained to Alan Burgess and his wife that, although the file on their daughter's disappearance would be kept open, the hunt for her was to be stepped down, in the absence of any untried lines of investigation. The security gates were still smartly painted in black, and the lawns on either side of the curved drive were still immaculate. A powerful car was parked in front of the house, facing towards the road.

The lifestyle of its inhabitants did not appear to have changed much either. When they arrived, Alan Burgess was standing on the steps of the bungalow, dressed in a business suit with a briefcase in his hand, clearly intent on leaving for work the moment they had delivered their message. Geraldine Naylor was not there. Her husband explained that she was in Peru finalising a deal for the importation of genuine Andean alpaca wool.

'Mr Burgess,' Jonah began, tipping his head back in an attempt to make eye contact, 'as I said on the phone, we have some news about your daughter Mollie. Do you think we could come in?'

'As you can see, I'm on my way out,' Burgess replied impatiently, coming down the steps and walking past Jonah to reach his car. He stood on the drive with his hand on the door of the silver Audi. 'I don't really understand why you couldn't have told me whatever it is over the phone.'

'We are investigating the death of a man in the grounds of Lichfield College the Wednesday before last,' Jonah told him. 'At the scene, we found traces of blood, which have now been identified as almost certainly belonging to Mollie. We believe that she was there and that she left the scene alive, possibly in the company of another woman, who also left traces of genetic material there.'

Alan Burgess froze in the act of opening the car door. His hand tightened on the handle and then dropped to his side; his mouth fell open. He stared round at Jonah and Bernie, and blinked several times.

'She's alive? He stammered at last. 'Are you sure?'

'Nothing is absolutely sure,' Jonah replied, pleased to have gained his full attention at last, 'but everything points towards that. Here's a picture of the man we think she was with last week.' He glanced towards Bernie who produced a photograph of Robin Hillier from her pocket and handed it to Burgess. 'Have you ever seen this man before?'

Burgess studied the photograph then offered it back to Bernie, shaking his head as he did so. 'No, never seen him before in my life.'

'Keep the picture,' Jonah instructed, 'and show it to your wife when she gets home. We think it's possible that Mollie could have been living with him since she disappeared. It would be useful if you could both think back to before then and see if you can remember him being around at all before that.'

Burgess nodded, slipping the picture into his jacket pocket. 'What happens now?'

'We will be putting out an appeal to the public to report any sightings of Mollie around the time that we now know she was in Oxford last week,' Jonah told him. 'It's important that your wife knows about this new evidence before that. How can we contact her?'

'Use her mobile number.' Burgess fumbled in his pocket and produced a business card headed "Naylor's Naturals: fine fabrics from around the world". He handed it to Bernie. 'You should get through to her on that.'

'Thank you Mr Burgess. We'll go now – unless you have any more questions?'

THE SECRET GARDENER

'No, no – that's fine. I need to get off myself anyway.' Burgess snapped back into the role of a busy professional with no time to waste chatting to police officers. He opened the door of his car and stood looking over it for a moment before getting in. 'Thank you for telling me about this. Please keep me informed.'

'This is Mollie Burgess,' Anna told her depleted team, as a photograph of a fair-haired girl appeared on the screen in front of them. 'She left home about three years ago and hasn't been seen since. Now, traces of her blood have been found on Robin Hillier's person and on the door leading from the Fellows' Garden at Lichfield College into Goose Lane. DCI Porter was the senior investigating officer, which is why I've invited him along today to fill you in on the background to the case.'

She sat down and Jonah took her place at the front of the room. He looked round. Many of the faces were familiar: Andy Lepage, of course, and most of the civilian staff who would be manning the telephone lines and studying CC-TV footage; but there were a few that he did not recognise, people who had joined the force since his retirement or who had been transferred from other departments.

THE SECRET GARDENER

'Mollie Burgess was fifteen when she left home,' he told them, 'which means that she is now eighteen. These are her parents.'

Portraits of Geraldine Naylor and Alan Burgess appeared on the screen alongside Mollie's photograph.

'Her mother, Geraldine, is the owner of *Naylor's Naturals*, which is a company that specialises in producing clothing and household textiles from natural fibres: wool, cotton, linen etcetera. She seems to spend most of her time jetting off around the world on business. Father, Alan, is an accountant and a partner in *Burgess Lipton*, which has offices in Thame. The day Mollie left home, they thought she was going out for a night at the pictures with a school friend. However, she took a bag of clothes with her and it looks very much as if she was planning to stay away from home.'

'Planning to stay with Hillier, do you think?' asked Andy.

'We don't know,' Jonah answered. 'Mollie's father didn't recognise him and we haven't found anything to link her with him. On the other hand, now that we know that she's alive and still in the Oxford area, it seems pretty clear that someone must have been keeping her hidden for the past three years. That could be Hillier or it could be the woman with the long black hair who was there in the Fellows' garden with them or it could be someone we don't know about yet.'

'Maybe Hillier abducted Mollie *and* the other woman,' Andy suggested. 'And they turned on him and stabbed him in order to get away.'

'I think we'd better interview Augusta Peckforton's neighbours again,' Anna agreed. 'If he was holding them, it must have been at her house. We could do with speaking to her sister as well, in case she saw any signs when she took it over. However, there's something else that may need to take priority over that. A call came through this morning from a witness who thinks she saw Hillier buying breakfast for two young women last Wednesday morning. She works in a coffee bar in the centre of Oxford. I want you to go over and take a statement and see if she recognises Mollie's photograph. There are CC-TV cameras in the street outside, so I've asked for tapes from the whole of last week to be sent over in case they're on those.'

'Why don't I do that?' suggested Jonah eagerly. 'In fact, why don't you ask the Chief Super to bring me into your team on a temporary basis, while you're so short of manpower? It's only good sense for me to help out, when I know all about the Mollie Burgess case.'

'Well, I can ask her,' Anna replied doubtfully. 'I'm seeing her in a few minutes anyway, as it happens. She's had the DCC on her back about that Sri Lankan girl who disappeared last year and wants to talk to me about it. If she's expecting me to take that on again as well as this, I hope she'll give me back Monica and Alice. I'll ask her if she can give you some sort of temporary ID. Without that, I don't see I can send you out to interview witnesses. It was OK with the Burgesses, because they already knew you.'

'Tell her I don't expect to get paid,' Jonah added hopefully. 'I'm happy to do it on a voluntary basis – like a Special Constable.'

'Meanwhile, how about you getting stuck in and going through some of the CC-TV footage,' suggested Bernie mischievously. She knew that Jonah's chief weakness, as a detective, was his impatience with the dull routine aspects of the job. 'There must be plenty of work to do there, if we've got a week's worth of tapes from several cameras.'

'Or I could go along with Andy and help interview the waitress,' Jonah said quickly, treating Anna to one of his most endearing smiles. She smiled back. It was difficult to refuse him when he was in this mood: like an eager puppy waiting to have a ball thrown.

'OK,' she conceded, 'I can't see any harm in that. 'And I *will* have a word with Alison about letting you on the team officially. And, talking of Alison, that's where I ought to be now.' She raised her eyes and looked round the room. 'OK guys, you know what to do. Let's catch up again at three this afternoon.'

'I couldn't swear to it,' Tamsin Docherty murmured as she stared down at the photograph that Andy held out. 'She looked a lot older, but then school uniform always makes people look young, doesn't it?'

'She *is* older now,' Jonah told

her. 'This photograph was taken three years ago.'

'Well then, I think it might be her, but … I still couldn't be sure. I wasn't really noticing that much.'

'What about this man?' Andy asked, replacing Mollie's photograph with a picture of Robin Hillier, which had been produced by enhancing the photograph on his driving licence.

'Yes,' Tamsin sounded more confident now. 'That's the man. I recognised him from the Facebook post the police put out. He came in with two girls – the one who might be the same as that picture you showed me, and a black woman – they sat down at one of the tables over there.'

THE SECRET GARDENER

She pointed towards a dark corner of the room well away from the windows. 'And he came over to the counter and ordered three coffees and bacon baguettes.'

'How did he pay?' asked Jonah.

'Cash.'

'And then he ate breakfast with the two women?' asked Andy. 'Did they go out together after that?'

'I suppose so,' Tamsin answered cautiously. 'I wasn't noticing. It's always quite busy at that time of day. We get a lot of office workers and university staff calling in for breakfast before they start work.'

'How did they seem together?' enquired Jonah. 'I mean – did the women seem frightened of the man at all? Or ... what sort of relationship did they seem to have with him – and with each other?'

'I really couldn't say,' Tamsin answered, looking rather uncomfortable. 'I mean – I only saw them for a few minutes. They did seem a bit nervy, I suppose. The black one in particular kept looking around as if she thought there might be someone they knew in the shop. And they kept whispering together while they were waiting for the man to come back with the food.'

'I see,' Andy nodded. 'Now, can you concentrate on the black woman for a minute? Can you describe her too me?'

'Well,' Tamsin considered the

question for a moment. 'Like I said, she was black – I mean she had dark skin.'

'How dark?' Andy probed. 'Like me? Or darker?'

Tamsin studied his face. Andy was the result of a love affair between a young college servant and a mature postgraduate student from Nigeria. His face was the colour of milk chocolate, his eyes were deep brown and his hair was jet black and frizzy.

'Darker than you,' she said at last, 'but her hair was straight, not Afro like yours. I thought that was odd, because usually … Well, anyway, that's why I remember, but I suppose she could've had it straightened. Some of them do, don't they?' She made a sharp intake of breath and then gabbled on, blushing and appearing flustered. 'I'm sorry. Was that rude? I didn't mean to … I mean … I don't really think of people as *us* and *them* – honestly!'

'I think we need to consider the possibility that Mollie Burgess and Amanda Jayakody are together,' Jonah told Anna, when the team reconvened that afternoon. 'The description that the waitress gave of the other woman could easily be her.'

THE SECRET GARDENER

'It'd be a bit of a coincidence, though,' Anna replied sceptically. 'Anyway, I'm here to tell you that the Chief Super has agreed to have you back temporarily. She's merging the three enquiries and she wants you to lead on the Mollie Burgess aspect. Arshad Khan is to have overall charge and specific responsibility for Pandora Birch. Her disappearance has enough similarities with the Mollie Birch case that there's at least a chance they're connected. I'm still in charge of Robin Hillier's murder, but now that the cases appear to be linked, I've got to keep DCI Khan informed about anything we do. You are reporting to me, but you need to keep him in the loop too.'

'And what about Amanda Jayakody?' persisted Jonah. 'Who's going to be looking for her?'

'The Chief Super agrees with me that it's most likely that she's lying low because her visa's expired and she's working illegally.'

'Which could mean that she's in danger of modern slavery,' Jonah insisted. 'So what are we doing about it?'

'Alison's got an appointment with the woman's father on Monday. She's not doing anything more about it until after that. I've filled her in with everything we found out last time and she'll decide who to deploy and how much resource we can afford. Now, please can we concentrate on our own enquiries and stop worrying about-'

'But Amanda's disappearance could be connected too,' Jonah interrupted. 'She could be the other woman who was with Hillier just before he was killed.'

'Or that may be someone completely different ,' Anna argued, beginning to wonder if having Jonah on the team was going to be more trouble than it was worth. She turned and raised her voice to address the room. 'Now, does anyone have anything useful to report?'

'Please ma'am,' one of the civilian staff raised her hand. 'I've got something on the CC-TV that might tell us who the other woman is. It's

Hillier and the two women caught on camera not far from the coffee shop last Wednesday morning.'

'That'll be worth seeing,' Jonah broke in eagerly. 'Can you get it up on the screen?'

A minute or so later, they were all watching intently as fuzzy figures moved along the street. The angle of the camera made it difficult to see faces, especially if the person of interest had a hat on or a hood up.

'That's him!' Andy called, as a tall man appeared at the bottom of the screen. 'That's the shirt he had on under his overalls when we found him.'

'And those are the two women,' Jonah added. 'Just behind him. It doesn't *look* as if he's forcing them to go with him. It's more as if he's leading the way and they're following.'

'They could easily get away from him if they wanted to, in this crowd,' Bernie agreed.

'But he might have some hold over them that makes them too scared to try,' Anna pointed out.

The figures moved up the screen, becoming obscured by others as more people followed them along the busy street.

'Are there any more cameras further up that road?' Anna asked.

'Yes,' confirmed another of the staff from behind a computer at the side of the room. 'But we haven't had time to look at the footage from there yet.'

'Well you'd better get on and do that,' Anna told him. 'What would be really useful would be a view of them from a camera that's facing the other way, so that there's a chance of seeing their faces. And meanwhile, Steff!' she turned back to the woman who had provided the images that they had been watching, 'see if you can get a couple of still pictures out of this – with the three of them together. And get them enhanced, will you? I'd like to put them out on the news together with pictures of Mollie Burgess and Robin Hillier. Surely *someone* must have seen where they went after this.'

THE SECRET GARDENER

'More to the point,' Jonah said drily. 'Did anyone see the two women later on, after they'd left Hillier for dead in the Fellows' Garden?'

8. DILEMMA

'Peter? Are you busy this afternoon?' Father Damien's voice was unusually tentative. 'I could really do with speaking with you. I need some advice. Could you come over?'

'Yes, that'll be no bother,' Peter assured him, wondering what this unexpected summons could be about. 'The grandkids are with their mum today, so I'm free as a bird. Shall I pop round right away?'

'If you don't mind. I wouldn't ask only it's a bit … well, I'll explain when you come.'

Peter locked the back door, scribbled a note for Bernie, in case he was still out when she and Jonah returned, and left the house. As he walked the short distance to St Cyprian's presbytery, he pondered on what it could possibly be that was so urgent and so secret. And what sort of advice could a priest of some twenty years' experience require from a convert who had joined the church little over a year before? Clearly, this must be a temporal rather than a spiritual matter, but on what subject could Peter be considered sufficiently expert to be the counsellor of choice?

Damien was waiting for him at

the door when he arrived. He ushered him through to the familiar study, where he had prepared Peter for his confirmation. There were two steaming mugs of coffee and a plate of homemade flapjacks (the gift of a parishioner) on the round table in the centre of the room. Peter sat down in his usual chair and pulled one of the mugs towards him. The priest took a seat on the opposite side of the table.

For several seconds neither spoke. Damien cleared his throat and opened his mouth, then seemed to change his mind and pushed the plate of biscuits towards Peter.

'Have one of these,' he urged. 'Deirdre seems to have surpassed herself this time. They're very good, but I mustn't eat them all myself.'

Peter took a flapjack but did not bite into it. Instead, he raised his eyes to look his friend in the eye.

'But you didn't call me over here in such a hurry just to help you eat up Deirdre's flapjacks, did you? What's up?'

'It's … you know this schoolgirl the police are appealing for information about?'

'Pandora Birch?'

'Pan-? No, not that one – the other one. Her picture was on the lunchtime news. At least … I think that was it. I didn't see it myself but … I had a phone call just now, from someone who's seen her.'

'Then they ought to contact the police,' Peter told him.

'I know, but it's not as simple as that. You see… she's a good Catholic and she doesn't want people to know … I mean …'

'I'm sorry,' Peter shook his head in bewilderment, 'I don't understand. What doesn't she want people to know?'

'That she was there.'

'Where?'

'At the ab-' Damien broke off suddenly and smiled ruefully across the table at Peter. 'I'm sorry. I'm not making a lot of sense, am I? I think I'd better go back and start the whole story from the beginning.'

'Yes. I think that might help,'

Peter said encouragingly, when his friend failed to continue. Damien took a deep breath and began.

'My sister, Bridget, is married with two kids. They live in Cumnor. She's a qualified nursery teacher, but at the moment she's a full-time mum. Her husband, Aidan, teaches at a Catholic high school in Swindon. She has a history of difficult pregnancies. Benedict – her youngest – had to be delivered very early to save her life. He still has lots of health problems as a result. She came to see me six weeks ago because she'd just discovered that she was expecting again ...'

'I'm frightened,' Bridget told her brother. 'I nearly died last time and the doctor says my kidney function still isn't back to a hundred percent. He's recommending an abortion, but …'

She looked pleadingly into his eyes, willing him to tell her that her circumstances warranted a bending of the church's usual strict stance on preservation of the life of the unborn child.

'We took precautions,' she continued, when he did not reply, 'but I suppose that probably only makes it worse. I mean, we were going against Catholic teaching, weren't we? Except that almost everybody does it, don't they?'

'Yes, I think you're probably right,' Damien agreed. 'Of course, they don't tell me about it, but Catholic families are certainly a lot smaller than they used to be. But, getting back to you – what does Aidan say?'

'I haven't told him yet. I only got the test result on Friday. He thinks it was just a routine one monitoring my kidneys – which it was, until this turned up! Oh Damien! I don't think I can bear to go through all that again! And there are the other kids to think about – especially Ben. He's way behind other children his age and his seizures aren't getting any better. He needs me – they both do! I just can't take the risk! That's why I came to see you. I was hoping you'd have an answer.'

'An answer to what, exactly?' asked Damien gently.

'I don't want to commit a mortal sin,' Bridget answered almost inaudibly, 'but I don't want to die either.'

'I'm sorry,' her brother sighed, leaning across to take her hands in his. 'I wish I could tell you otherwise, but the church's teaching is clear. It isn't permitted to sacrifice one life in order to save another.'

'Do you really think that God wants me to die, rather than ...?' Bridget asked in a whisper.

'No. I'm sure He doesn't,' Damien came back immediately. 'He wants the best for you *and* your baby.'

'And what about Marie and Ben? What about Aidan? I know he wouldn't be able to cope – even just if I have to be in hospital for weeks the way I was with Ben.'

'God loves them too. I'm sure of it.'

'So why …? Why doesn't He …? Why didn't He stop me getting so ill when I was expecting Ben? Why doesn't He cure Ben's epilepsy?'

'I think He usually leaves that to the doctors.'

'The doctors say I ought to have an abortion.'

They sat together for several minutes without speaking.

'So, you think I ought to go through with it and trust God that everything will be OK?' Bridget asked at last. 'You don't think there's any … loophole, for this sort of situation?'

'I don't know – honestly, I don't. At the end of the day it's for you and Aidan to decide. You asked me what the church's teaching is, and I can only tell you that, according to Catholic doctrine, the life of the unborn child has exactly the same value as the life of anyone else – including the mother. I'm sorry, I wish I could tell you differently, but that's what the Church has always accepted.'

'I know,' Bridget agreed

miserably. 'And I don't *want* to kill my baby. I'm just so frightened,' her voice dropped to a whisper again. 'I'm so frightened that we'll both die and Aidan will be left with Marie and Ben, and he won't be able to cope. Ben needs so much help and I'm the only one who … no that's not fair. Aidan's very good with both of them, but …'

'Young children need their mother,' Damien finished for her. 'I – I -,' he broke off in confusion. Then, after gathering his thoughts, 'if it's any consolation, I wouldn't think badly of you if you decided an abortion was the only solution. And I'm sure God would understand too. Think about Jesus and the woman found in adultery.'

'But he said to her "go and sin no more", didn't he? And if I go ahead with something *knowing* it's a mortal sin ...'

'Only in the eyes of the Church,' her brother said gently. 'There are plenty of people – good Christian people – who would say that you have a right to take into account your own safety and the interests of your other children. I'm really not the best person for you to have come to. As a priest, I've got to give you the party line, but as your brother, I – I – I wouldn't blame you if – if your conscience told you something different.'

'But the baby wouldn't be

baptised,' Bridget moaned. 'That's why, if I could be sure that *they*'d be OK, I'd take the risk with myself. I'm just scared that I might be putting Aidan and the kids through hell for nothing, if we both die and the baby goes to limbo.'

'Well, you can set your mind at rest about that at any rate,' Damien told her, relieved to be able to offer a small crumb of comfort. 'Pope Benedict gave his approval to a report by the International Theological Commission, which said that there's no such place as limbo and no reason to believe that God won't draw unbaptised infants to Himself in eternity, just the same as any baptised Christian. He has a loving plan for them; we just can't know what it is.'

'Really? Are you sure?'

'Absolutely,' Damien said firmly. 'Baptism isn't some sort of magic. It's all symbolic, and I've known lots of people who've never been baptised who deserve to go to heaven a whole lot more than some of the Catholic serial offenders that it's been my pleasure to minister to in prisons!'

'So, what do you think I ought to do?' asked Bridget, after thinking about this for a few moments.

'First off, you need to talk to Aidan,' Damien replied, speaking quietly but firmly. 'Whatever you decide, it has to be something that both of you are comfortable with – or at least, maybe not comfortable, but you have to agree that what you're doing is … the least worst option, I suppose.'

'OK.' Bridget got up. 'I'd better go now. I left the kids with Mum, but it's not fair to expect her to cope with Ben for more than a couple of hours. He's so demanding.'

'Did you tell her why you were coming here?'

'No. Actually, I didn't even tell her this is where I am. I said I needed to shop for some new shoes – so I suppose I'd better try and pick some up in Oxford before I go back. I don't want her to know about this – you won't tell her, will you? I just *know* she'd be upset that I'd even *thought* about you-know-what!'

'Don't worry. I'll treat what you've told me as being under the seal of the confessional,' Damien promised.

Bridget picked up her handbag and made for the door. 'Thank you for listening. I feel a lot better now.'

'I'm just sorry I couldn't give you a proper answer.' Damien dismissed her thanks with a wave of his hand. 'Just remember – I won't be judging you, whatever you and Aidan decide in the end.'

Damien gathered up the two empty mugs and got to his feet.

THE SECRET GARDENER

'I think I need a re-fill. How about you?'

Peter followed the priest out to the kitchen, where they poured more coffee from a percolator on the working surface next to the sink and added milk from the fridge.

'As I said, that was all six weeks ago, and I hadn't heard from Bridget since – until this afternoon.'

'So she didn't tell you what she and her husband had decided?' asked Peter.

'No. I don't think I was expecting her to. Or at least, only if they were keeping the baby. By this time, I had a pretty shrewd idea that they must have gone for the abortion, because otherwise there'd have been an announcement of the prospect of a *happy event*, but even so, I wasn't sure.'

He led the way back to the study, carrying one mug in each hand.

'And now?' prompted Peter.

'That's where this girl I was telling you about comes in.' Damien slumped down into the chair and rested his elbows on the table, cradling the coffee mug in his hands. 'That's where Bridget saw her – in the abortion clinic.'

'And she doesn't want to talk to the police, in case it gets out that she was there having a termination,' Peter exclaimed, understanding at last.

'That's right. She saw the photo

on the lunchtime news and she's convinced that it's the same girl as she saw in the waiting room there. 'She rang me right away, because I'm the only other person – apart from Aidan and her doctor – who knows anything about it. She's worried about our parents – or any of their friends – getting to hear. I asked her for permission to talk to you, in confidence. She wants to do the right thing, but …Would the police keep it all confidential, do you think?'

'Up to a point,' Peter answered cautiously. 'I mean – there wouldn't be any need for them to release her name during the enquiry. It would only be if they needed her to give evidence in court ...'

'Is that likely?'

'I shouldn't think so, but I couldn't actually rule it out. It all depends exactly what she saw and whether any offence was being committed at the time.'

'If she told you all about it, could you pass on the information to the police without involving her directly?' Damien suggested. 'Could you keep her name out if it, do you think?'

'I suppose so,' Peter said slowly, 'but I couldn't give her any cast iron guarantees that they wouldn't need to interview her formally later – if it did come to a prosecution and her evidence was necessary for it to succeed.'

'I understand. Will you do it then? Tomorrow's Saturday, so Aidan'll be at home to look after the kids. If I ask her to come over here in the morning, could you come round and have a chat with her?'

'Yes, of course, anything to help – just so long as she understands I can only do my best regarding keeping her name out of it.'

'Good. I'll ring her right away. I know it'll be a weight off her mind to have told someone officially. She was anxious not to be the person who prevented the girl being found.'

'Yes, the girl.' Peter put out his hand to prevent Damien picking up his phone. 'Can we just be clear which girl it is that we're talking about? You said it wasn't Pandora Birch. I'm not aware of any other girl's photo being circulated.'

'I haven't seen it either,' Damien confessed. 'Bridget said it was new on the news today, but that it was an old case that had been re-opened.'

'Mollie Burgess?' hazarded Peter.

'Yes! That's the name. So you do know about it?'

'It was one of Jonah's cases, before he retired,' Peter told him. 'And now, they're looking into it again, because traces of her blood have turned up on a murder victim – the man who was found in Lichfield College last week.'

'What day last week?'

THE SECRET GARDENER

'He was found early Thursday morning, presumed killed Wednesday night.'

'And Bridget saw the girl – Mollie – on the Monday afternoon,' Damien observed thoughtfully

'Two days before she's known to have been in the Fellows' Garden at Lichfield with a man, who later turns up dead, and another unidentified woman,' Peter finished. 'The police certainly need to know exactly what your sister saw at that clinic.'

9. WITNESS EVIDENCE

Peter arrived early at St Cyprian's the next day and slipped into the church before his appointment with Damien and his sister was due. For Bernie's benefit, he had invented a harmless fiction involving a couple of renegades from the Youth Club, to explain why he needed to commit perhaps the whole morning to a meeting at the presbytery. Now he was hoping for a few minutes to himself before what he anticipated would be a difficult interview.

He pulled the door closed behind

him and stood for a moment, waiting for his eyes to adjust to the relative darkness within. Soft light filtered through the large stained glass window on his left and dappled the floor ahead of him with kaleidoscope colours. He hastened across to the far side of the church and then turned to go down the left-hand aisle, past the confession room and the small side chapel to the front of the main seating area. He sat down on the front pew and bowed his head briefly in prayer.

Then he raised his head again and gazed up at a statue of the Virgin Mary, which stood against the pillar that separated the side chapel from the body of the church. 'What would you do?' he asked her. 'What can I say to her?'

The virgin stared back with the expression of wistful anxiety that she always had on her face. Peter got up and went closer. She was almost life size and standing on a plinth, so her face was level with his. Her skin was a warm brown colour, similar to that of Peter's children, Hannah and Eddie. She was holding the infant Christ who, seemingly far more serene and confident than his mother, had his right hand raised, delivering a blessing.

'It must have been risky for you, too,' Peter murmured. 'It was always risky for women in those days. Were you frightened? But I suppose you'd had an angel promising you that it was all going to turn out OK. Did you believe him? Did you sometimes hope it had all just been a dream and you wouldn't have to go through with it?'

He put out his hand and stroked the cold painted plaster of her blue gown. He tried to imagine what it must have been like for Bridget and her husband having to choose between risking her life and destroying their unborn child. What if he and Angie had faced that dilemma when she was expecting Eddie? He knew what he would have wanted. He would have put Angie's safety above every other consideration. Losing the baby would have been a blow, but compared with the anguish of Angie's death …!

But it would have had to be Angie's decision in the end, and she would most likely have taken the opposite view. She would have wanted to leave it in God's hands and trusted that whatever happened was his will.

'You'll put in a good word for Bridget, won't you?' Peter whispered. 'You understand she was only acting for the best – for her family.'

There was the sound of a door opening and soft footsteps on the tiled floor. Peter looked round to see Father Damien entering the church from the passageway that connected it to the presbytery.

'Bridget's here,' he told Peter. 'Are you ready or shall I tell her to give you a few more minutes?'

'It's OK. I'll come now.'

Peter followed his friend back down the corridor, past the choir vestry and the church office and into the priest's home. This time, Damien led him into the lounge where his sister was sitting, looking very nervous, on an easy chair near a window overlooking the garden at the back of the house. She got up when they entered and took a step towards them, holding out her hand.

'Peter, this is my sister Bridget,' Damien introduced them. 'Bridget –

DI Peter Johns, or at least he used to be a DI before he retired to be a full-time childminder and house-husband!'

'Pleased to meet you,' Bridget murmured, glancing nervously up at Peter as they shook hands, and then dropping her eyes again abruptly. They were brown, like her brother's and there was something about the set of her jaw that was similar too, but her hair, fastened in an austere coil at the nape of her neck, was a much paler shade than his.

'Me too,' Peter muttered back, then, a little louder. 'I mean, thank you for coming forward and I hope I can help.'

'Why don't you two sit down and

get to know each other while I get us some coffee?' suggested Damien, disappearing in the direction of the kitchen without waiting for an answer.

Peter held out his arm inviting Bridget to return to her seat. Then he pulled another chair round so that he was sitting close and at an angle where he could look her in the eye.

'It's a terrible thing to lose a child,' Peter said tentatively.

Bridget nodded, seemed to be about to speak then changed her mind. She sat, staring down at her hands, which were clasped together in her lap.

'I know the police officer who tried to find Mollie Burgess when she left home three years ago,' Peter tried again. 'He's back on the case again, now that we know she's still alive. If you know anything about her movements in the last couple of weeks, you can tell me and I'll pass it on. You won't need to go to the police station or sign a statement or anything.'

'And you won't need to tell them my name?' Bridget asked in a whisper.

'No. I can just say it was someone who spoke to your brother. They'll just assume it's one of his parishioners – or even,' he added, seeing Bridget about to raise an objection, 'a complete stranger who decided to confide in a priest because they didn't want to go to the police.'

'I see.' Bridget sat in silence thinking this over.

'Damien told me you have two children,' Peter began again. 'A girl and a boy – is that right?'

'Yes.' Bridget brightened up a little. 'Marie's four and Benedict's three. Their father's looking after them this morning.'

'They're just a year older than my grandchildren,' Peter told her. 'It's hard work having two kids so close together. I know, because I get to have them four or five days most weeks. Their mum has to work or she might not be allowed to stay in the country.'

'That's dreadful! Would they really separate a mother from her children like that?'

'I hope not, but we don't want to take the risk of finding out. Her visa is based on her being in a shortage occupation'

'Here we are!' Damien declared cheerily, coming in and setting down a tray on a low table standing against the wall under the window. He gave a mug of coffee each to Peter and Bridget and then offered round the inevitable plate of flapjacks. 'Shall I stay, or would you rather I left you to it?'

'I think I'd prefer you to be here – if that's alright with you, Bridget?' Peter answered.

THE SECRET GARDENER

Bridget nodded. 'Fine by me.'

They sat nibbling their biscuits and sipping their coffee. After a while, Peter took the lead.

'Bridget,' he said softly, leaning towards her a little, 'you told Damien that you'd seen Mollie Burgess, the girl who's been missing for three years. Could you tell me about it, please?'

'It was in the waiting room at the – the abortion clinic,' Bridget answered, going red and lowering her eyes. 'I – you – I suppose you know why I was there?'

'You brother told me what a difficult decision it was for you,' Peter assured her quietly. 'I'm glad my wife and I were never in such an awful situation. I was thinking about it just now. I honestly don't know what we'd have done.'

'I felt awful about it,' Bridget confessed. 'It felt like I was committing a murder, but Marie had chicken pox and Benedict's fits got worse and he was admitted to hospital for three days and I decided that I just couldn't risk … I was afraid I might be in hospital for weeks, the way I was when I was having Ben. And then it would have all been down to Aidan and my mum and dad to cope. And then my blood pressure was up and there was protein in my urine and the doctor said …' her voice dropped, becoming almost inaudible. 'I was a coward. I didn't want to die.'

'I don't think you were a coward,' Peter said quietly. 'I think it was very brave of you to put your family first.'

'But I killed my baby! Maybe if I'd just waited a few more weeks they could've delivered her early – like they did with Ben – and she'd have survived.'

'But you don't know that,' Peter insisted softly. 'It might have gone the other way and you might both have died. And you were only trying to do what was best for your children, and your husband, and your mum and dad. I'm just a very new Catholic and I don't know what the clever theologians would say, but from where I'm looking, there doesn't seem to be a right thing for you to do, and you just did the best you could.'

'And I think Peter's right,' Damien backed him up, speaking quietly but firmly. 'I've been looking into it. If you'd had cancer and needed a hysterectomy to save your life, the Church would allow it. I don't see that this is any different.'

'Do you really think so?' Bridget looked hopefully across at her brother, who nodded.

'I do. And I also believe that God is bigger than the Church and I'm sure He understands exactly why you did it and doesn't blame you at all.'

'I haven't been to Mass since,'

Bridget mumbled. 'I didn't feel I could.'

'Have you talked to your own priest about it?' Damien asked.

'No. I didn't know how to ... I mean: how could I confess a mortal sin when I'm not really sorry I did it?'

'I'll give you absolution,' Damien promised. 'I won't have you feeling like an outcast when you were only doing your best. But maybe we ought to move on now. Peter came to hear about that missing girl that you saw.'

'Yes, of course.' Bridget turned towards Peter. 'As I said, I was there in the waiting room, very nervous and hoping nobody I knew would come along – not that I thought they would, because it's not the sort of place … but you never know, one of the mums from nursery could've worked there or something. Anyway, this girl came in. She looked even more terrified than I felt. There was an older woman with her. Her mother I suppose, although they didn't look much alike.'

'Could you describe her to me?' Peter asked, getting out a small notebook and a pencil from his pocket.

'She had bleached blond hair and lots of makeup on her face,' Bridget told him. 'And I particularly noticed a tattoo of a parrot on her hand.'

'That's useful to know,' Peter

said encouragingly. 'Do you happen to remember which hand?'

'Her ... her right I think,' Bridget screwed up her face in concentration as she pictured the scene in her mind. 'Yes. I'm sure of it. I noticed it when she reached across to wipe the girl's face with a tissue. She'd been crying I think and her mascara had run.'

'OK. Good. And you're sure it was Mollie Burgess that you saw – the girl that the police put out an appeal about yesterday?'

'Yes. I'm quite sure. She hadn't changed much from the picture on the news and I know her name was Mollie because the other woman called her that.'

'And did Mollie use the woman's name at all?' asked Peter hopefully.

'No.' Bridget shook her head. 'I did hear them talking about someone called "Zack" though.'

'That's interesting. Could you tell what his relationship was to Mollie or the other woman?'

'Not really. The woman seemed to be using him as a sort of threat to force Mollie to do what she wanted. I heard her say something like, "if you don't co-operate, Zack will be angry, and you know what that means, don't you?" or something like that. The poor girl looked scared stiff.'

'So you're pretty sure the girl was there to have a termination?' Peter asked.

'Yes. Definitely. They called me in and took my history, and did a scan to check the age of the foetus. Then they sent me back out again to wait for the doctor who was going to … It was a medical abortion: the doctor gave me a tablet to take and then I had to take another one the next day. Anyway, when I came out, the waiting room was empty, but then the girl – Mollie – came back. She looked terribly young and vulnerable and the woman seemed to be angry with her about something. I felt sorry for her. She was painfully thin and quite obviously pregnant. I remember wondering if she could possibly be less than twenty-four weeks, but maybe it just showed more because she was so skinny.'

'What you've told us is tremendously helpful,' Peter assured her earnestly. 'With your permission, I'll pass it on to the police team. There should be no need from them to talk to you. They can contact the clinic and they'll be able to confirm everything. They should have a record of whatever name she booked in under, and an address and family doctor. With any luck, this will mean they'll be able to track her down without you being involved at all.'

'I do hope so!' Bridget breathed wholeheartedly. 'I've kept thinking about how worried her poor parents must be, not knowing where she's been all these years and probably fearing the worst.'

'Yes,' Peter agreed, remembering Bernie's description of Mollie's mother and father and wondering how much thought they had really been giving to their absent daughter among their busy lives. 'It will be a great weight off their minds if your evidence helps us to find her.'

Jonah was very excited to hear Bridget's story, when Peter related it to him over lunch. True to his promise, Peter kept her identity secret, explaining that the witness was a Catholic who did not want it to be known that she had visited an abortion clinic. Passing the information on officially was more difficult. Knowing that she was off-duty for the weekend, Peter rang Anna at home, only to be told by her daughter Jessica that she was away, and was keeping her mobile switched off.

'She's having a *Romantic Weekend* away with Dad,' Jessica explained in tones of deep disgust. 'They're trying to patch things up so he can come back and live with us again. It's their wedding anniversary tomorrow and Dad has this crazy idea that it would be an appropriate time for them to get back together.'

'Maybe it's not such a crazy idea,' Peter suggested gently. 'I expect your mum would find it a help having someone else to look after Donna.'

'She's got me!' Jessica protested indignantly. 'I'm eighteen now. I'm an adult and I know Donna far better than Dad does, because I've been looking after her right from the day she was born.'

'And you've done a really great job of it,' Peter agreed, 'but you can't be there all the time, can you? You'll have to go to lectures and tutorials and things when you start at uni next term. Don't you think it would be useful to have your dad there, working from home the way he used to when you were Donna's age?'

'Well he needn't think he can just swan back in here and start running the house again,' Jessica retorted. 'We've got our routine all sorted. He's going to have to fit in with the way we do things now.'

'I'm sure he understands that,' Peter said, continuing his attempt to reconcile the teenager with her father's possible return to the family home. 'And if he doesn't, I'm sure your mum will see that he does before she lets him back. And I'm sure,' he added as an afterthought as a new idea struck him, 'that Donna will always see *you* as her second mum however much time your dad spends with her.'

Silence. Peter got the impression that Jessica was unconvinced but was reluctant to contradict him.

'Well, I'll tell Mum you rang,' she said abruptly. 'Now, I'd better go. Donna's nappy needs changing.'

'This is Charles,' Sally Pearson told Lucy when she opened the door to them that afternoon. 'Charles – this is Lucy. I think I mentioned her to you. Her father and stepfather were both police officers, and her mum – Oh! Here she is!' she broke off as Bernie appeared from the direction of the kitchen. 'Bernie, let me introduce Charles Jayakody.'

Bernie hurried down the hall to greet the visitors. They were very different from one another in appearance. Sally's pale skin looked positively washed-out alongside her companion's deep brown face and hands. Her greying fair hair contrasted with his neatly trimmed thick black thatch. He was dressed austerely in a black suit over a black shirt with a clerical collar, while she was in "civvies", comprising a gaily-coloured blue and white striped blouse and light blue trousers.

'I'm very pleased to meet you Charles,' Bernie said, holding out her hand, 'although I'm sorry about the reason you're over here. Come and take a seat in the kitchen. The tea's nearly ready.'

She turned to lead the way and almost collided with Jonah's wheelchair, as he emerged from his private quarters, eager to meet the visitors. She stopped and turned back to speak to Charles.

'Let me introduce ex-DCI Jonah Porter. Jonah, this is Charles Jayakody.'

'He used to be in Thames Valley CID and he still has close contact with people there,' Sally added. 'That's why I asked him to report Amanda's disappearance last year.'

Jonah smiled up at Charles, who smiled back a little nervously and mumbled something inconsequential. Sally had briefed him in advance not to offer his hand and, bereft of this traditional routine, he was unsure how to greet a paralysed man in a wheelchair. Jonah studied his face. Yes, assuming that his daughter had a similarly dark complexion, she might well fit the description that the waitress had given of the woman who had accompanied Robin Hillier and Mollie Burgess to the coffee shop ten days ago.

'Well, let's not all stand around here in the hall,' Bernie said, breaking into his thoughts. 'Come and sit down.'

She led the way to the kitchen, where Peter was putting the finishing touches to a salad, which he quickly finished and placed in the centre of the large table. Bernie ushered her guests to their places while Jonah positioned his wheelchair at the end of the table and Lucy sat down next to him. Soon they were all tucking in to slices of fresh bread accompanied by cheese, hard-boiled eggs and a variety of cooked meats.

As soon as the food had been passed round and everyone was eating, Jonah turned to address Charles.

'Sally tells me you're meeting Chief Superintendent Brown on Monday.'

'That's right,' Charles confirmed. 'I had a short telephone

conversation with her yesterday afternoon and she assured me that she had one of her best officers in charge of finding Amanda.'

'Anna Davenport? Yes, I'd agree that you can rely on her,' Peter commented from across the table.

'No. That wasn't the name. It was a man – DCI Khan. She assured me that he was very experienced, but-,' he broke off as he noticed the silence that had descended on the room at his mention of the chief inspector's name. 'What is it? Is there something wrong?'

'No, not at all,' Peter said hastily. 'Arshad Khan has a very good reputation.'

'But he suffers somewhat from

being expected to take on every case that involves an ethnic minority of any sort,' Jonah added. 'And at the moment he's very busy with an urgent missing person enquiry concerning a teenage girl who disappeared only last week and may well have been abducted.'

'So, are you saying he won't have time to look for Amanda?' Charles asked anxiously.

'No, that's not what he means at all,' Peter said quickly. 'It's just that he'll need to delegate things to more junior officers – which would happen anyway as a matter of course. The Senior Investigating Officer co-ordinates the investigation: he doesn't do all the leg-work.'

'But there's something you aren't telling me, isn't there?' Charles persisted, looking round at each of them in turn.

'OK,' Bernie sighed. 'I suppose you'd better know. It's nothing really. It's just that there's a bit of history between him and Peter.'

'It really isn't anything you should be worried about,' Peter hastened to add. 'It's my problem, not anyone else's. I'm sure you can rely on him to find your daughter if it's humanly possible.'

'But what exactly ...?' asked Charles, looking towards Bernie.

'Peter's first wife was a West Indian,' Bernie explained, trying to tell the story as briefly as possible.

'She was killed in a racist attack sixteen years ago. Arshad Khan was on the team that investigated her murder. He was a raw detective sergeant at the time and thought he was an expert on ethnic minorities.'

'Probably because everyone around him assumed he must be,' Peter put in. 'There were hardly any non-white officers on the force in those days.'

'Anyway, he said some pretty crass things to Peter about him not understanding what it was like for his wife to be a black woman in a white society, and managed to create the impression that Peter was implicated in her death, through negligence if not directly.'

'Years later,' Jonah added, taking up the story, 'he was also involved in investigating the abduction of Peter's baby granddaughter, Abigail, and he put his foot in it again, this time with Peter's son, Eddie.'

'Your granddaughter was taken?' Charles exclaimed, turning to Peter with a look of surprise and sympathy on his face.

'And she was found safe and well within just a few days,' Peter replied at once.

'Mind you – it felt more like months!' Lucy contributed with a grin. 'We can laugh about it now, but it was awful while it was going on.'

'And this Arshad Khan found

her?' Charles asked hopefully.

'Well, he was part of the team that did,' Bernie told him. 'Police work's never just down to one person. It was actually Jonah who was heading up the investigation. It was one of his last before he retired.'

'I've just been called in to help with another of those cases – one which looked to have been a failure but has now got a new lease of life,' Jonah commented, taking the opportunity to steer the conversation round to his current preoccupation. 'It's another missing girl. She went off three years ago and hadn't been seen since – until just over a week ago. We now think that her disappearance is linked to a case

that DCI Davenport is leading on –
which is why I thought that she
would be the most appropriate
person to look into what happened to
your daughter too. The cases have
certain similarities.'

'But DCI Khan is a very
competent detective too,' Peter put
in quickly, worried lest Charles
should think that he was being
fobbed off with a second-rate officer.
'His team has a good clear-up rate.'

'And I don't suppose *you*'ll have
any trouble with him,' Lucy added,
unthinkingly, 'with you both being …
I'm sorry, that didn't come out right,'
she mumbled, going red in the face
and busying herself with her food.

'Khan's a good officer,' Peter

repeated, determined not to allow his personal animosity to prejudice Charles' opinion. 'It's just that he's been given so many racially motivated crimes to deal with that he tends to see racism everywhere, even when it isn't there.'

'And he gets given all the cases involving ethnic minorities because a lot of white officers are afraid of causing offence by saying or doing the wrong thing,' Bernie added.

Charles thought about this for a few moments and then turned back to Jonah.

'You said there were similarities between this other girl's disappearance and what happened to Amanda. What exactly do you mean?'

'Why don't I tell you about Mollie Burgess and let you decide whether that resonates with what we know about Amanda?'

'Go on,' Charles nodded.

'Mollie Burgess left home of her own volition, taking with her a bag of clothes, including her riding boots, jodhpurs and riding hat, which made us think that she might have been promised a job working with horses. However, we checked all the stables for miles around and none of them had seen her. She had a mobile phone with her, but it was permanently switched off and her service provider reported that no calls were made or received from about an hour after she left the house. During the weeks leading up to her disappearance, she made a large number of calls to a pay-as-you-go mobile phone, which was also never used after that time. We think that was probably her kidnapper, grooming her to come away with him – or her. Despite extensive searching and numerous appeals for help, she wasn't seen again for three years.'

'Yes,' Charles said thoughtfully. 'I can see some similarities. In particular, the fact that they both thought that they were being offered employment. That was the last thing we heard from Amanda. She had been offered a job and they were sure that they could get her a visa to allow her to stay in England, but the police told me that the company she was going to work for didn't exist!'

'That's right,' Jonah confirmed. 'I checked it out myself. It looks as if she was duped into handing over her passport – supposedly for them to obtain permission to employ a non-EU national – and then she'd be stuck, unable to prove her identity or to get back home, and probably scared stiff of the consequences of being here illegally. And that's what's going to make finding her so difficult. She'll be deliberately trying to keep out of sight.'

'But you say you've recently made progress with finding this other girl,' Charles commented hopefully, 'even after three years.'

'Yes,' admitted Jonah, 'but more through luck than judgement. Some of her blood turned up at the scene of a murder last week and subsequently witnesses came forward who had seen her with the murder victim the day before. That at least means that she's still alive.'

'And that she's allowed out sometimes,' Peter added. 'So there's a chance she'll be seen again.'

'Except that, with all the publicity recently, her minders will probably keep her off the streets for a while,' Jonah responded. 'We're not out of the woods with Mollie Burgess by any means, but at least we've got something to work on now.'

'And Amanda?' Charles asked anxiously. 'Do you have anything to work on to find her?'

'Not much,' Jonah admitted, 'but that doesn't mean that we'll give up. And it isn't impossible that finding Mollie will help to find Amanda. Mollie has also been seen recently with another young woman. That could be suggestive of a large-scale Modern Slavery business targeting vulnerable young women in Oxford.'

Jonah was keen to see the new appeals for information, which Anna had arranged to have broadcast. So after their meal, they gathered in the living room to watch the television news. As usual, the headlines were all about Brexit and the Conservative Party leadership contest, but just before the end of the bulletin there was a brief recap on the Lichfield College murder and its connection with Mollie Burgess.

'More video footage has been released of the victim on the day before he was killed,' the newsreader announced over a rather poor quality picture of a crowded street. 'The police are asking people to come forward if they have seen him, or either of the two women who can be seen with him here, any time in the last three weeks.'

They watched as the footage was repeated, this time with circles superimposed to identify Robin Hillier and the two women. Hillier strode ahead and then turned and looked back, as if checking that the women were keeping up with him. One was small and slim with curly blond hair. The other was taller and had long black hair. The fair-haired figure pushed through the crowds to reach Hillier. Then she too glanced back momentarily giving them a brief glimpse of her face.

'That's Mollie Burgess,' Jonah announced, 'but we don't know who the other woman is.'

'I do,' answered Charles. 'It's Amanda. I'm sure of it.'

THE SECRET GARDENER

'How can you be so sure?' Sally asked at once. 'It didn't show her face.'

'She's my daughter. I know what she looks like. I know the way she walks and the way she holds her head. I'm sure that's Amanda. We must tell the police right away.'

'The officer in charge of this case is away for the weekend,' Peter told him, hoping that a delay might encourage Charles to reflect on the unlikelihood that his daughter would have been caught on the same video clip as the missing teenager. 'It would be better to wait until Monday, when she'll be back.'

'But that would waste time!' Charles protested. 'Surely the police need to act now to find her.'

'Those pictures are from ten days ago,' Peter reminded him. 'The man that you saw there was killed a few hours after that was taken. Nobody knows what happened to the two women after that.'

'Peter's right,' Bernie agreed. 'There really isn't any great hurry to tell them that the other woman is Amanda, because they're already doing everything they can to find both Mollie and the other woman. That's why they put out these pictures. They're hoping that someone may have seen them more recently.'

'I still think I ought to tell the police at once,' Charles insisted.

'What about DCI Khan? Is he away too? Why should I not tell him?'

'You could,' Jonah admitted, 'but Anna knows more about it, and her team are collating responses to this appeal for information. In a way, you already have informed the police, because I'm leading on re-opening the Mollie Burgess case.'

'In that case, what are you going to do about Amanda?' Charles demanded.

'I'm going to ring Sergeant Lepage right away,' Jonah told him. 'He's holding the fort until Anna gets back. He'll be able to tell us if they've made any progress in finding out where Mollie and Amanda went after Robin Hillier was killed.'

He studied Charles' face, which bore an expression of dissatisfaction and impatience, and decided that it would be better if he were not present to overhear this conversation. He excused himself and left the room to make the call to Andy in private.

A few minutes later he returned, smiling but with some anxiety in his eyes. Everyone looked expectantly towards him.

'Andy tells me that they've had a phone call from someone who's seen them,' he began.

'When? Where?' demanded Charles at once. 'Are they safe? Are they still-'

'The caller wouldn't give a name

and rang off without saying much,' Jonah continued. 'They're trying to trace the call, but no success so far. The caller alleges that there are rooms being used as a brothel above one of the bars in the centre of Oxford. He's one of the punters, which is why he wouldn't give his name. He recognised Mollie and said that he'd seen a dark-skinned woman with long black hair who may have been the other girl in the CC-TV pictures. Andy's planning to spend the evening in the bar watching what goes on, in the hope of spotting something that would justify a raid on the premises.'

'Surely knowing that two kidnapped girls are being kept there is enough?' blurted out Charles indignantly. 'Why wait any longer?'

'The police need to know more about what they're dealing with before they go in,' Peter explained.

'At the moment, they've only got one anonymous tip-off to go on,' Jonah agreed. 'If they send in the big guns prematurely, the people in charge may get away and escape justice.'

'And, without knowing more about the set-up, we can't even be sure of releasing the girls,' Peter added. 'What if they aren't kept there all the time? If a police operation goes off half-cock, they could be spirited away to the other end of the country before we can locate them.'

'So the smart thing to do,' Jonah concluded, 'is to wait while Andy does his reconnaissance and then make a plan to rescue the girls once we know exactly what's going on in there. I've invited him for lunch tomorrow, so that he can bring me up to speed with whatever he finds out.'

'You'll be welcome to come too,' Bernie told Charles. 'Then you can meet Andy and hear what he has to say. And you'll probably have information about Amanda that you can give him to help them find her,' she added, hoping to convince him that everything that could be done would be done and that his journey to England had not been a waste of time.

'Bernie's right,' Jonah affirmed. 'This could be the breakthrough that we've been waiting for, but we need to be careful not to rush in guns blazing and just frighten them off. It's like reeling in a fish: if you go too fast, it's liable to get away.'

'Do you think that other woman could be Charles's Amanda?' Bernie asked Peter in bed that night.

'I doubt it. I'd say it's just wishful thinking, prompted mainly by Jonah having drawn attention to the similarities between her disappearance and the Mollie

Burgess case.'

'And I don't see the two cases are that similar,' Bernie agreed. 'They were so different in age when they disappeared for a start. And, as I remember it, we discounted the idea of Mollie going for a job at a stables quite early on and concentrated on the idea that she went to live with a boyfriend of some kind.'

'That's right,' Peter murmured, putting his arm round Bernie and drawing her closer. 'The only common feature, in my opinion, is that they both went voluntarily. They weren't running away from home; they were running *to* something, but I don't think it was the same something in the two cases.'

10. IDENTIFYING FEATURES

Sally Pearson was also concerned that Charles might have built up false hopes that his daughter had been seen recently and might soon be found alive and well. She counselled him seriously the following morning not to mention having recognised her in the video on the television news when speaking to people at church that morning.

'I know you're sure it's her,' she argued gently, 'but to most people it was just a blurry video of a woman with dark hair seen from behind. It'll be much better not to say anything until the police have had a chance to confirm that it really was Amanda.'

She watched his face as Charles nodded his agreement. The sadness and expression of betrayal told her that he understood only too well that she did not really believe that the woman on the news had been his daughter. She was humouring him, and he knew it.

The service that morning was led by an old friend of Bernie's, one of the "Local Preachers" upon whom the Methodist church relies to fill its pulpits. Stan Corbridge was a Geordie who had worked as a welder in the shipyards on the Tyne for more years than he cared to remember. Now retired, his two great passions in life were his flock of racing pigeons (housed in a loft at the bottom of Bernie's extensive garden) and his lay preaching ministry.

Sally dropped Charles off outside the church in Cowley Road before going on to take a communion service at one of the other Methodist churches in the area. Bernie was waiting for him outside, Lucy and Jonah having already gone in to find a row of three seats where Jonah's wheelchair could also be accommodated. Peter, having already attended Mass at St Cyprian's that morning, was at home preparing the lunch. The welcomer on the door greeted Charles warmly and gave him a hymnbook and a notice sheet.

'I hope you'll stay for coffee afterwards,' she added. 'I know there are lots of people who would like a chance to talk to you. We were all so sorry to hear about your daughter. Is there any news?'

'Nothing definite,' Charles answered carefully, remembering Sally's warning. 'I have an appointment with the police tomorrow, so I may know more after that.'

It was the Sunday following the annual Methodist Conference, at which new leaders for the Methodist

Church of Great Britain are installed in office and matters of doctrine, order and discipline are debated. Stan's prayers focussed on the new President and Vice-President, and for healing within the church following a controversial, and sometimes heated, debate on the subject of whether same-sex marriages should be permitted in Methodist churches in Britain; but he also remembered missing persons including Pandora, Mollie and Amanda. He spoke feelingly to Charles as they filed out past him on the way to coffee in the hall.

'Losing a child is the worst thing that can happen to any parent,' he said as he shook Charles's hand.

'And to lose one and not be sure what happened or where they are must be ten times worse.'

'Stan's son, Stephen, took his own life at the age of twenty-one,' Bernie explained, when they were settled round a table with mugs of coffee in front of them. 'He was their only child. It was quite devastating for him and Sylvia – that's his wife.'

'Like Amanda,' Charles nodded sadly. 'We – I – don't have any other children either.'

The after-service coffee was a rather hurried affair, because everyone was keen to leave before the Cowley Road Carnival got underway. This annual event brought together the varied communities of East Oxford in a celebration of cultural diversity. The road outside the church would be closed to traffic for the procession and the church itself had been designated as a "quiet zone" where anyone who was overwhelmed by the noise and crowds could retreat for some time out.

Bernie, glad that she had resisted invitations to take a leading role in any of the festivities, led the retreat back to their car and off home as soon as politeness allowed. It was good that so many people wanted to express their sympathy to Charles, but the longer he was there and the more people he spoke to, the more likely it was that he would let slip his conviction that his daughter was the other woman in the police videos.

Andy was already there when she and Charles arrived back at the house in Headington. (Lucy had opted for lunch at the carnival where "delicious treats from all around the world" were promised.) He shook hands with Charles and assured him that the police would be making every effort to find his daughter. Then, as they sat in the back garden with glasses of fruit juice, Jonah began his inquisition.

'OK, Andy,' he said briskly, 'Let's have it. How did you get on at the bar last night? Any sign of the missing girls?'

THE SECRET GARDENER

'I didn't see them, if that's what you mean,' Andy replied, grinning at his old boss's enthusiasm for the investigation. 'But I do think there's something going on there – something not quite right. I hung around for about four hours, mostly just watching. There was a young barmaid called Tiffany who saw me on my own and came over to talk a couple of times. She made a few suggestive remarks – like she thought maybe I was hoping to pick up a girl but was too shy to ask – but she left me alone after a while when I didn't respond.'

'Is that all?' Jonah sounded disappointed.

'No. I got the impression that a lot

of the punters were regulars. They made jokes with Tiffany and with an older woman, who I think was Tiffany's mother. There was a lot of coming and going and most of it was men on their own – not groups of mates having a drink together. And every so often, one of them would go off to a room somewhere at the back, with Stacey – that's the older woman – and then she'd come back without them. I managed to get close enough on one occasion to overhear one of them asking if Rita was in tonight. Stacey said yes, but she was busy right now. Then Stacey said she'd give him a nod when Rita was free. The man took a drink and a bag of peanuts and went and sat at a table next to the door into the back room.'

'Was this Stacey running the show?' Jonah asked.

'The licensee name over the door was *Zachary Pimm*,' Andy told him. 'I assume it was him in charge of the bar, but I rather fancy it was Stacey who ran whatever little side-line it is they've got going on in that back room.'

'Zachary?' queried Peter, knocking over his orange juice in surprise at hearing this name. 'Did people call him Zack, by any chance?'

'Yes, they did – why?'

'It's just that Bridge- I mean the woman who told Father Damien she'd seen Mollie Burgess at the abortion clinic – said that her minder talked to her about someone called Zack, who would be angry if she didn't do what she was told,' Peter explained.

'And now that anonymous tip-off says Mollie Burgess is working as a prostitute in a brothel attached to this Zachary Pimm's bar,' Jonah declared triumphantly. 'It all fits! Somehow, he or one of his associates lures Mollie away with some promise about working with horses or, thinking about those posh frocks she took with her, maybe as a fashion model, and then forces her into prostitution.'

'And do you think that's what

happened to Amanda too?' Charles asked anxiously.

There was a long silence as everyone struggled to think what to say in answer to this.

'I'm sorry,' Peter answered at last. 'I think it may be – unless you were mistaken and she isn't the woman who was with Mollie the Wednesday before last.'

'I was not mistaken,' Charles repeated doggedly. 'I know my daughter. I'm sure it was her.'

'I'm sorry – what's all this about Mollie Burgess and an abortion clinic?' Andy asked in a puzzled voice.

Everyone looked towards Peter.

'One of Father Damien's flock –

you remember Father Damien, the priest at St Cyprian's? Well, as I said, a woman who doesn't want to be identified came to him and told him she'd seen Mollie Burgess attending an abortion clinic a few days before Robin Hillier's death.'

'And she says she overheard them talking about someone called Zack?' Andy queried.

'That's right,' Peter confirmed. 'She agreed to meet me so long as I kept her name out of it. She described the woman that Mollie was with, too.'

'And?' demanded Jonah impatiently. 'What did she look like? Could it have been either of the women Andy saw in Pimm's bar?'

'She said bleached blond hair and a lot of makeup.' Peter repeated Bridget's words as precisely as he could remember. 'And she had a tattoo on her hand.'

'What of?' asked Andy excitedly.

'A parrot,' Peter told him. 'At least that's what she thought it was.'

'A red parrot?' demanded Andy, 'with a black beak and yellow streaks in its tail?'

'Dunno,' Peter shrugged. 'She just said *a parrot.*'

'It must be her!' Andy declared. 'It'd be too much of a coincidence not to be. That's Stacey, I'm sure of it!'

'What I don't understand,' Bernie said, after a short pause, 'is where

Robin Hillier comes into all this. Was he working for this Zachary Pimm bloke? And if so, why was he living in that store room in Lichfield College? And why on earth would he have taken the girls there?'

'Maybe he was supposed to be moving them to a new location,' Andy suggested. 'They must have spun some sort of story for the clinic as to who Mollie was. They could have been trying to get her away from the area before anyone started checking up on her.'

'But then, why allow her to be seen in public in her home town for the first time in three years?' objected Jonah.

'OK then,' Andy tried again.

'Suppose the girls got away and he was trying to get them back again.'

'The video didn't look like two kidnap victims and their captor,' Jonah commented. 'And the waitress from the café said he left them on their own while he ordered breakfast. It sounds more like three friends together – or a man and his two daughters.'

'Maybe he was helping them get away from Zack and his associates,' Bernie suggested.

'In that case, where are they now?' asked Andy. 'And why haven't they gone to the police?'

'Afraid of being accused of killing Hillier maybe,' Jonah speculated. 'Perhaps he lured them away promising to help them and then attacked them in the Fellows' Garden after dark.'

'Ye-es,' Peter mused. 'I suppose that would fit the facts. Are you suggesting that they fought back and that's how he got killed?'

'As you say, that would fit the facts,' Jonah agreed.

'OK, so let's get this straight,' Peter said, trying to get the sequence of events clear in his mind. 'You're suggesting that Mollie and Amanda – if it is Amanda that we've seen with her – were being held by Zachary Pimm and this woman Stacey and forced to work as prostitutes. Mollie falls pregnant and Stacey takes her to an abortion clinic

– that was the Monday before Hillier died. A day or two after that, she escapes along with another girl – let's assume it *is* Amanda for the time being – and Hillier befriends them.'

'Or pretends to,' added Jonah.

'Hang on a minute!' Andy called out suddenly, remembering what Gavin had related to them from the rough sleepers. 'I'm not so sure that the girl we're calling Amanda was one of Zachary Pimm's prostitutes.'

'What then?' asked Charles hopefully.

'Gav Hughes says that one of the homeless guys that he's chummy with told him that Hillier had a black girlfriend,' Andy explained. 'We've no evidence linking Mollie with Amanda except them having been seen together in Hillier's company. Could she and Hillier have been working together to get Mollie out of Pimm's clutches?'

'But, if the woman in the video really is Amanda Jayakody, where's she been for the last year?' Jonah demanded. 'Is Hillier supposed to have been hiding her all that time?'

'My daughter would never have consented to live with a man in the manner that you're suggesting,' Charles interjected. 'And she would have let us know where she was, unless she was being forcibly prevented.'

'OK, let's not get hung up on the

details,' Peter said. 'Let's just concentrate on Mollie for the time being. She escapes from Pimm – either on her own or with another girl – and meets Hillier, who gives her breakfast on Wednesday morning. By Wednesday lunchtime, he's down at the railway station – have I got that right, Andy?'

Andy nodded and Peter resumed, 'looking out for someone getting off a train from the north somewhere. So where has he left Mollie and the other girl?'

'Hidden in the store room at Lichfield?' suggested Andy.

'A bit risky,' Bernie objected. 'What if one of the real gardeners came in looking for a trowel or something?'

'There's another room in there,' Andy told them, thinking about his exploration of the store room with Ruby and Anna. 'It didn't look as if anyone ever went in there. It was full of old empty boxes.'

'OK. Let's assume they were holed-up in there for the rest of the day,' Peter nodded. 'Now, what about Hillier? Do we know who he was waiting for or whether he found them?'

'We're sort of assuming it must have been Mariella Peckforton,' Andy replied, 'and he won't have met her at the station, because she came down the day before and stayed at Holy Cross College overnight.

However, he may possibly have run into her later, because one of the porters remembers letting her into the Fellows' Garden at Lichfield on the Wednesday afternoon.'

'What time?' snapped Jonah.

'He couldn't remember, but late-ish. He said it wasn't long before dinner.'

'So she could've been there when Hillier got back from the station,' Jonah murmured thoughtfully. 'Perhaps they arranged to meet again after dinner.'

'And they had an argument and she killed him!' Andy broke in.

'But then where do the girls come in?' Peter asked.

'And would a sixty-something

female academic be able to stab to death a well-built man used to manual work?' added Bernie sceptically.

'And the knife,' Jonah put in. 'What about that? Where did it come from and where's it gone now?'

'I don't understand!' Charles lamented when everyone else paused to think. 'Who are all these people? What have they got to do with Amanda?'

Jonah, who as usual had all the facts at his fingertips, gave Charles a brief résumé of the Robin Hillier murder case. When he came to the discovery of long black hairs at the crime scene, Charles stopped him.

'Do they have DNA from the

hair?' he demanded urgently. 'Could they test it to see if it's Amanda's?'

'Yes, I'm sure they said they'd got a DNA profile from it,' Andy answered.

'And if you were to give them a sample, they could check for a familial match,' Jonah added excitedly. 'I'll get Anna on to it first thing tomorrow. What time's your meeting with the Chief Super?'

'Not until the afternoon,' Charles told him glumly.

'Never mind about that then,' Jonah grinned. 'That gives us the whole morning to get on with things before she hands you over to DCI Khan.'

'Are you sure about doing that?'

Peter intervened, knowing that there was no chance of changing Jonah's mind but feeling obliged to make the attempt. 'A few hours won't make all that much difference and Alison may feel you're undermining her authority.'

'But if it helps to clear up a murder and two missing persons,' Jonah countered, 'she ought to be grateful. And Khan clearly has as much as he can handle with trying to find Pandora Birch or he wouldn't have been scrounging officers from Anna's team.'

He turned to address Charles.

'Don't worry. We're on the case now. We'll get that DNA test done first thing tomorrow. At least then

THE SECRET GARDENER

we'll know if Amanda really is mixed up with the death of this Secret Gardener guy, or if we're going to have to start from scratch looking for her.'

11. THE PACE QUICKENS

True to his word, Jonah presented Charles to Anna in her private office the next morning before she even had time to fill the coffee maker. She listened patiently as he explained the circumstances of his daughter's disappearance and his certainty that she was the unknown woman seen accompanying Mollie Burgess along an Oxford street on the morning of the day that Robin Hillier met his death.

'I brought these pictures of Amanda,' he finished, holding out a cardboard wallet of photographs. 'Surely someone must have seen her. Can't you put them out and ask people to call in, like you did for this other girl?'

'Certainly we can,' Anna answered gently, but I really ought to wait until you've spoken to Chief Superintendent Brown. It's up to her to decide who will be in charge of looking for your daughter.'

'But you're in charge of investigating Hillier's murder,' Jonah interjected. 'So you have the authority to look into whether or not the dark-haired woman who was with him on the day that he died could have been Amanda Jayakody. You'll be perfectly justified in taking a DNA sample from her father to check against the profile you've got from the hairs that she left behind.'

'OK,' Anna conceded. 'I'll arrange for that to be done.'

She pressed a button on her desk and spoke to her secretary. 'Could you send someone in here to escort Mr Jayakody down to have a DNA swab taken? And send Andy Lepage in too while you're about it.'

'And I could take one of those pictures round to the coffee shop where they had breakfast that morning,' Jonah resumed as soon as she looked up again. 'She recognised Hillier and thought she recognised Mollie. Maybe she'll be able to tell us if the other woman was

Amanda.'

There was a knock at the door and Stella Gilbert looked nervously in. This was the first time she had been summoned to a DCI's room.

'Come in, constable!' Anna called out. 'This is Mr Charles Jayakody. His daughter has been reported missing and we need a DNA sample from him to match with some traces that we think may have come from her. I'd like you to take him down to have that done.'

'Yes ma'am.' Stella looked towards Charles. 'Come with me please, Mr Jayakody. And don't worry: it's a very simple procedure.'

'Do you have anywhere to go?' Anna asked him, as he got up to leave. 'Until you're appointment with Superintendent Brown this afternoon, I mean?'

'I'm staying with friends,' he explained. 'One of them is waiting for me in reception.'

'Good. Well, I may see you later then.'

Stella and Charles left the room, making space for Andy to slip in.

'Charlene said you wanted to see me,' he greeted Anna. 'Has Peter told you about Mollie's visit to the abortion clinic?'

'No. I've been too busy listening to Jonah crowing about how he was right when he said the dark-skinned girl in the café might have been the same one that went missing a year ago,' Anna answered with a wry smile. 'Her father has been in here just now offering to give a DNA sample and giving us these photos.'

'I know,' Andy grinned back. 'He had me over at Bernie's place talking to him yesterday. It still strikes me as far too much of a coincidence, but the father was absolutely adamant that he'd recognised her from the CC-TV.'

'Well, now I'd like you to take these photos and show them to the waitress in the coffee shop where Hillier's supposed to have bought breakfast for Mollie Burgess and this other girl,' Anna instructed him, holding out the folder of pictures. 'See if she recognises her. Then come back here and tell me what Jonah's going on about when he says you spent Saturday night in a bar on the lookout for prostitutes.'

'Right you are!' Andy took the photographs and headed out of the door.

Anna turned to look at Peter. 'Now, what's all this about Mollie Burgess and the abortion clinic?'

'Do you remember Father Damien Rowland, from St Cyprian's in Headington?'

'No, I don't think I know him.' Anna looked puzzled.

'He found a body under the organ at his church,' Jonah told her.[8]

---

[8] You can read about this in *Organ*

'Surely you must – no, of course! You were on maternity leave. It was the Easter after Donna was born.'

'Anyway,' Peter continued, 'that's neither here nor there. The point is: one of his flock came to see him because she'd recognised the picture of Mollie that you put out on the news. She didn't want to go to the police because … well, she didn't want people to know that she'd been at the abortion clinic. Abortion is absolutely forbidden by the Catholic Church and lots of her family and friends would have … well, she just didn't want anyone to know.'

Failure © 2018 Judy Ford ISBN: 978-1-911083-38-2

'And this Father Damien told you about it?' asked Anna.

'Yes, but he also persuaded her to agree to meet me, which she did,' Peter told her. 'I interviewed her and she told me what she'd seen and gave me permission to pass it on to you – just so long as I didn't have to reveal her name. I warned her that she might have to give evidence in court, but I said we'd try to avoid it coming to that.'

'But you do know her name, if we need to get in touch with her?' Anna asked sharply.

'Oh yes!' Peter assured her. 'I know exactly who she is, but I promised to try to keep her out of things.'

'OK. So what exactly did she see?' Anna asked, sitting back in her chair and folding her hands in her lap.

'On the Monday, two days before Hillier was killed, she was in the waiting room of an abortion clinic – and yes, I can tell you which one – when she saw a teenager, whom she later recognised as Mollie Burgess, with a woman whom she assumed at the time must be her mother,' Peter began. 'She seemed to be very upset and anxious – but then that's not that surprising considering the circumstances – and her "mother" didn't seem to be very sympathetic.'

'Go on,' Anna encouraged when

Peter paused for breath.

'I asked her to describe the older woman,' he resumed. 'She said her hair had been bleached and there were some darker roots showing, which isn't much to go on. But the most significant thing was that she had a tattoo visible on her right hand.'

'And Andy Lepage has seen a woman with a tattoo that matches her description,' Jonah cut in excitedly. 'So we think we may know who she is.'

Anna raised her eyebrows in surprise and looked towards Peter enquiringly.

'My witness overheard this woman telling Mollie that someone called Zack would be angry if she didn't do as she was told,' he continued. 'She got the impression that Mollie was frightened of going through with the abortion, but even more frightened of "Zack", whoever he was. Anyway, she came away from the clinic, leaving Mollie and her minder there, and didn't think any more about it until she saw the video of Mollie with Hillier on the television news.'

'And meanwhile,' Jonah interjected before Anna could respond, 'an anonymous caller claims to have seen Mollie in a brothel behind a bar run by one Zack Pimm!'

'Whose partner appears to be a

woman called Stacey with bleached blond hair and a tattoo of a red parrot on her hand,' Bernie added triumphantly.

'My, my!' Anna exclaimed, looking round at them all. 'You have all been busy bees while I was off. Anyone would think I'd been gone for a fortnight, not just two days.'

'How was the romantic weekend?' Peter asked with genuine concern. 'Jess seemed to think Philip was trying to patch things up with you.'

'He's coming back,' Anna replied succinctly. 'Jess won't like it, but I hope she'll come round. Marcus will hardly notice the difference, I don't suppose. He's out with his mates more often than at home.'

'And what about you?' Peter probed gently.

'I'll have my childcare problems solved,' Anna shrugged. 'That's about where we're up to at the moment. We'll just see how things go. Now, I'd better get on to that clinic and see what they know about Mollie Burgess.'

The receptionist at the clinic confirmed that a young woman answering Mollie's description had attended on the day in question. She had registered under the name of Rovena Miftari. She had presented an Albanian passport as proof of identity and confirmation that she was over eighteen. She had been assessed by a doctor and sent home with a further appointment for the next day. She failed to attend and had not been seen or heard from again.

'How did she pay?' Anna asked. 'I mean, if she was an Albanian national, she wouldn't be entitled to free treatment, would she?'

'She brought cash with her for the initial consultation. Since she didn't come back, I don't know how she was planning to pay for the procedure.'

Anna asked to speak to the doctor who had seen "Rovena". The receptionist was reluctant at first, but gave way when Anna told her that the young woman was suspected of being the victim of kidnapping and sexual exploitation. The doctor admitted to having been in two minds about allowing the abortion to go ahead.

'The scan indicated a 24-week gestation,' she said nervously, 'but the girl was very insistent that she hadn't made a mistake with the dates and it couldn't be more than 22 weeks. And then her social worker told us about how she'd been raped repeatedly by her father before she finally managed to escape from the family home. She had marks on her wrists where he used to tie her up for hours, or so they told me. In the end, my colleague and I decided to give her the benefit of the doubt and we signed the forms. She seemed so young and scared and … it just seemed to be the least worst option.'

'And you asked her to come back the following day?' Anna asked.

'Yes. Because it was so far into the pregnancy, a medical abortion wasn't really practicable; so we booked her in for a surgical abortion the next day. It needed to be as soon as possible because we knew we were already verging on the legal limit.'

'I see.' Anna thought for a moment. 'You said just now that she had her social worker with her. Did she give her name?'

'Yes. And she showed me an ID badge with the local authority logo on it. I was convinced she was genuine,' the doctor replied defensively.

'And the name was ...?' Anna prompted.

'I can't remember,' the doctor gabbled. 'I was running late. I just checked that the ID looked OK and then concentrated on the patient. She was very nervous and hardly spoke at all. Maybe her English wasn't that good. The social worker said she'd come from Albania with her parents and been kept at home since, hardly going out. It all sounded very ... well, I thought it was a good thing Social Services had got charge of her at last and I hoped we'd be able to give her a fresh start in life without … without the millstone of a baby conceived through incest to remind her of it all.'

'Alright,' Anna said grudgingly. 'You can save the excuses for later – if we establish that your so-called social worker is the imposter that we think she is. Just think back and try to remember if they said anything that might give us a clue as to where the girl was living or where the two of them were heading when they left the clinic.'

'Reception will have her address,' the doctor answered, suddenly adopting a very formal manner. 'As I said, the girl hardly spoke during the consultation. She just nodded to confirm what the social worker said and showed me a diary where she'd noted down the start of her last period, when I questioned her dates. Naturally we'll co-operate with any police investigation, but I can assure you that everything we did was in good faith based on the facts as we knew them.'

After finishing the call, Anna looked round at the others.

'Well, there we have it. According to the clinic, the girl that your witness identified as Mollie Burgess is an Albanian national currently living in a hostel for homeless women under the supervision of Social Services. We'd better check that story out first before jumping to any conclusions.'

Further telephone calls established that Oxfordshire Social Services had nobody on their books by the name of Rovena Mitfari. The homeless hostel also denied all knowledge of her. It looked increasingly likely that Bridget could have been correct in thinking that the young woman whom she had seen was the missing schoolgirl Mollie Burgess.

'Presumably she's been kept somewhere out of sight for the last three years,' Peter murmured. 'I wonder how many other girls they've got there. It looks like a highly professional modern slavery business with young women lured away from their homes and forced into the sex industry.'

'It's awful to think of something like that going on under our noses, here in Oxford,' Anna agreed with feeling. 'How could we have failed to pick up what was going on in Pimm's bar?'

There was a knock on the door and Andy Lepage entered.

'It looks like Charles Jayakody was right!' he declared, smiling round at them all. 'Tamsin Docherty is fairly confident that the other woman with Hillier that Wednesday morning *was* Amanda. She says she paid special attention to her because she was so different from anyone she'd seen before. Of course, it's possible that she'd have said the same about any exceptionally dark-skinned Asian, but on balance I'm inclined to accept her identification.'

'OK.' Anna looked down at her notes. 'So we've got Amanda and Mollie both being held by Zack Pimm and this Stacey woman, who may or may not be his wife, but where does Robin Hillier come into all this? And who killed him? We seem to be making good progress with both of these missing persons enquiries, but no headway at all in solving his murder.'

'I'd say the question is-,' Jonah began, but he was interrupted by the ringing of the telephone on Anna's desk.

'I'm sorry,' Anna's secretary said apologetically. 'I know you're in a meeting, but I've got a Professor Peckforton on the line who's demanding to speak to the person in charge of the Robin Hillier murder enquiry. She won't talk to anyone else and she insists that she has important information for you. Can I put her through?'

'Yes. Go ahead.' Anna switched to speakerphone and waited for the connection to be made. 'DCI Davenport here, how can I help you?'

'My name is Professor Mariella Peckforton,' came the response in the clear, commanding tones of someone used to being in a position of authority. 'I understand that you are in charge of investigating the murder of Robin Hillier.'

'Yes. That's right,' Anna confirmed.

'You asked for people to contact you with information about his movements. I believe that I may have been one of the last people to speak to him before he died.'

'Really? What makes you think that?'

'He was killed during the night of Wednesday 26th June – is that correct?'

'That's right,' Anna agreed.

'Well I had a conversation with him that evening.'

'What time?'

'Just before I went back to my room to dress for dinner, so that must have been half past six or maybe twenty to seven.'

'I see. And you say you had a conversation with him. How did that come about?'

'Presumably you are aware that he had been living in my sister's house for a number of years before she died?'

'Yes.'

'I was the executor of her will and inherited the house, which was the home where we both grew up. Robin Hillier was still living there when she died, so naturally I met him when I went down to deal with her estate. I let him stay on there until the house was sold, and he did a good job of keeping it in order and showing potential purchasers around etc. etc.'

'Did he tell you where he was planning to go after that?' Jonah asked.

'Who's that?' Mariella demanded suspiciously. 'Are you still there Inspector Davenport?'

'That was DCI Jonah Porter,' Anna replied hastily. 'He's leading on a related investigation into a missing girl, who was seen with Robin Hillier shortly before he died and may well have been with him when he was killed. We'd both like to know whether he gave you a forwarding address after he left your sister's house.'

'No, he didn't. There would have been no point, seeing as the house was sold. However, I do know where he went, because he told me all about it when we met that evening.'

'Yes. Tell me about that evening,' Anna said encouragingly. 'How did you come to meet? Was it arranged or by chance?'

'Oh completely fortuitous. I was invited to talk about my research by an old friend of mine and I stayed overnight at my old college – Holy Cross, which is just across the road from Lichfield, as I'm sure you are aware. We were finished by about four, so I had a few hours free before dinner. I decided to go round to

Lichfield to have a look at the bench that they'd erected in Augusta's memory. I suppose you've probably seen her will?'

'Yes,' Anna replied. 'We were surprised that she didn't leave anything to Robin Hillier. We wondered if she wasn't able to leave him the house, because it had been your family home.'

'No. There was nothing like that. She bought me out of it years ago, when I moved up to Durham. She could have left it to whomever she chose. To be honest, I'm surprised she didn't give it all to the college, but maybe her lawyers told her that I might contest the will if she ignored her only living relative entirely. But to get back to that Wednesday afternoon, I thought I'd better check up on that bench, seeing as I was executor and it was a condition of Augusta's will that the college put it up; so I went round to the porter's lodge and asked to be let in to the Fellows' Garden. A young woman took me across, opened the gate for me and told me I could stay as long as I liked and to be careful to pull the gate closed properly when I left.'

'And this was about four o'clock?' Anna queried.

'It would have been about half past by then or maybe more like quarter to five. Anyway, I walked around a bit and looked at the flowers and then I found the bench and sat down on it. It was quite sunny and pleasant there, so I got out a book to read. It was perhaps half an hour later that I looked up and saw Robin Hillier trimming the edge of the lawn with long-handled edging shears. After a while, he looked up and I could see that he recognised me, so I said good afternoon to him and asked him how he was getting on.'

'I see. And then he told you what he'd been doing since he left your sister's house?'

'Not immediately. I commented that he was back in his old job, and he said, no, he was just doing a few odd-jobs in return for somewhere to sleep at night until he found somewhere more permanent.'

'That's interesting,' Anna commented. 'So he gave you the impression that this was a proper arrangement with the college authorities, did he? Work in exchange for accommodation?'

'That's how he made it sound,' Mariella agreed, 'but when he told me that he was sleeping in the tool shed under the chapel, I started to suspect that he wasn't being completely straightforward with me. Anyway, eventually he admitted that he was having trouble finding a place to rent because of having no previous landlord to give him a reference and no current address. I offered to give him a reference as the owner of the house that he'd looked after between when my sister died and when the new owners moved in. And I told him I'd speak to the college authorities and see if they had a room they could let him stay in for a few weeks, so that he had an address to give when he was applying for places to live. I told him that Augusta had left a lot of money to the college and I could dress it up as a verbal request that she'd given to me before she died.'

'And why did you offer to do all this for a man you hardly knew?' asked Anna.

'I considered that I owed it to him,' Mariella replied. 'Or, to be more precise, I considered that Augusta owed it to him. In fact she owed him a lot more than just a helping hand to a rented flat, but that was the best I could do for the time being at least.'

'And why did you think that?' Anna pressed her.

'As soon as I realised that he wasn't just a paid care-giver, I knew exactly how it must have been for him.' There was a note of bitterness in Mariella's voice now. 'Until that afternoon, I hadn't been aware that he'd been living with her for over thirty years. In all the letters she wrote to me, she never mentioned him once! But as soon as he told me, I could see that he was just another of her victims.'

'Another?' asked Anna sharply.

'Another, apart from who else?'

'Me, principally,' Mariella declared unexpectedly, 'although there may have been others.'

'Could you explain that?'

'Augusta was nine years my elder. From an early age, she used to bully me and boss me about. Our parents died when I was thirteen and she became my legal guardian. That made things considerably worse. She became ever more autocratic. Everything had to be done exactly as she decided. It often seemed that she would deliberately disagree with me about things in order to overrule what I wanted and impose her will on me.'

'So, you'd say that she was

controlling?' queried Anna.

'Exactly!' Mariella agreed. 'And that's exactly how that poor man described it to me in the garden that evening. He wasn't complaining. I think he still loved her, the poor fool! He was just explaining how he'd ended up in the situation he was in.'

'Homeless, you mean?'

'And with no money except a small pension from his gardening job,' Mariella agreed. 'Apparently, all the time he was living with Augusta, she insisted that his salary – and later his pension – was paid directly into their joint bank account each month. And then she transferred it into an account in her sole name and gave him small amounts of pocket money.'

'He used to pay the mortgage on his wife's house, until it was paid off,' Anna commented, 'so she must have allowed him to keep that.'

'He was married?' Mariella exclaimed in surprise. 'I had no idea.'

'Yes,' Anna told her. 'Married with two young children when he first went to live with your sister.'

'She'll have realised that the wife could get lawyers involved.' Her calm apparently restored, Mariella resumed her story. 'She was very calculating in her cruelty. She knew exactly how far she could go without provoking interference from the authorities or anyone outside the family. I wish I'd known before. Quite a substantial part of her estate must have rightfully belonged to him.'

'What time was it that you left the Fellow's Garden after your conversation with Robin Hillier?' Anna asked when it began to seem as if Mariella had no more to tell them about him.

'As I told you before, it was just before dinner – about half past six or a little later. Robin let me out through the gate into Goose Lane, seeing as I was staying at Holy Cross. The last I saw of him was as he closed it behind me.'

'One more thing,' Anna said, hurrying to prevent Mariella ringing off now that she had imparted what she had to say. 'Did you see any sign of a young woman – or possibly two young women – in the garden with Robin Hillier? He had been seen in the company of two women, early that day, one with curly blond hair and the other dark-skinned. We believe that they may have been present when he was killed.'

'No,' Mariella answered decisively. 'He was quite alone when I saw him.'

'Thank you,' Anna drew the conversation to a close. 'What you've told us is very useful. If you think of anything else-'

'There's another incident you ought to know about,' Mariella interrupted. 'It happened later that night, as I was on my way to my room after dinner.'

'Oh?'

'One of the domestic staff stopped me and asked if I was any relation of Augusta Peckforton. I didn't realise at the time, but now you tell me Robin Hillier was married, I suppose it was probably his wife.'

'What makes you say that?'

'The things she asked. She started off by trying to hand me an envelope, which she said had a note in it for Augusta. She seemed taken aback when I told her Augusta had been dead for some months. Then, when she'd taken that in, she started asking after Robin Hillier.'

Mariella paused as if debating whether to say any more.

'What sort of things did she ask?' prompted Anna.

'She wanted to know where he was and if I could get a message to him.' Mariella hesitated again. 'I tried to avoid telling her anything, because, as I told you, I didn't know who she was or why she wanted him, but she was persistent and I was tired and didn't want a scene, so in the end I told her that she might well find him working in the gardens of Lichfield College. Then she seemed satisfied and went off towards the college kitchens and I didn't see any more of her.'

'I see,' Anna murmured. 'That's

very interesting. Thank you. Now, before we let you go, is there anything else we ought to know about Robin Hillier or his-'

'What did she look like?' Jonah cut in before Anna could wind up the conversation. 'The woman who accosted Professor Peckforton. It would help if we could be sure that it really was Mrs Hillier.'

Anna was about to relay this question to Mariella, but she was there first, having heard Jonah's voice through the telephone.

'Sixties, I should think, grey hair, slightly shorter than me, so about five foot five or six, wearing black trousers and a white shirt with a Holy Cross tabard over them. I'm sorry, I didn't notice anything else.'

'Thank you. That's useful,' Anna said to Mariella. 'Now, I won't take up any more of your time. Thank you very much for ringing. Your information is very useful.'

She ended the call and turned to face Jonah and the others.

'Based on that description, it certainly could have been Robin's wife. I think it definitely rules out either of his daughters, so unless he had some sort of relationship with another member of the domestic staff at Holy Cross, the chances are we now know that Mrs Hillier was keen to find her husband and had just been told where he was the night he died.'

'She could have taken a knife with her from the college kitchen, slipped across Goose Lane into the Fellows' Garden, stabbed him and then put the knife back,' Andy added excitedly. 'It all fits!'

'Except that Professor Peckforton told us that Robin closed the door behind her when she left,' commented Jonah. 'And it locks automatically, so how did his wife get into the garden?'

'Perhaps she knocked on the door and Hillier opened it for her,' Andy suggested. 'It stays light late at this time of year. He could've still been outside working in the garden.'

'But equally well, Mariella Peckforton could've done it herself,'

Bernie interjected. 'We only have her word for it that Jill Hillier spoke to her after dinner. She could have made all that up to cover up the fact that *she* went back that night and killed Hillier. She carefully avoided claiming it was Mrs Hillier, so if she denies having met Mariella, Mariella can say it must've been another woman.'

'But what motive could she have?' asked Anna wearily. 'Hillier's wife stood to gain financially by his death – although she claims not to have been sure about that – and she had the most reason to be angry with him over his behaviour towards her.'

'Jill Hillier *and* her daughters,' Jonah concurred. 'If she denies having done it, and we can't find any forensic evidence to link her to the crime scene, it's going to be hard to prove that she killed him herself and didn't just pass the information about his whereabouts to one of them and then they did it.'

'We'd better interview Jill Hillier again,' Anna decided, 'but we also need someone to go over to the abortion clinic and follow up on this Rovena Mitfari. They must have kept her contact details and probably a photocopy of her passport, seeing as she was supposed to be going back there. And then there's Pimm's bar. It looks likely that he and this Stacey woman must be holding Mollie and Amanda and goodness knows how many other young women at the back of there somewhere, but how are we going to flush them out and get the evidence to secure a conviction? We need more information before we go in all guns blazing in case we only make things worse for the girls. I only wish I had more officers available to do the groundwork.'

'Can't you hand over Pimm's bar to DCI Khan?' suggested Andy. 'He's supposed to be looking for Amanda.'

'But *I'm* in charge of finding Mollie,' Jonah cut in. 'And it's Mollie who's been positively identified at Pimm's. We're only assuming that Amanda was there too, because they've been seen together since.'

'Isn't the way in to arrest Stacey and question her about her visit to the abortion clinic?' asked Bernie. 'Get the staff from there to confirm that she was the "social worker" who accompanied Rovena Mitfari to her appointment, and then ask her to produce this Rovena and explain what their relationship really is.'

'The trouble is, we don't know how many other women Stacey and Zack may be holding in the rooms above his bar,' Anna pointed out. 'If we arrest Stacey, Zack and his mates may spirit them away somewhere and we'll never find them.'

She sighed and looked round at

the others, trying to prioritise the work in her mind and to allocate jobs among her remaining team members.

'What do you think, Peter?' she asked at last. 'You've been very quiet. Where would you start?'

'I was just thinking about Amanda and Mollie,' Peter answered. 'What are we doing to find them? We think we know that they were being held by Zack and Stacey up until the day Mollie was taken to the clinic, but they seem to have got away from them by the morning of the day Hillier was killed, because he was giving them breakfast with no sign of their minders. If we raid Pimm's bar, we may release any other prisoners they've got holed up in there, but those two young women are still going to be out on the streets somewhere, and in danger of being picked up and exploited by other unscrupulous characters.'

'Peter's right,' Bernie backed him up. 'Mollie and Amanda ought to be the first priority. Robin Hillier's already dead. Nothing worse can happen to him.'

'And the other girls that Zack and Stacey have got in that back room of theirs,' Andy added decidedly. 'Judging by the number of men Stacey was showing through there, they must have a good few of them still held there, even with Mollie and

Amanda gone.'

12. TANGLED TALES

Anna leaned back in her seat and closed her eyes while she went through in her mind all the things that needed to be done, and tried to work out the best way of distributing the work. She had better visit the abortion clinic herself, she decided, and she would ask Peter to go with her, since he had heard first hand from the woman who had seen Mollie there. That left Social Services, Jill Hillier and the homeless community, which all needed to be tackled, as well as some discreet enquiries about Zachary Pimm and his associates, which must be done without allowing him to know that he was under police scrutiny.

'OK,' she said at last. 'Andy: you go round to Jill Hillier and ask her about this conversation she's supposed to have had with Mariella Peckforton.'

'Right you are!' Andy got up to leave.

'But before you go,' Anna called him back. 'Get some people running checks on Zachary Pimm, this Stacey, if they can find her, and … was it Tiffany you said the other woman in the bar was called?'

'OK. Is that it?'

'For now. When you get back from Jill Hillier's, see if you can trace any Albanian nationals with the name of Rovena Mitfari or any social workers with parrot tattoos on their hands.'

'Right you are,' Andy repeated, heading for the door. 'See you later!'

'Jonah,' Anna continued. 'Can I leave you to pick up Gavin and get him to take you round to speak to the rough sleepers to find out if any of them have seen two young women together on the streets in the last few days?'

'At your service,' Jonah smiled back.

'And Peter?' Anna turned to her friend with an apologetic look on her face. 'Do you mind coming with me to the abortion clinic?'

'So long as I'm back by two,' Peter acquiesced. 'Crystal's on a late shift today, so I've got the grandkids from half past.'

'We'll get off right away then. It's probably as well not to give them too much time in any case. They must have realised that there was something wrong and they may be busy covering up anything that could be construed as a failure of due diligence on their part.'

'Mrs Hillier,' Andy began, looking across the cluttered sitting room towards Jill, who was perched on the edge of her chair, nervously trying to light a cigarette. 'Why didn't you tell us that you met Augusta Peckforton's sister the night your husband died?'

'You didn't ask,' she mumbled, still struggling with the cigarette in her mouth.

'And you pretended that you didn't know where your husband was,' Andy persisted. 'Why was that?'

'I didn't!' Jill's voice rose and her hand shook as she put the cigarette lighter down on a small table in front of her.

'Professor Peckforton says that she told you he was working in the gardens of Lichfield College.'

'Oh that! I thought you meant I was supposed to know where he was living. I'm sure that was what you asked me about last time.' She leaned back a little and sucked hard on the cigarette.

'You also told us that you didn't know that Augusta Peckforton had died,' Andy went on relentlessly. 'Why did you do that – when her sister had told you about it less than two days before we interviewed you?'

'I forgot,' Jill mumbled. 'You got me up out of bed. I'm not a morning person. It takes me a while to get going – especially when I've been working late.'

'It's a rather strange thing to have forgotten,' Andy commented. 'Are you sure you weren't just trying to mislead us into believing that you hadn't seen your husband for years, when in fact you'd spoken to him only a couple of days before?'

'What d'you mean?' Jill suddenly appeared more alert than Andy had seen her before. She leaned forward and stubbed out her cigarette in the ashtray that lay next to the lighter. 'Who says I saw Robin before he died? It's a lie, whoever it was!'

'Professor Peckforton told us that you accosted her the night Robin Hillier died and asked her where he was. She also said that she told you to look for him in the gardens at Lichfield College, and that, after that, you went off. I'm deducing that you most likely headed straight across to Lichfield in order to see your husband.'

'I couldn't,' Jill said in a low, sulky voice. 'The college was locked up for the night.'

'So you did try to see him?'

'I went across and tried the gate on Goose Lane, and then I went round to the front and tried there, but both gates were locked.'

'That's better!' Andy said encouragingly. 'Now we're getting somewhere. What did you do after that?'

'I just went home,' Jill shrugged and reached for another cigarette.

'No point hanging around the streets any longer.'

'No,' Andy agreed. He leaned forward and tried to catch her eye, but she became suddenly very busy with the cigarette lighter. 'Professor Peckforton also told us that you tried to give her a note to give to her sister. Do you still have it?'

'No!' Jill's eyes opened wide and she dragged hard on the cigarette in her mouth, giving Andy the impression that she was alarmed at this line of questioning. Then she took it out, exhaled in a cloud of smoke and gulped in another breath before adding, 'I threw it away.'

'Do you mind telling me what was in it?'

'Yes, I do. It was private.'

'But it was presumably about your husband, who is the subject of a murder enquiry, so I need to know,' Andy pressed her. 'What was it that you wanted to say to Augusta Peckforton?'

'I – I –,' Jill stammered looking round the room wildly and taking quick, nervous sucks on the cigarette. 'I – I – just wanted to talk to her. I wanted to ask her … Imogen's struggling at the moment – for money, I mean. Her wages don't go far with two kids growing up and I don't have anything much to spare or I'd help her out.'

'You were hoping she would help your daughter financially?'

'Or just let Robin know, so he could. I know he'd've wanted to help if he knew, but she hasn't – hadn't – let him see either of the girls for months! I can't understand why he put up with it! She – she – well I don't know. He always was easily led. He always saw the best in people and often that meant he let them lead him up the garden path.'

'She manipulated him?' Andy suggested.

'That's right,' Jill nodded. 'That's the word: manipulated. That's why, when I saw the name *Peckforton* on the list for high table, I thought I'd try to get a note through to her, to try to … I was hoping even she might see that a man ought to help his own daughter.'

Anna and Peter meanwhile, were speaking to the receptionist at the abortion clinic.

'I don't know any more than I told you over the phone,' she insisted. 'I have her records, here on the computer. Rovena Mitfari booked for an initial consultation on Monday the twenty-fourth of June, and for a surgical termination on Tuesday the twenty-fifth. Here's the scanned image we took of her passport to confirm her identity and age.'

She turned her computer screen round so that Anna and Peter could see the passport, which stated that its holder was Rovena Mitfari, date of birth 2nd April 1999, place of birth Tirana. The photograph was of a young woman with shoulder-length brown hair and tanned skin.

'Could you print us off a copy of that?' Anna asked.

'Of course.' The receptionist took hold of the computer mouse and a few clicks later, they could hear the sound of a printer whirring into action beneath the counter.

'She arrived the first day with a woman who said she was her social worker,' she continued, handing over the printout. 'She showed me her ID. It looked fine to me. In any case, the girl was over eighteen so she could sign for herself. She didn't need to have had anyone with her.'

'Did you make a note of the social worker's name?' Anna asked, already confident of receiving a negative answer.

'No. As I said, her presence wasn't necessary. I treated her as just a friend of the patient, coming with her for moral support. Women often like to do that. It's not for us to check up on who they are or keep records of their names.'

'Of course, but do you happen to remember what it was?' Peter asked. 'We haven't been able to find anyone matching her description working for Social Services.'

'No, sorry.' The receptionist

shook her head. 'Like I said, I didn't take much notice of her.'

'We have a witness who says that the girl appeared to be frightened,' Peter told her. 'Was that how she seemed to you?'

'I didn't notice particularly. Patients often seem that way – it's a difficult time for them, especially the young ones.'

'My witness got the impression that she was frightened of the woman she was with,' Peter persisted. 'The woman who claimed to be a social worker. Did it strike you like that at all?'

'I can't say it did. It's not up to me to psychoanalyse people.'

'OK.' Anna took charge again.

'Now we need to speak to all the other staff who saw her that morning.'

'That will be the sonographer who did her scan and the doctor who assessed her and took her consent for the surgical procedure. I'll just check who they were.' She busied herself with mouse and keyboard for a few seconds before looking up at Anna again. 'Yes. They're both in again today. Dr Garston is with a patient at the moment, but it looks as if the sonographer's free. Shall I give her a buzz?'

'If you don't mind.'

The receptionist pressed buttons and spoke through an intercom. 'Hi Mel! I've got the police here wanting to talk to you about that Albanian girl we had in a couple of weeks ago. Is it OK for me to send them in now?'

The muffled response was presumably in the affirmative because the receptionist immediately turned to them and pointed them in the direction of the sonography room. Anna went ahead down a short corridor and in through a door on the right.

Peter looked round the room. There was a couch standing against one wall, with an ultrasound machine on wheels next to it. On the other side of the room, a woman in a white uniform tunic sat at a desk. She turned her chair at the sound of their entry and got up to greet them.

'Hello! I'm Melanie Roberts. What can I do for you?'

'DCI Anna Davenport and DI Peter Johns,' Anna replied briskly, holding up her warrant card. 'We need to ask you some questions about a woman who came here two weeks ago. She gave her name as Rovena Mitfari, but we have reason to believe that she was using a false passport and that she may really have been this girl.'

She held up a photograph of Mollie Burgess. Mel leaned forward and studied it.

'Yes,' she murmured, looking up again. 'It could have been her. Isn't this the girl that's been on the news recently? The one that's supposed to be mixed up in a murder or something?'

'That's right,' Anna nodded. 'Her name's Mollie Burgess. She disappeared from home three years ago, and now we have evidence to link her to the death of a man in central Oxford, which took place shortly after Rovena Mitfari came here. A witness came forward who is convinced that she saw her here. We're trying to trace her, partly because of a possible connection with the murder, but mostly because she's been missing since she was fifteen and it looks as if she's been abducted and forced into sex work.'

'That's awful!' Mel's eyes widened in horror. 'Well, I couldn't be absolutely sure it was her, but it certainly could have been.'

'More likely than this woman?' asked Anna, holding out the photocopy of Rovena Mitfari's passport.

'Yes, I think so,' Mel studied the picture carefully. 'Of course, passport photographs never look very realistic, do they? And a lot depends on how people do their hair and that sort of thing. I suppose, she could've bleached her hair and had it curled since that photo was taken, but … Yes, the girl I saw a fortnight ago had much lighter hair and it was curly – more like in that other photo you showed me.'

'Good,' Anna said, putting the

pictures away. 'That's very helpful. Now tell me: how did she seem? Was she nervous? How did she interact with the woman who came with her?'

'Yes, I'd say she was very nervous,' Mel confirmed, 'but that's not unusual.'

'Did she speak with an accent at all?' asked Peter, keen to establish beyond doubt that this was Mollie and not an Albanian immigrant.

'She hardly spoke at all. She just nodded when I explained about the ultrasound. As far as I can remember, the only thing she said the whole time she was here was when she saw the image on the screen, while I was measuring to assess the age of the foetus. She said, "Is that my baby?" And then the other woman told her not to ask stupid questions and she started crying. It was my fault. I shouldn't have let her see it. Women often get emotional if they see the image when it's a relatively late abortion. The worst is when it's a foetal abnormality that hasn't been picked up until very late.'

'Did you get the impression that she – the girl I mean – actually wanted an abortion?' Peter asked, watching Mel's face closely. 'Or could she have been acting under duress – from the other woman who came with her, for example?'

'That's not for me to say,' Mel

answered quickly. 'The doctors make the final decision. I just do the ultrasound and send them a report. They will have talked it through with the patient and obtained informed consent.'

'But, if I were to tell you that she didn't come back for her second appointment,' Peter persisted, 'would that surprise you?'

'Not really,' Mel admitted, 'but then, I would never be surprised about that,' she added hastily. 'It's a very emotional time for a woman and a big step for her to take.'

'Now, about the other woman,' Anna asked. 'Did she tell you her name?'

'Not that I remember.' Mel shook

her head. 'She didn't speak much either.'

'Could you describe her to me?'

'I'm not sure I could. She was only here for a few minutes and she wasn't even one of the patients. I didn't really …'

'Have ago,' Anna encouraged. 'Think back. Was she taller or shorter than the girl she was accompanying, for example?'

'Taller, I think – but don't hold me to that! I could be wrong.' Mel paused and seemed to be thinking. 'Her hair was platinum blond with dark roots just starting to show. She was wearing a jacket and a knee-length full skirt and sensible shoes – just the sort of thing you'd expect a social worker to wear – but she had a lot of makeup on, which isn't.'

'Good. Thank you,' Anna noted down this description, and then looked up at Mel again. 'You didn't happen to notice her hands by any chance, did you?'

'No?' Mel stared back with a puzzled expression. 'Why would I?'

'Other witnesses have noticed a distinctive tattoo on her right hand,' Anna explained. 'I just wondered if you'd seen it too, that's all.'

'No,' Mel repeated. 'I don't remember seeing anything like that.'

'OK,' Anna smiled back. 'Now, is there anything else you can remember about either of the women? Anything they said – to one another or to you? Anything about their appearance or the way they behaved that was in any way unusual?'

'No.' Mel shook her head again. 'It was just another routine scan. I'm sorry.'

'Never mind.' Anna handed her a card. 'If you do remember anything else, give me a ring on this number.'

She turned to go. Peter followed her out into the corridor and back to the reception desk. There were several women in the waiting area: one on her own, sitting away from the others, apparently engrossed in reading a magazine; a teenager with an older woman beside her, both of them looking both nervous and embarrassed; and two friends talking together in low voices. Peter felt very much out of place as they looked towards him, apparently wondering what a man could be doing in this all-female enclave. The receptionist looked up as they approached.

'Dr Garston can see you now,' she said. 'Back down the way you've come and it's first on the left.'

Still conscious of the eyes of half a dozen women on him, Peter turned and led the way back along the corridor and into the doctor's room. As in the sonography room, there was a couch standing against one wall and a desk opposite. Dr Louise Garston was a small woman with close-cropped black hair and striking dark brown eyes beneath thick black eyebrows, which contrasted with her pale complexion. She got up as they entered and shook hands with each of them in turn.

'Please – sit down,' she said, gesturing towards two metal-framed chairs with plastic cushioned seats. 'Diane tells me you want to talk about Rovena Mitfari, the Albanian girl who came here back on the twenty-fourth. Is that right?'

'Yes,' Anna confirmed. 'We have reason to believe that she wasn't who she claimed to be. Another witness has told us that she was in fact this woman.' She held out the picture of Mollie Burgess. 'What do *you* think? Could this have been her?'

The doctor took the photograph and studied it carefully. Then she handed it back.

'It could have been,' she said, 'but I couldn't swear to it. Who is this?'

'This is Mollie Burgess,' Anna told her. 'She went missing three years ago, aged fifteen. We now have reason to believe that she was being held captive somewhere in the Oxford area and being forced to work as a prostitute. She has recently been seen on the streets with another young woman and an older man, who has been discovered dead.'

'Well the woman she came here with was older – mid forties at least, I'd say.'

'No. We think that was a different woman,' Anna agreed. 'We suspect that her so-called *social worker* was one of her captors, who came with her to make sure that she didn't escape and didn't confide in anyone here. Could you describe her to me?'

'Fair hair: straight, about shoulder length maybe a bit longer.' The doctor thought for a moment. 'She had heavy black-framed glasses on and lots of makeup. If she took those off, I doubt I'd recognise her.'

'How did Rovena – or the woman who was calling herself Rovena –

behave towards her?' asked Peter. 'What sort of relationship did they seem to have?'

'I couldn't say. Rovena hardly said a word all through the consultation. I had to press her really hard to confirm that she understood what the procedure was and what it would involve for her. I have to admit ...' Dr Garston paused and looked nervously across at Peter and Anna. 'I have to admit, I was uneasy about allowing her to proceed, but there was the social worker telling me this dreadful story about her being raped by her own father and ...' she paused again and her face went rather red. 'Well, of course, that explained why the girl was so traumatised and couldn't speak for herself, and … and I knew that if we didn't act at once it would be too late, because she was already twenty-two weeks. So … so I signed the form and one of my colleagues counter-signed it and we arranged to do the procedure the next day.'

'I see.' Anna paused for just long enough to allow the doctor to start wondering whether she was planning to report her for misconduct or to prosecute her for signing off an abortion beyond the legal limit. 'And how did they seem when they left?'

'What do you mean?'

'What mood were they each in? What sort of atmosphere was there between the two of them?'

'I don't really know. I'm not sure what you're getting at.'

'Was there any possibility that the girl was under any sort of duress from the older woman?' Peter intervened.

'No! I told you: she said she was her social worker and I assumed that she was acting in the girl's best interests,' the doctor replied defensively.

'OK. Let's leave it at that.' Anna got up to go. She put one of her cards down on the desk. 'Ring this number if you think of anything else that might help us find either of them.'

Jonah and Bernie were having an interesting – if unproductive – time with Constable Hughes, touring various locations in the city where he knew the local homeless people might be found. Most shook their heads and denied any knowledge of Hillier or his female companions. None had anything further to add to their sparse recollections of Hillier's behaviour in the days leading up to his death. None of them admitted to recognising either Mollie or Amanda from their photographs.

Finally, Gavin introduced them to the man who had talked about Hillier having a black girlfriend. Craig Manson was younger and fitter-looking than most of the homeless men that they had met. He had a shaved head and a scar on the left-hand side of his cheek. He was dressed in combat trousers and jacket, and carried a military-style rucksack on his back, which he set down on the floor next to his chair when Gavin invited him into a coffee bar for a drink and a chat.

'What happened to you?' he asked Jonah, while they were waiting for Bernie to return with the coffee.

'I got a bullet in the neck ten years back,' Jonah answered laconically.

'You been in the military then? Which regiment?'

'No. The police. Someone

objected to me putting away a fraudster and they tried to pay me back.'

'That's terrible,' Craig said with feeling. 'I mean it's bad enough when you're on active service. But you know you've got to expect that sort of thing in a war zone, but back here in Oxford ...' his voice tailed off and he sat in silence shaking his head and nervously picking at rough edges on his fingernails.

'But I got the last laugh,' Jonah went on. 'With friends like Bernie and technology like this chair, I was able to go back to my job as a detective for another nine years, before they finally pensioned me off. And even now – as you can see –

they keep asking me back to help out.'

'I wish it was like that in the services,' Craig responded bitterly. 'While you're there, it's all *we're all one big happy family* and *the regiment looks after its own* and all that; but once you've been discharged, nobody wants to know you.'

'You're an ex-army man then? Jonah asked.

'Yes. The Mercian Regiment – armoured infantry. I served in Iraq and Afghanistan.'

'And now?'

'Like I said, nobody wants to know. I've had a few jobs, but I keep being told I don't fit in. I get these flash-backs – you know: someone bangs a door and I'm diving for cover. It upsets people and they tell me to leave.'

'It must be difficult,' Jonah nodded, 'adjusting to being back in civilian life after the sorts of things you must've seen and done.'

'Too right, it is!' Craig agreed vehemently. 'And it's easier for everyone just to tell you to get lost and go and be someone else's problem.'

'Here you are!' Bernie announced, arriving back with the drinks. 'Yours was the Americano, wasn't it? I brought sugar in case you want it.'

She put down a cup and saucer

on the table in front of Craig and then turned her attention to Jonah. She had his drink in his own plastic beaker with a lid and a drinking straw poking out of the top. She flapped up a tray attachment on the arm of his chair and set the coffee down on it, adjusting the angle of the straw so that he could reach it easily with his mouth. Gavin meanwhile, following behind her, set down two more cups of coffee on the table before sitting down opposite Craig.

'How're you keeping then?' he asked conversationally.

'Alright,' Craig mumbled back. 'You know.'

'This here is DCI Porter,' Gavin told him, nodding towards Jonah.

'He's interested in what you told me about Robin Hillier having a girlfriend.'

'How well did you know Hillier?' Jonah asked. 'I get the impression he kept himself to himself and didn't have much to do with other homeless people. Is that right?'

'Yeah. I reckon he didn't rate us. He hadn't been on the streets for long. I reckon he didn't really believe it was happening to him – d'you know what I mean?'

'Yes. I think I can understand that.'

'That's how it is for the first few weeks,' Craig went on. 'You keep thinking: it's just for one night, and then I'll find somewhere. And then it's another night and another and before you know it …'

'Can you remember where you saw this girlfriend of his?' Jonah probed gently.

'No.' Craig shook his head. Then he screwed up his eyes and seemed to be thinking. 'Or … yes! I know! It was in the covered market. It'd come on to rain and there were crowds of people in there sheltering.'

'And you saw them there together?' Jonah asked eagerly. 'Robin Hillier and … can you describe the woman?'

'She was black,' Craig shrugged. 'That's all I noticed.'

'Could she have been this woman?' Jonah made the screen

attached to his chair rotate so that Craig could see a photograph of Amanda displayed on it.'

'It could've been,' Craig muttered dismissively. 'They all look the same to me. Look!' he continued in a louder voice. 'I don't know, do I? I just saw she had her hand through his arm, like they were … and I noticed it 'cos I'd never seen him with a woman before. He headed off with her out on to the High and that's the last I saw of them – OK?'

'Can you remember what day that was?' Jonah asked calmly.

'No. All my days are the same. I don't keep count of time. It's not like I have to be in the office by nine, is it?'

THE SECRET GARDENER

'Try and think,' Gavin urged gently. 'I talked to you last Monday. Robin was killed the Wednesday night before that. So the latest you could've seen him in the market was that Wednesday afternoon.'

'Well, maybe that's when it was then – or it could've been longer ago. I just don't remember, OK?'

'OK then,' Jonah said equably. 'If you don't know which day it was can you remember what time of day you saw them? Was it before lunchtime or after?'

'Dunno. I don't always get any lunch,' Craig mumbled. 'It was busy, like I said, so not very early, I reckon.'

'We think that this black woman

was going round with another girl,' Jonah told him. 'Did she seem to be with anyone when you saw her?'

'Only Hillier. I told you – I thought she must be his girl. I noticed 'cos it seemed strange: him and a black girl. He was quite old too and I'd never seen him with *anyone* before – no mates, no nothing!'

'And you've never seen this woman at all?' Jonah persisted, bringing up a photograph of Mollie Burgess on to the screen. 'We think she's probably out on the streets somewhere, probably with the black woman that you saw with Hillier.'

Craig glanced briefly at the screen and then shook his head. 'Nope!' he declared. 'Never seen her in my life!' He finished his coffee and then looked round at them all. 'Are we done now?'

'Yes, I think so,' Jonah replied with a note of disappointment in his voice. 'If you do remember which day it was you saw Hillier in the covered market, please tell PC Hughes, will you? It could be important.'

Anna clapped her hands to call the room to order. Her team had reconvened to compare notes and consider their next move. Peter had returned home to his grandchildren. Gavin was back in the more familiar world of uniformed policing. However, Jonah and Bernie were still present, albeit with Bernie keeping a close watch on the clock, poised to tell her friend that it was time to call it a day and leave the case to those who were being paid to wear themselves out in the cause of public safety.

'Let's just re-cap on what we know about Mollie and Amanda's movements in the last two weeks,' Anna began. She clicked a button to bring up a map of central Oxford on the screen. 'We believe that they were being held by the owner of this bar, one Zachary Pimm and his accomplice, Stacey.'

'I've got some more on them,' a

voice called out from halfway down the room. 'Stacey is Pimm's wife, and they have a daughter called Tiffany.'

'That'll be the barmaid I saw,' Andy nodded. 'She was called Tiffany.'

'Quite a nice little family business,' Jonah observed drily.

'I'm not sure about that,' Jennifer Moorehouse replied from behind her computer desk. 'They don't own the bar. They just run it for a limited company headed up by a John Lockhart. He's a director of several small and medium-sized businesses, mostly in the entertainment sector.'

'Do any of them have a police

record?' Anna asked.

'Not as far as I could find,' Jennifer shook her head.

'OK. Thanks. That's useful information.' Anna turned back to the screen and once more pointed to the location of Pimm's bar. 'We know that Mollie was still in Stacey's custody on Monday the twenty-fourth, because they were seen together at the abortion clinic. However, by early on the Wednesday, Mollie seems to have got away from Stacey, because she was with Amanda Jayakody and Robin Hillier having breakfast in this café here.'

'What we don't know,' Jonah continued, taking up the story, 'is when exactly they escaped, what role Hillier played in it or where they are now.'

'And we also don't know who killed Hillier or why,' added Andy. 'His wife admits to trying to find him that night – after lying about not knowing where he was or even that he wasn't living with Augusta Peckforton any longer. Could she still be lying when she says she couldn't get into the Fellows' Garden to see him?'

'Or Mariella could've stabbed him before dinner,' Bernie suggested, 'and he just took a long time to die. She might have been afraid he'd tell the world how Augusta had treated him and sully her sister's name.'

'Except that she seemed to be quite open with us about Augusta's behaviour and to consider herself to be a victim as well,' Jonah pointed out. 'Personally, my money would be on the murder being somehow connected with those two girls that he'd befriended – if he did befriend them, and it wasn't that he'd caught them and was intent on taking them back to Pimm and Co.'

'Which brings us back to what we're going to do about Pimm and that brothel that he seems to be running behind his bar,' Anna cut in. 'I think it's time we went in there with a search warrant. The difficult thing is deciding when to do it. If we wait until night-time, we'll end up arresting a whole load of clients who won't be best pleased at being identified and will clog up the system while we work out who's done anything illegal and who hasn't – and it'll be easier for the professional criminals to get away in the confusion. On the other hand, we can't be sure they don't have somewhere else that they keep the girls during the day, so there might be nothing for us to find.'

'The most important thing is to make sure they're all there when you do go in,' Jonah said decisively. 'Otherwise, the ringleaders could scarper when they hear you're on to them. So I'd wait until after opening time, if I were you. And make sure you've got plenty of backup to prevent them making a run for it.'

'Plenty of backup may be a tall order in the present climate,' Anna muttered, 'but I think you're right. I'll organise a search warrant right away and get as many uniformed officers as I can muster to surround the place. It'll be easier to do that without attracting attention at night when everyone expects to see a lot of police on the streets.'

13. POLICE RAID

'I've got people deployed on all sides of the building,' Inspector Jordan Fox reported to Anna as he joined her in a shop doorway fifty yards or so from Pimm's bar. 'They've got all the exits covered, including an emergency fire door from the first floor on to the next-door roof. Shall I send the search team in now?'

'OK. Don't worry about letting the customers in the bar go – just don't let Pimm or any of the staff get away.'

Fox gave a signal and half a

dozen uniformed police emerged from a van, parked in the shadows of a narrow side street, and followed him across the road to the bar. They stood just inside the entrance, barring the way out, while Fox strode up to the bar brandishing the warrant in his hand.

'Are you Zachary Pimm?' he demanded, putting it down on the counter in front of a middle-aged man with a round red face, who was smiling across at a customer as he served him a pint. The smile instantly vanished when he saw Fox's uniform. Then he carefully adjusted his features to register affable surprise, as if an officer with a search warrant was both incomprehensible and of no consequence.

'Yes,' he replied calmly. 'What can I do for you?'

'I have a warrant to search these premises,' Fox said coldly, 'and DCI Davenport would like to ask you a few questions.'

'Why? What am I supposed to have done?' Pimm asked, affecting an air of innocent indignation.

'I'll let Inspector Davenport explain it all to you down at the station,' Fox replied. 'Now, if you wouldn't mind coming round here, a couple of my officers will show you to our van.'

'Certainly officer,' Pimm smiled back ingratiatingly. 'Just give me a moment to fetch my coat and I'll be right with you.'

Out of the corner of his eye, Fox became aware of movement at the other end of the bar. A woman was sidling nonchalantly towards a door at the back of the room.

'Mrs Pimm?' he called out to her. 'Don't go. We'd like you to accompany your husband to the police station to help us clear up a few things.'

Ignoring his words, the woman made a dash for the door and slipped through it. Two uniformed officers were after her in a flash. There was a sound of raised voices in the back room accompanied by noises of furniture being moved on a hard floor and a crash of broken glass.

'That's it!' Fox shouted. 'Appleton! Arrest Mr Pimm and take him out to the van. The rest of you, search the premises and don't let anyone leave without my say-so.'

Sergeant Appleton, tall and muscular with fair hair and pale blue eyes, hastened round to the back of the bar and snapped handcuffs on to Pimm's wrists.

'There's no need for that,' Pimm protested. 'I don't know what this is all about, but I'll come quietly. I've got nothing to hide.'

Appleton handed him over to two constables who bundled him outside and into the waiting police van. Then he followed Fox through the door into the back room.

The scene that greeted them was chaotic. The woman whom Fox had seen leaving the bar, was struggling and screaming in the hands of two female officers, who managed to handcuff her just as he entered. A younger woman, who had attempted to leave through a fire exit, was now being firmly escorted back inside by PC Melanie Stanton and her German Shepherd Dog, PD Q, who had been guarding the back of the building. Two wooden chairs lay on their sides, where they had been knocked over in the scuffle. Behind them, a table was strewn with overturned glasses, some of which had rolled on to the floor and shattered.

A plump man in a smart business suit collided with Appleton in his haste to get through the door back into the bar. Appleton caught him around the chest and set him down unceremoniously on one of the few chairs still remaining upright. The man attempted to get up again, but the police officer pushed him back down.

'Just stay there,' he commanded. 'I'll deal with you in a moment.'

'But I have to go,' the man protested, struggling back to his feet. 'My wife will be expecting me home. I don't know what this is all about, but it's nothing to do with me. I'm just a customer, here for a couple of drinks and a game of cards with a few mates.'

'Cards? Mates?' Fox demanded, coming across and standing over the man. 'Where are they? I don't see them.'

'The others have already gone. I was just … look, here's my card.' The man thrust a business card into his hand. 'Ring me at the office tomorrow if you need to talk to me, but I really must get off now.'

'I'm sorry, sir,' Fox pocketed the card and then looked over the man's head towards a young police constable, one of a team who had just entered the room from the bar. 'Take this gentleman out to the van, will you, Timpson? His name's Gerald Gatley – Councillor Gerald Gatley. I'm sure he'll be delighted to tell you all about why he was here and what he was doing and who he was with. Let him have a little chat with DCI Davenport and then she can decide whether to let him go home.'

He watched as PC Ben Timpson led Gatley back through the door leading to the bar. Then he surveyed the room again. In a corner, not far from the door by which they had entered, he saw a staircase going upwards, presumably to rooms above this one and probably above the bar too. He nudged Appleton and pointed towards it.

'Get up there,' he commanded. 'My guess is that's where they keep the girls. Take the rest of the lads with you – and go carefully. Remember, the chances are the women are the victims in all of this.'

Appleton disappeared up the stairs followed by three constables. Fox looked round the room again. Along the wall to the left stood a long red sofa, occupied by four scantily-clad young women, who stared round in bewilderment and cowered away from the turbulent activity going on in front of them. Fox studied their faces. None of them looked like the pictures that he had been shown of Mollie Burgess and Amanda Jayakody.

THE SECRET GARDENER

Two of them were small and dark-complexioned, but Mediterranean rather than Asian or African. They looked so similar to one another that he suspected they might be twins. The third had the appearance of an Amazon by contrast. She was tall and athletic-looking with pale skin, golden hair and stunning blue eyes. Perhaps a Viking princess rather than an Amazon, he decided. Finally, his eyes rested on the fourth figure. She too was of below average height. Her long hair was straight and fell down over her chest, but did not reach far enough to cover her small breasts partially encased in a black bra beneath a white-lace bodice. It was blond, but there was a thin line of a darker colour showing at the roots. Her eyes were deep brown and frightened.

'Don't be afraid.' Trainee Constable Stella Gilbert had followed Melanie into the room and was now making a beeline for the sofa. 'We're here to help you. Do you have a coat or a dressing gown you could put on, so we can take you somewhere safe, away from all this fuss and bother?'

'We can't leave,' the Viking Princess told her in a thin voice quite out of keeping with her imperious persona. 'Zack will be angry with us if we-'

'Zack is under arrest,' Fox told

her. 'So is Stacey, and,' he turned to address the young woman whom Melanie had now handcuffed and subdued, 'Tiffany, I presume?'

'Yes,' she nodded. 'Tiffany Pimm, but none of this is anything to do with me! I just do what I'm told – ask anyone. It's Dad and Mum run the place. I just pull pints and clean tables.'

'Save that for DCI Davenport,' Fox snapped. 'OK Mel, take her away. There's a van waiting for them outside. And then you can stand Q down. I don't think anyone else is going to try to make a run for it.'

'OK,' Melanie answered, taking Tiffany firmly by the arm. 'I'll put Q back in the van, but shall I get

Wesley out and have him go over the place? The chances are, in a setup like this there'll be some drugs around the place.'

'Better wait 'til we've got everyone out,' Fox decided after a moment's thought. 'Keep him on standby and I'll let you know when to send him in.'

Melanie nodded quickly and then pushed Tiffany towards the door. Fox stood surveying the wrecked room and listening to sounds of shouting and banging overhead. Then he turned his attention back to the red sofa and its occupants.

'It's alright,' Stella coaxed, kneeling down on the floor and smiling towards the young women.

THE SECRET GARDENER

'We'll look after you now. If you could all just find something to put on over those clothes – and some more comfortable shoes,' she added, looking down and realising that the women would find it difficult even to walk as far as the police van in the high heels that they were wearing.

The women gazed back unspeaking, with bewildered expressions on their faces. Eventually one of the twins plucked up courage to plead in a foreign accent that Stella could not place, 'please! Leave us here. Do not put us in prison.'

'Nobody's going to put you in prison,' Stella assured her earnestly. 'Like I said, we're here to help you.

Please! Just get some clothes on and we'll take you somewhere safe, where you can tell us all about what's been happening to you. It's Zack who may be going to prison, not you. Please! Trust me.'

She got to her feet and put out her arm, gesturing to them also to rise. They stared back, still cowering against the sofa. Then the Viking Princess relaxed a little and seemed about to get up, but before she could do so there was a disturbance in the corner of the room where the staircase lay. Stella looked up and saw a line of men in various stages of undress descending the stairs and entering the room. They were followed by Appleton and three constables.

'There are ten or a dozen girls up there,' he reported, 'and one of them answers to the description of Mollie Burgess.'

'OK.' Fox looked the men up and down. They were clearly clients and not part of Pimm's gang. 'Take them back into the bar and get their names and addresses, then let them go. The girls are more important than these losers.'

It took a long time, but eventually they had the groups sorted. The punters were questioned on the premises and then released. Zack, Stacey and Tiffany were taken back to the police station and put in cells for the night. Thirteen young women were found places in secure accommodation overnight under the supervision of Social Services. Tomorrow would be time enough for them to tell their stories and for the process of reuniting them with their families to begin.

Anna watched as Mollie and Amanda were driven away together. Should she contact their parents that night to let them know that their daughters were safe? No, she decided, far better to wait until they were rested and washed clean of the exaggerated makeup and pungent perfume designed to make them more attractive to Zachary's clients, and wearing clothing less likely to shock their nearest and dearest.

Better also to prepare their families to hear what they would have to tell them about their life since their disappearances.

She looked at her watch: still the right side of midnight. The operation had gone more smoothly and more quickly than she had dared to hope. She would have the luxury of some sleep in her own bed that night after all, and Jessica would be able to relinquish responsibility for baby Donna for a few hours. Things would certainly be better when Philip moved back in with them – or at least, she hoped they would. She turned to Fox, who was standing next to her also watching the van drive away.

'Can I leave you to finish tidying things up here? I could do with getting off home. It's going to be a busy day tomorrow.'

'No problem. I don't think there's a lot more to do. We've got everybody out, it's just a matter of sweeping the place for drugs and going over it with a toothcomb for evidence that those girls were trafficked.'

'Good. I'll get off then.' Anna took one final look round before heading back to her car. The street was eerily quiet and deserted. There were no late-night revellers, no students heading back to their colleges after an evening out, just two constables standing guard to keep onlookers away and Mel Stanton, now accompanied by drugs dog PD Wesley, an eager liver-and-white Springer spaniel, on their way into the building to sniff out further evidence with which to incriminate Zack and his associates.

It had been a good night's work, but the hard part was still to come. They had cleared up two missing persons enquiries, but it was still uncertain how these were linked to the death of Robin Hillier. She would let Jonah know that Mollie Burgess had been found, first thing in the morning. There was no point disturbing him during the night. He would probably want to be the one to tell her parents that she was safe.

She had better report to DCI Khan first thing in the morning as well, to let him know that Amanda Jayakody had also been recovered, safe and well. Jonah had been right, after all, when he said that the two cases might be linked. That only left Pandora Birch. Anna could not decide whether to be glad or sorry that she had not been found among the young women in the rooms above Pimm's bar. It would have been a dreadful thing for a sixteen-year-old to have been forced into the life that they had endured, but at least then her ordeal would have been over and her frantic parents would be able to receive her back, however damaged she might be by the experience. It would be a difficult day for them – and for DCI Khan – when the news broke that Mollie and Amanda had been found, and yet their own daughter was still missing with nobody able to say whether the hunt for her would ever bear fruit.

14. CLOSING IN

'Now Mollie, don't be afraid,' Anna began, looking across the table and wishing that the interview room were more homely and comfortable. The grey walls and Spartan furnishing might be appropriate for questioning hardened criminals but it was not conducive to putting at ease a frightened teenager who had just been rescued from a three-year ordeal of sexual exploitation. 'We're here to help you. Nobody can hurt you now and nobody is going to criticise you for anything you've done. We just want to know exactly what happened. Do you understand?'

Mollie glanced nervously towards the social worker who sat next to her; then she looked back at Anna and Jonah on the other side of the table and nodded.

'Good.' Anna smiled in what she hoped was a reassuring way. 'Now, please can you think back to three years ago when you left home? You told your dad that you were going to the pictures with a friend. Do you remember that?'

Mollie nodded nervously.

'It was Ella Campbell,' Jonah added. 'We talked to her, and she told us that you hadn't arranged to go to the cinema with her at all. I'm guessing that's because you had other plans and you didn't think your dad would approve of them. Am I right?'

Mollie nodded again.

'Do you mind telling us about them?' Jonah pursued gently.

'I – I was going to live with Harry,' Mollie replied after a long pause.

'Harry?' Jonah enquired.

'He was my boyfriend – at least … at least that's what I thought he was. He had this lovely house in the country with stables and everything!' Suddenly a dam seemed to burst and the words came tumbling out of her mouth in a torrent of indignation. 'He told me he loved me and he wanted us always to be together. He said Mum and Dad wouldn't understand, because he was so much older than me, so it would be better if we didn't tell them. He – at first it was great. He was at home all day and we just chilled together or went riding. He gave me lots of presents too – new clothes and stuff and he said one of the horses was mine. He was so-o-o good with horses! But then he started going away – sometimes overnight. He said it was business. I asked for money to go shopping, but he said I mustn't go out because Mum and Dad might see me and make me go back home. He locked me in! He actually locked me in the house and wouldn't let me go out – not even to see the horses!'

'Does Harry have another name?' Anna asked when Mollie finally paused for breath.

'Lockhart. He used to say, as soon as I was eighteen we'd get married and I'd be Mrs Lockhart.' Molly screwed up her face in an expression of disgust. 'I used to think that would be so wonderful! He gave me an engagement ring – a real diamond ring! And he said we were going to live together in that big house forever.'

'Didn't you think of letting your Mum and Dad know you were alright?' Anna asked, trying not to sound judgemental. 'I know you didn't want them to take you back, but didn't you know they'd be worried about you?'

'I don't suppose Mum even noticed!' Mollie retorted. Then, looking a little shamefaced, she went on, 'actually I did try to ring them, but my phone wasn't working. I think maybe Harry broke it deliberately. He said he'd get me a new one, but he never did.'

In the next room, DCI Arshad Khan was interviewing Amanda Jayakody, assisted by DC Alice Ray.

'So you thought you were being offered a job?'

'That's right,' Amanda confirmed with a wry smile. 'I realise now how naïve and stupid I was not to check it out more thoroughly first. I was just so excited when I got this message on LinkedIn[9] saying that they'd seen my profile and thought I was just what they wanted for their graduate scheme, that I never thought. I just went along to the interview and … I even believed them when they said they needed to keep my passport so that they could apply for a visa for me to stay in Britain. I can't believe I let them take me in like that!'

---

[9] LinkedIn is a subsidiary company of the Microsoft Corporation. It provides a platform for professional networking, including job search.

'Can you describe the men who interviewed you?' Arshad asked. 'Did they tell you their names?'

'There was a youngish man called Harry. He said he was in charge of the graduate recruitment scheme. And there was an older man who talked about all the benefits of working for the company – pension schemes and health insurance and stuff – and showed pictures of the place out in the country where they ran their induction course. And there was a woman who said she was from Human Resources. She didn't say much. She just took notes.'

'Is that all you can remember about them?' Arshad pressed her gently. 'No more names? Or any more about what they looked like?'

'I can't remember, sorry.' Amanda shook her head. 'Harry was quite tall with dark brown hair – quite long – and big brown eyes, like …,' she paused and smiled, 'like Bambi's in the Disney film. I suppose you'd say he was tall, dark and handsome – and didn't he know it!'

'How d'you mean?' Alice asked sharply.

'He was in charge of the "induction programme",' Amanda explained. 'They weren't lying about the country mansion. A car picked us up in the centre of Oxford – that's me and two other new graduates, both women, which with hindsight ought to have made me suspicious – and took us out there. For a few days, it all seemed quite kosher – lots of team-building exercises and that sort of thing – just long enough for us all to let our families know that we were all set up with a job and everything was fine.'

'And then?' Arshad asked.

'Our mobile phones mysteriously disappeared. We asked for out passports back, but they were never given to us. At first, they said that the visa process was taking longer than they expected, and then they said that we owed them money for applying on our behalf and we'd get our papers back after we'd worked for long enough to pay back the debt.

'So the others were also foreign nationals?' Arshad queried.

'That's right. I suppose that ought to have rung alarm bells too, but it didn't. If I thought about it at all, I thought maybe they were hoping to pay us a little less because we didn't have as much choice as British citizens did.'

'You mean you had to have a job that satisfied the immigration rules?' asked Alice.

'That's right,' Amanda nodded. 'And we had to have one fast or we'd have to go home, and it would be more difficult to get a job applying from abroad. One of the others was Chinese and the other was from

Nigeria, I think. I don't know what happened to them. After a few weeks we were separated and I was taken to that place in Oxford where the police found us yesterday.'

'Did you try to escape?' Alice asked wonderingly. 'I mean: you're bright and educated. Couldn't you have found a way to get out and go to the police?'

'They told us we would be put in jail as illegal immigrants if we tried to run to the authorities.'

'But that's not true!' Alice began, but Arshad silenced her with a look.

'You don't know what it was like,' Amanda said earnestly, leaning forward to look Alice in the eye, 'being kept shut up in those rooms day and night and never meeting anyone except Zack and Harry and Stacey – and the "clients", of course! And being told all the time that we owed money – for the visas that we never saw and for food and clothes and rent. I know it sounds stupid now, but we believed every word they said – and anyway, if anyone questioned it or stepped out of line, Zack would punish them.'

'How?' Arshad asked.

'It depended,' Amanda shrugged. 'Sometimes he just slapped them about the face; sometimes it was solitary confinement without food; sometimes he punished all of us to try to turn us against whoever it was who'd annoyed him. We soon learned not to try anything.'

'But you and Mollie did escape in the end,' Arshad said gently. 'How did that come about?'

'Mollie was desperate. Did you know she's pregnant? Do you know about them trying to make her have an abortion?'

Arshad nodded. 'Yes. Someone recognised her there – at the abortion clinic. That's how we found you.'

'She was terrified by what they'd told her at the clinic about what they were going to do to her. She said she'd do anything to stop them. She had all sorts of mad ideas for getting away. In the end, I said I'd go with her. I thought she'd end up getting herself killed if she went on her own. Some of the other girls created a diversion and we managed to slip out of the back way.'

'Is this your passport?' Andy asked, holding out the photocopy that the receptionist at the abortion clinic had given to Anna. He was interviewing one of the girls who had been sitting on the red sofa in the room behind Pimm's Bar. At his side sat Stella Gilbert, very nervous at being part of a CID operation for the first time.

'Yes!' The young woman on the other side of the table looked up at him with a puzzled frown on her face. 'Where did you get this?' she asked in strongly accented English.

'It was presented at a clinic as identification for this woman.' Andy put down a photograph of Mollie on the table.

'Mollie?' Rovena Mitfari looked at him in surprise. 'But why? And how could they …?'

'She was a Missing Person,' Andy explained. 'Her name had been in the papers and on TV. They were afraid someone might recognise it. And the clinic would've wanted to know her doctor's name and address. They had to make out she was a foreign national or people might manage to join the dots and work out who she was.'

'And the people at the clinic? They believed that she was me?' Rovena asked in amazement.

'Yes,' Andy nodded. 'The passport was issued five years ago. I suppose they thought her appearance had changed. I'm not sure that I would have recognised *you* from that photograph,' he added, studying the girl's face. 'Your hair's much longer now, for example. Now, can you tell us how Stacey came to have your passport in the first place?'

'The woman who took them from us must have given it to her.'

'What woman was this?' Andy asked.

THE SECRET GARDENER

'In Tirana. We called her Agnesa. She never said what her last name was.'

'Tell us what happened,' Andy urged gently.

'She told us she could get us jobs in England. She said the pay was three, four, five times what we were earning in Albania. She said first we must learn good English. She could arrange lessons. She said they were free, but then afterwards she said we had to pay for them out of our wages after we came to England.'

'When you say *we*,' Andy interrupted, 'who else do you mean?'

'There were about twenty of us in the class. I started going with my friend Drita. We worked together in a shop where lots of tourists come, so we thought our English was quite good, but Agnesa said we needed lessons before we could work in England. So we went to her "free" classes. At the end, she said that she had jobs for us all and they would pay for our travel to England, but if we did not go, we had to pay for the classes. It was a lot of money and we thought the jobs in England sounded good, so we decided to go.'

'Just you and Drita?' queried Andy. 'Or did the others go too?'

'I think all the class. One or two said they did not want to go, but when Agnesa told us how much we owed, I think they went as well. We did not have any choice. The classes were so expensive.'

'Then Harry started bringing men home with him,' Mollie continued. 'He said they were "business associates" and I had to be nice to them because if I wasn't it might lose him a lot of money.'

'And by "being nice" he meant you had to go to bed with them?' asked Anna.

Mollie nodded. 'Some of them were quite nice about it, but some of them were horrid and rough and wanted me to do all sorts of – of – weird things. I knew it was wrong, but I was frightened so I did them.

And sometimes, if they were pleased with me, Harry would be nice to me afterwards and let me ride the horses again and tell me how much he loved me and that it would all be better when we were married and what a pity I was still too young.'

'Couldn't you have got away?' Anna asked, struck by the mention of horse riding. 'I mean: when you were riding, how could he have stopped you riding off and finding your way home, or to a police station?'

'But I didn't want to leave him!' Mollie protested in wide-eyed astonishment. 'I loved him! I just wished he didn't keep going off and leaving me shut in and bringing his friends back and expecting me to …'

'And how did you end up working for Zack Pimm?' Anna enquired. 'Was he one of the men that Harry brought back to the house with him?

'Yes,' Mollie nodded. 'He'd been a few times. Then one day Harry told me we were going for an outing in his car. I thought it was funny, 'cos we never went out. Harry was afraid someone might recognise me and tell the police. He said they'd put me in prison because I'd been having sex when I was under-age.'

'But that's ridiculous!' Anna exploded. 'And you believed him?'

'I knew it was against the law,' Mollie replied earnestly. 'They told us that at school. But I was so much in love with Harry that I didn't think about it until it was too late.'

'Those laws are there to protect girls like you,' Jonah told her gently. 'It's Harry who'll go to jail, not you, but we don't know where he is. Can you tell us where this country house is that he kept you in?'

'No. Sorry.' Mollie shook her head. 'We came into Oxford on the Southern by-pass and then along Botley Road. That's all I know.'

'How long did it take to get to Oxford?' Jonah asked.

'I don't know. I don't have a watch.'

'But it wasn't so far you had to stop on the way?' Jonah persisted.

'No.'

THE SECRET GARDENER

'Do you remember seeing anything on the way? Any landmarks? Or anything unusual that might help us to work out where you were coming from?' he pressed her gently.

'It was dark. I didn't see much. I don't remember anything until we got to the big roundabout at Botley.'

* * *

'Don't be afraid, Drita,' Monica said, looking across the table with what she hoped was a kindly smile. 'You're not in any trouble. We're here to help you.'

'But I should not be here,' the young Albanian answered fearfully.

'They told me that you have severe punishments for people who enter Britain without the proper papers. They showed us pictures!'

'If you're here illegally then you may be deported,' Joshua Pitchfork told her, 'but that's all.'

'You won't lock me up in the dark or force me to work to pay for my fare back to Albania?'

'No,' Monica assured her. 'Whatever they told you, you're safe now, but we need you to answer our questions so that we can make sure they don't do this to any more people. So now, tell me about the set-up at Pimm's bar. You all lived upstairs, is that right?'

'Yes,' Drita nodded. 'There were

two big rooms where we were kept while the bar was closed, and five small ones for – for what they called *entertaining* the men that came. You know what that means?'

'Yes,' Monica agreed, 'I know what that means.'

'Stacey was in charge of us. We had to do what she said or Zack would come and ...,' she hesitated. When she began again, she spoke slowly, picking her words with care. 'He was very ... careful. He knew how to hurt us without leaving a mark. He ... he did not want his ... property ... to lose its value.'

'So, when a man wanted one of you to *entertain* him, he would ask Stacey?' queried Joshua. 'Is that how it worked?'

'I am not sure. Stacey and Tiffany would be serving in the bar, I think, and the men would speak to them – but you have to remember, we were not allowed out there. We had to stay upstairs or in the back. Four of us would sit on the sofa in the back room and wait, and when a man came through he would choose one of us.'

'I see,' Monica said encouragingly. 'And then I suppose you – or whoever was chosen – took them upstairs?'

'Yes. They paid Stacey and she told us what we had to do – there were different things that they could pay for – and which room. Then we went upstairs with them. Stacey would ring a bell in the room to tell us that it was time for them to go. Sometimes they got angry and wanted longer, but we had to send them back or Zack would charge us for the extra time.'

'Charge you?' asked Joshua in astonishment. 'How could he do that? Where did you get the money from?'

'We had no money,' Drita sighed. 'We were paid an amount for each client, but we never saw the money. We owed so much for the English lessons and the fare from Albania and for food and clothes and our rooms.'

'You mean – however many

clients you had, you could never pay off the debt?' Monica suggested.

'Exactly!' Drita agreed. 'There was no way out, so we just did as we were told and …' she shrugged. 'When you have no hope, you stop feeling anything.'

'They gave us contraceptive injections,' Amanda explained, 'and they provided condoms, but some of the men didn't like them, and we were told not to argue with the clients or upset them. Mollie used to hate the injections, because she was afraid of needles. She used to try to get out of it. Maybe she succeeded and that's how she got pregnant. I don't know.'

'Did she want to keep the baby?' Alice asked. 'Is that why she went to the clinic so late?'

'I don't think she realised for a long time,' Amanda shook her head. 'And then she was too scared to say anything. She knew Stacey would be angry with her, so she tried to hide it. Of course, that only made Stacey even more angry when she found out.'

'And then Stacey took her to the clinic and she was booked to have an abortion the next day,' Arshad took over the questioning, 'but she never went back. What happened?'

'Mollie was distraught when they

got back from the clinic. She was terrified by what the doctor said was going to happen to her if she went back. She said she'd rather die than go through with it. In the end, we all agreed to help her to get away. Just before opening time that night, some of the other girls made a diversion. They had a big fight in one of the rooms upstairs. Stacey and Zack both came up to sort things out, and Mollie and I managed to slip downstairs and get out through the back door. I couldn't believe it was so easy!'

'Why didn't you go straight to the police?' Arshad asked, 'or to Mollie's home?'

'We were afraid. Mollie said that

what we had been doing was illegal and we'd be sent to jail. And I thought I'd be sent to jail for not having a visa to stay here.'

'So where did you go?' asked Alice.

'We just wandered around, trying to get as far away from the bar as we could. It was still light and there were quiet a lot of people about so we tried to sort of mingle with the crowd. Then it got late and we didn't know where to go to sleep. There were some homeless people lying in shop doorways, but we didn't like the look of them, so we just kept on walking.'

'All night?' enquired Arshad.

'No. We got so tired, we just had to find somewhere we could rest, and then I remembered there was a funny cubby-hole place in the wall of Lichfield College – that's my college, I used to be a student there. So we headed off down Goose Lane to see if it would do for us to settle down for the night, but there was a man already sleeping there.'

'Did you speak to him?' Arshad asked sharply, remembering the report that he had read of Doug Finney's story. 'Did he see you?'

'I don't think so. We turned back as soon as we saw him there and went to look for somewhere else to sleep. That was when we bumped into Robin.'

'Robin Hillier?' asked Alice excitedly.

THE SECRET GARDENER

'That's right,' Amanda nodded and smiled sadly. 'He was nice. He took us through a gate into the Fellows' Garden. It was funny: I'd been living in Lichfield College for three years, but I'd never been in that garden until then! He told us he was one of the gardeners and he had a place where we could sleep in there. It seemed strange, but beggars can't be choosers and he didn't look dangerous, so we went in with him and sat down in a funny room under the college chapel.'

'The store room?' Alice queried.

'That's right. There were lots of gardening tools there and weed killer and that sort of thing. He ...,' Amanda paused for a few seconds before continuing, 'he showed us how to make a bed out of bags of compost, and he got out a sleeping bag and a pillow from a cupboard. He made Mollie take the sleeping bag and he found a roll of funny white stuff that he called fleece and unrolled some of it to make a sort of blanket for me. He told us to lie down and get some sleep and he'd be back in the morning. Then he left.'

'And did he come back?' Arshad asked.

'Yes. I didn't expect to be able to sleep, because the bags of compost weren't very comfy and it was cold, but we were so dead tired that we soon dropped off and we didn't wake until Robin came back. He opened the door and the sunlight came streaming in. He said it was time for breakfast and he took us to a coffee shop and bought us bacon baguettes.'

'The waitress recognised Mollie,' Alice told her. 'That's one of the things that helped us to find you.'

'OK,' Jonah said, looking searchingly towards Mollie, 'you and Amanda came back to spend another night in the Fellows' Garden, but something happened that night, didn't it? Tell us about it.'

'It was awful!' Mollie declared, staring round with eyes wide. 'It was really bad luck! Zack and Harry came after us just as we were turning into Goose Lane. I don't know if they'd been out looking for us or if it was just bad luck, but anyway they came after us and nearly caught us, but Robin was there holding the gate open and we got inside OK. We ran for our lives and went and hid in the store room, but they fought with Robin and knocked him down, and then they came after us.'

'So Robin was defending the two of you against Zack and Harry?' Anna asked.

'That's right,' Mollie nodded, 'but it was two against one and he couldn't keep them out. We hid in the little room at the back where the roof comes down low, but they came in and found us and dragged us out.'

'Was that how you got that graze on your face?' Jonah enquired.

'Yes. Zack got hold of me and pulled me out through that little low door and he bashed my head against the wall on the way. My nose started bleeding and the blood ran down into my mouth.'

'And you wiped it away and got blood on your hands,' Jonah murmured. 'But sorry, I interrupted you – go on.'

'Harry grabbed Amanda by her hair and pulled her out too. They dragged us out of the store room and across the grass and that's when …

that's when …,' she gulped and put her hand across her mouth.

'Yes?' Anna encouraged. 'That's when what happened?'

'That's – that's when I saw Robin. He was lying on the path with his head in the flowers and – and – and there was blood everywhere!'

'Did you get down and try to help him?' Jonah asked, still intent on reconciling her story with the forensic evidence from the crime scene.

'No. I couldn't. Zack had hold of me. He held my arms behind my back and sort of bent me down over Robin and said something like, "see what happens to people who get in our way!" like he was threatening us.

I think Robin was dead. He never moved or anything.'

'And after that, it was just back to normal,' Amanda concluded. 'Zack "disciplined" us in front of the other girls as an example to them and added a fine to the amount we owed him, for his "trouble" as he put it in having to come after us, and then the next night we were both back on the red sofa like before.'

'Was there any more talk of Mollie having an abortion?' Alice asked.

'No.' Amanda shook her head. 'I think they got scared after the doctor said she might be beyond the limit. I think they were afraid if they went back again, there might be more questions asked – or maybe they were scared that Mollie would say something. Besides,' she added with a bitter little laugh, 'it turns out there are some men who get a thrill from having sex with a pregnant girl. One of the others told me some of the regulars were asking for Mollie specially while she was away. I don't know what they were planning to do with the baby when it was born, but I think they'd decided that Mollie's condition could be exploited for their benefit.'

'I see.' Arshad sat back in his chair and pondered on all that he had heard. 'Thank you, Miss Jayakody. We'll get all this typed up in the form of a statement for you to sign – unless there's anything else you think we ought to know?'

Amanda shook her head.

'In that case, we'll stop here.' Arshad got to his feet. 'Your father is outside. I'll take you to him and you can wait together while we prepare the statement.'

'It looks like a multi-faceted modern slavery business,' Jonah observed. 'They've got three distinct sources of women coming in: girls like Mollie being seduced by Harry Lockhart, overseas graduates like Amanda, desperate for a job in the UK, and the likes of Rovena and Drita who are recruited in their home countries and brought over here.'

They had reconvened to compare notes after interviewing all the women who had been held in the rooms above Pimm's bar. The Albanians and other foreign nationals had been taken away by representatives from the Salvation Army's Modern Slavery Unit. Amanda and her father had been allowed to return with Sally Pearson to the manse. Mollie was waiting in another room in the police station while a social worker explained to her parents what had happened to her. She drew her feet up on to her chair and hugged her knees with her arms, dreading the impending reunion. Dad would be angry with her, she was sure, and Mum? There was bound to be some important business meeting that she was missing in order to be here!

'We need to find this Harry Lockhart,' Arshad declared. 'I think it's highly likely that he's holding Pandora Birch. Her disappearance looks very similar to what Mollie Burgess described to you.'

'We've got people working on that,' Anna told him, 'and they're also checking the Land Registry for that country house of his that Mollie told us about. Unfortunately, she couldn't give us much help with its location and the area south of Oxford is teaming with big houses with their own stables.'

'Meanwhile,' Jonah said, 'we'd better get on with interviewing Zack Pimm and the others, before their lawyers start quoting habeas corpus at us. I'd like to talk to him first – if that's OK with everyone?'

'I'd like to question him too,' Arshad put in quickly. 'It seems to me, he's the most likely to lead us to Harry Lockhart.'

'And there must be other people involved – the man and woman who interviewed Amanda Jayakody, for example,' Anna agreed, 'and other places where they're keeping the girls. He may be able to help us with all of that.'

'OK,' Jonah replied equably. 'How about you and I interview him together, Arshad? It'll be better to have a female officer present for Stacey and Tiffany in any case. They'll be less likely to try to claim they were intimidated then.'

'Andy and I will take Stacey,' Anna decided. 'It's a pity Peter can't be here. He knows more about what happened at the abortion clinic than the rest of us. Monica! I'd like you and Alice to interview Tiffany. Try to catch her off-guard. She seems to be trying to say that she was only doing what her mum and dad told her. Play along with that and see if you can get her to give anything away.'

'OK, I admit it,' Zack said, smiling across the table at Arshad and Jonah. 'I did turn a blind eye to what them girls was doing. But look at it this way: if I hadn't've let them use my rooms they'd still've been doing it, just out on the streets. And everyone knows how dangerous that can be for them! I was helping to keep them safe, like a kind uncle – see what I mean?'

'Very philanthropic of you,' Jonah replied drily. 'And I suppose your *protection* was just thrown in for nothing, so long as they paid the rent for those squalid rooms you kept them in during the day?'

'You trying to make out I was ripping them off?' Zack continued to smile. 'If they was squalid it's only 'cos them girls didn't look after them properly. I gave them everything they needed: food, clothes, a roof over their heads, and so long as they paid the rent I didn't ask them no questions – know what I mean?'

'I know exactly what you mean,' Jonah replied coldly. 'And I'm sure that you are aware that it is illegal for prostitutes to work together in that way.'

'And it is also illegal for anyone else to profit by it,' Arshad added grimly.

'But, like I said, I wasn't profiting by it. I was just charging them a fair rent for the rooms. I can't help it if they bring men back there, can I?' Zack maintained his air of amiability, smiling round at each of them in turn.

'So they're lying when they say that your wife supervises them and takes money from their clients?' Jonah asked, fixing Zack with a glacial stare.

'Look here,' Zack leaned forward and gave Jonah and Arshad a *we're-all-men-of-the-world* look, 'I don't know any of the details, right? You and me both know this sort of thing goes on, and where's the harm in it? We both know there'd be a lot more rape out there if there weren't girls like mine willing to satisfy men's needs at a fair price, know what I mean? It's the oldest profession, ain't it? They was independent professionals and if they decided to let my Stacey look after their earnings for them while they was on the job, so to speak, that's their lookout – nothing to do with me.'

'Tell me about Harry Lockhart,' Arshad said, suddenly changing tack.

'Harry Lockhart?' queried Zack, adjusting his smile to indicate that the name was unfamiliar to him.

'That's right,' Arshad said coldly, 'the guy whose father owns your bar and several other business premises across the region. Where might I find him?'

'Search me,' Zack shrugged. 'They don't come here much. They leave me to run the place.'

'He has a country house, somewhere to the south of here,' Jonah told him. 'Do you know the address?'

'No idea!' Zack shook his head. 'We don't hang out together. It's just a business arrangement.'

'You were together the Wednesday before last,' Jonah said drily, 'when you followed Mollie Burgess and Amanda Jayakody into the Fellows' Garden at Lichfield College.'

'Who told you that?' Zack's voice

rose and his smile was replaced by a look of consternation. 'That's a bloody lie! Them fucking girls! That's all the thanks I get for looking after them! You don't believe them, do you? That sort – they'd make up anything if they thought it'd get you on their side.'

'I thought they were professionals doing a public service,' Jonah replied smoothly. 'Isn't that what you just told us?'

'Well, yeah – up to a point,' Zack was sounding far less sure of himself now. 'But that don't mean you can trust what they say. I never went in that garden and I never stabbed no gardener neither!'

'Who said anything about

anyone being stabbed?' Arshad demanded with icy calm.

'I read about it in the papers. That's what all this is about, isn't it? Some bloke got himself killed a couple of weeks back – that was in Lichfield College, wasn't it? You're trying to pin it on me, and those girls are helping you by telling lies about me!'

'Perhaps Harry could clear all this up for us,' Jonah suggested amiably. 'If you could just try to remember where he lives …?'

* * *

'No comment,' Stacey muttered for the tenth time, staring sullenly at

Anna across the table.

Anna looked down at her notes and sighed.

'Mrs Pimm,' she said, after a brief pause, 'we've interviewed the women that you were holding in those rooms above the bar. They've told us all about what was going on. You are going to be charged with various offences under the modern Slavery Act 2015 and the Sexual Offences Act 1956 whether you answer my questions or not. Don't you think you might as well co-operate with us in finding all the other links in the chain, so that we can stop this happening to any more vulnerable young women?'

'No comment,' Stacey replied

emotionlessly.

* * *

'You will tell the judge it was nothing to do with me, won't you?' Tiffany asked anxiously. 'I was only doing what Mum and Dad told me I had to. I never knew where them girls came from. They told me never to talk to them. I just a served drinks in the bar. It was Mum who-'

'OK, let's leave all that for the moment,' Monica cut across her. 'We're more interested in the people behind all this. Harry Lockhart, for instance – what do you know about him?'

'He comes to see Dad

sometimes,' Tiffany shrugged. 'They have what they call *business meetings* in dad's office, out the back of the bar.'

'Have you ever been to his house?'

'What, Harry's house? No.'

'Do you know where it is? Do you have an address?' Monica persisted.

'No. No – honestly I don't!' Tiffany's eyes flashed backwards and forwards between Monica and Alice. 'Look, I'd tell you if I knew, but I don't. Dad always said the less I knew the better. I'm sorry.'

'When was the last time Harry was here?' Alice asked.

'I – I don't know. Last week or the

week before, I'm not sure.'

'Two of the women ran away the week before last,' Monica told her. 'Do you remember that?'

'Yes. I remember.'

'Care to tell us about it?' Monica prompted.

'Well …,' Tiffany thought for a few moments. 'I was in the bar getting things ready, because it was nearly opening time. I heard a lot of screaming and banging coming from upstairs. Dad was there with me behind the bar. He told me to carry on while he went up to sort it out. I did as I was told. After a while things quietened down and Dad came back and we got on with opening up.'

'And then what?' asked Alice.

THE SECRET GARDENER

'When did you realise the girls were gone?'

'Not 'til later. Mum came in from the back, and went and whispered something to Dad, which made him wild and he stormed out to the back room and there was some shouting and that. Mum told me to mind the bar, and then she followed him. After a bit, they both came back and Dad pretended everything was OK and started joking with the customers and that. But after closing, he went ballistic! Shouting at the girls and throwing things. That's when I found out what it was all about.'

'Mollie and Amanda had gone?' queried Monica.

'That's right. Dad went out to look

for them, and Mum locked the girls in their rooms and then went out too. I just went to bed and tried to go to sleep. I don't know nothing about what happened after that.'

'Did your dad tell Harry Lockhart what had happened?' Monica probed. 'Did he come over to help look for them?'

'I dunno.' At the mention of Lockhart's name, Tiffany's eyes widened and she appeared scared. 'All I know is, the next night Dad left me and Mum looking after the bar on our own, and he went off out looking for them again. And then, just before closing time, he was back – him and Harry – with the two of them. They came in the back way and up the stairs and locked them in the bathroom, and then Dad came back and helped us shut up shop. Harry stayed in the back, in Dad's office. I didn't see him again. I don't know anything about him.'

'But you do know that he and your dad went out on that Wednesday night and came back with Mollie and Amanda?' Alice demanded sharply.

'I don't know about Wednesday,' Tiffany mumbled. 'It was two or three weeks back. That's all I remember.'

15. CRIMINAL CHARGES

'The trafficked women from Albania have been handed over to Victim Support,' Joshua Pitchfork reported when they reconvened to compare notes following the interviews. 'And Mollie and Amanda are both back with their parents. At least,' he corrected himself with a grimace of disapproval, 'I should say with their fathers. *Mrs* Burgess has had to rush off to catch a plane to Brazil.'

'Will they be deported?' Bernie wondered aloud. 'The Albanian women, I mean. Will they be sent back right away? Or will they be allowed to stay, at least until they've given evidence to convict Pimm and the others?'

'Do we know where this Harry Lockhart is yet?' Arshad demanded cutting across her musing. 'That has to be our number one priority. If we can't find him before he gets wind of the raid on Pimm's bar, he'll have spirited Pandora away somewhere and possibly even skipped the country.'

There was a general shaking of heads around the room. Jennifer Moorehouse raised her hand and Arshad nodded to her to speak.

'I've got two addresses for *John* Lockhart, the owner of the bar,' she told them. 'A flat in Canary Wharf and a house in Cornwall. Didn't you say Harry was his son?'

'But neither of those can be this country house where Mollie was held,' Arshad argued. 'Hasn't *anyone* got a lead on that?'

'Yes, I think I've found it.'

Everyone's eyes turned towards the voice, which came from behind a computer screen in a corner of the room.

'Peter!' Bernie exclaimed. 'What are you doing here?'

'Anna said you were short-staffed, so I thought I'd lend a hand. I've been trawling the electoral roll and I've found a Harold Edwin Lockhart, aged 27, living at a place called Lugmore Grange, down towards Newbury. Cross-referencing with the Land Registry, the place is owned by a John Lockhart, who appears to be the same as the one Jennifer was talking about – the guy who runs the company that owns the bar.'

'Good old Peter!' Jonah exclaimed warmly. 'You always were good at slogging through paperwork. That must be the one. I know that area. There are lots of stables there, and lots of horsey people.'

'Yes. Well done, Johns,' Arshad agreed. 'Give me the full address and I'll get off down there right away. Anna! I want you to get a warrant to search the house and grounds and put together a team to do it. Andy, come with me! We may not have much time to get Pandora out of there.'

'Our car's just outside,' Jonah interjected, before Andy could get to his feet. 'There's room for all of us, and old Peter can navigate, seeing as he's the one who knows where we're going.'

'Is that OK with you, Johns?' Arshad turned to look at Peter.

'Fine by me,' Peter replied in an expressionless voice that did not give any hint as to his feelings about the proposal. He turned to speak to Anna. 'The address is on the screen,' he told her. 'From the satellite picture, it looks as if there are a good few other buildings in addition to the house, so make sure the warrant covers the lot.'

Bernie drove, with Peter sitting next to her to give directions, while Arshad and Andy sat in the back with Jonah. A little more than half an hour later, they slowed to a crawl in a narrow lane with tall hedges on either side.

'It can't be far now,' Peter told them. 'There should be a gateway on the left just up here. Yes! There it is! Just before that telegraph pole.'

Bernie signalled left and pulled in next to a line of wheelie bins in a variety of different colour schemes.

Above those, a notice announced that this was the entrance to Lugmore Grange. A warning sign in smaller lettering informed them that this was private property and there was no right of way for the public.

'Go on!' Arshad urged. 'What are you waiting for?'

Bernie turned the car into a rough track, which led upwards between grassy fields bounded by post-and-rail fences towards a cluster of stone buildings. Seeing several horses grazing in the field to their right Bernie commented, 'very nice little place he's got! Rather more than just "room for a pony" here!'

The track ended in a yard

surrounded by farm buildings. Bales of hay were visible in a barn to their left. On the right, a building with an open front housed three cars: a brand new sporty model, a Range Rover and a sleek Mercedes. Bernie parked their car and they all got out and looked around.

'That must be the house over there,' Arshad called out, pointing across landscaped gardens beyond a narrow wrought iron gate.

'Yes,' agreed Jonah,' peering through the gate at a path that wound past borders of shrubs and herbaceous plants to an imposing white-painted house. 'I'm surprised they don't have more security. It looks as if you can just walk in.'

'I suppose they're relying on being too remote for anyone to find them,' Arshad murmured. Then, more briskly, 'OK, let's go and pay Harry Lockhart esquire a visit, shall we?'

'It looks as if the stables are round the back of this barn,' Bernie put in, as Arshad depressed the latch to open the gate. 'While you're talking to Harry Lockhart, why don't Peter and I have a look round them? It might look like over-kill if all five of us descend on him at once.'

'OK.' Arshad turned to look at her. 'Yes. That's probably a good idea. Judging by what Mollie told us about her first few days here, you might even find Pandora with the horses.'

'Take this, Andy,' Bernie said, holding out the portable ramp, which they carried with them to enable Jonah's wheelchair to negotiate steps and other obstacles. 'You know how to set it up, don't you?'

Andy took the ramp and set off through the gate, leading the way up the path with long loping strides. Arshad waited, holding the gate for Jonah's wheelchair to pass through. Then he came through himself and turned to check that the latch had closed properly behind him. He watched as Bernie and Peter disappeared behind the barn before turning round again and falling in beside Jonah, who was already following Andy along the path.

'Was that genuine or just a ploy to get Johns away from me?' Arshad asked in a low voice.

'Was what a ploy?' Jonah responded with a puzzled frown. 'I don't get what you're-'

'Mrs Johns,' Arshad expanded. 'Does she really think they'll find anything in the stables or is she afraid …? Look, I know I upset his son a couple of years ago when I had to question him about his baby's abduction, but-'

'Peter doesn't bear a grudge,' Jonah cut in. 'He's not like that, and he knows you were only doing what you had to do. But you do need to realise that, in Peter's eyes – and

Bernie's perfectly fine with it – there can only ever be one Mrs Johns, and that's Angie. Our Bernie's "Dr Fazakerley" if you insist on being formal.'

'That's where the trouble started,' Arshad confided. 'I suppose they'll have told you. I do realise I went a bit over the top back then, when his first wife was killed. I'd only recently been made up to sergeant and I was very full of myself and thought I knew it all. What can I do to-?'

'You don't have to,' Jonah interrupted. 'I told you: old Peter doesn't bear grudges. He's the closest I've ever come across to a truly good human being. He doesn't blame you.'

'Then why do I always feel that he and his wife are giving me the cold shoulder?'

'Probably your own guilty conscience,' Jonah replied glibly. Then, more seriously and in a lower voice, 'Look: you need to remember that the only person that old Peter ever blames for things is himself. That was what was so hurtful about the things you said to him about how he didn't understand what it was like for his wife and kids being black or mixed race. You implied that he was partly to blame for what happened to Angie – and he believed you!'

'I never meant-,' Arshad began indignantly. Then he stopped short and gave a sigh. 'No,' he admitted, 'I suppose at the time I probably did think …So, what can I do to put things right with him?'

'I told you – nothing.'

'But-'

'Shall I ring the bell, sir?' Andy, who was standing on the doorstep waiting for them as they approached the house, pointed up at a brass bell hanging on a bracket over the front door, with a leather loop dangling from its clapper.

'Yes. Go ahead!' Arshad nodded.

Andy sounded the bell vigorously, then set about positioning the ramp to enable Jonah to drive his wheelchair up on to the broad step in front of the house. They stood waiting for what seemed like a long time before the door opened and a tall, dark-skinned woman with prominent cheek-bones and liquid brown eyes looked out.

'Good afternoon,' she greeted them in a strong accent, which reminded Jonah of a Ghanaian minister who had visited their church some years before. 'Can I help you?'

'We're from the police,' Arshad informed her briskly. 'DCI Khan, DCI Porter and DS Lepage. Is Mr Harold Lockhart at home?'

A look of alarm flashed across the woman's face, but she answered calmly, 'Please wait here. I will go and see.'

'It's important that we speak to him,' Arshad called through the closing door as she turned to go.

'Another of the trafficked women, d'you think?' suggested Jonah as they waited for her to return.

'Or maybe one of the graduates recruited on their so-called training scheme,' Arshad nodded. 'Didn't Amanda say there was an African woman on the induction course that she went on?'

'Yes, that's right,' Jonah agreed. 'I bet Harry Lockhart gets to keep any of the girls he fancies, to be his domestics-cum-concubines!'

'How much longer before we try a forced entry?' asked Andy.

'Ring the bell again,' Jonah

instructed. 'Let them know we mean business.'

Andy gave another spirited ring of the bell. Before the sound had died away, the door opened again and the woman was back.

'Mr Lockhart will see you now,' she told them stiffly. 'Please, follow me.'

She led the way into a large room furnished with expensive-looking leather chairs and sofas. As they entered, a young man in jodhpurs and a roll-neck sweater got up from one of the large armchairs and walked over to a mahogany drinks cabinet on top of which stood an array of bottles and decanters.

'Drink anyone?' he greeted them

cheerily, smiling to reveal a row of perfect white teeth. His dark brown hair fell across his eyes and he pushed it back with the long artistic fingers of a tanned left hand, while holding up a whisky decanter in his right.

'No thank you,' answered Arshad curtly.

'On duty, eh?' Harry smiled back. 'You don't mind if I do?' he continued, pouring out a measure of whisky into a glass, adding ice from an insulated bucket and then wandering languidly back to resume his seat. 'Please,' he said waving his glass in the direction of his guests. 'Sit down and tell me what this is all about.'

'We need to ask you some questions about the abduction and false imprisonment of Mollie Burgess and Amanda Jayakody,' Jonah told him, 'and also about the murder of Robin Hillier two weeks ago.'

'Ask away!' Harry smiled back complacently. 'I don't know what you think I have to do with any of that, but by all means, ask your questions.'

'Where were you on Wednesday the twenty-sixth of June between six in the evening and midnight?' Jonah demanded.

'Let me see ...,' Harry murmured, leaning back in his chair and running his hands through his long hair. 'That's the Wednesday before last, isn't it? You know, I rather fancy I was here all evening that day. My housekeeper will know.'

He reached out and gave a tug on an old-fashioned bell-pull, which hung down to the right of a large marble fireplace. Jonah noticed that the mantelpiece had several silver cups displayed on it, as well as two large framed photographs of Harry, sitting astride a magnificent strawberry roan, shaking hands with what he assumed must be dignitaries from the horsey world.

'Yes sir?' The African woman appeared at the door of the room.

'Can you remember whether I was in to dinner the Wednesday before last?' Harry asked her. 'That's

June the twenty-sixth.'

'Wednesday? Yes, sir. You dined alone. I served avocado followed by a lamb chop and then ice cream for dessert, because it was the start of this hot spell.'

'Thank you, Rosemary,' Harry smiled indulgently. 'And what time was that?'

'Seven-thirty on the dot, as usual,' the woman answered promptly. 'I cleared the table at about eight-fifteen and brought you coffee here in the lounge just after that. You wanted to watch the highlights of the cricket world cup.'

'And I was in all night, wasn't I?'

'Yes sir.' You had a night-cap at about eleven forty-five and then had a shower and went to bed. I locked up at midnight and then went to bed myself.'

'That's very interesting,' Jonah said smoothly. 'Particularly in view of the fact that we have two witnesses who are confident that you were in Goose Lane, Oxford sometime between eight and midnight that night.'

'Witnesses?' Harry asked, looking round innocently.

'Molly Burgess and Amanda Jayakody,' Jonah replied impassively. 'You must remember Mollie. She lived here with you for several months back in 2016.'

'That's all, Rosemary,' Harry snapped, glancing quickly across at the black woman who was still standing in the doorway. 'You can go now.' Then, smiling pleasantly towards Jonah, he replied calmly, 'I'm sorry. You're mistaken there – or rather your witnesses must be mistaken.'

The woman backed out pulling the door closed as she did so, but Arshad was too quick for her. He leaped up and took hold of the handle, wrenching the door wide open.

'No, don't go,' he instructed. 'You recognised those names, didn't you?'

'Of course I did,' the woman protested, her eyes flickering anxiously in Harry's direction. 'I heard them on the radio. The police are out looking for them, I believe.'

'I think they meant more to you than that,' Arshad insisted. 'I think you know one or both of them personally.'

'No!' Rosemary insisted doggedly. 'I heard the names on the radio, that's all. Now, I need to go. I have work to do.'

'Not yet,' Arshad took a photograph out of his pocket and thrust it in front of the woman's face. 'Have a look at this picture. Have you ever seen this girl before?'

Rosemary studied the image for several seconds. Then she looked up at Arshad. 'No,' she said firmly. 'I've never seen her. Can I go now, please?'

'Very well,' Arshad muttered, putting away the photograph and returning to his seat.

'Perhaps we could talk about Zachary Pimm and the business that he runs for you in Oxford,' Jonah said smoothly.

'Now, that's not quite accurate,' Harry interjected. 'The bar is owned by my father. I'm not directly involved at all.'

'But you do know Pimm, don't you?' Jonah persisted. 'He's been to visit you here, for example, hasn't he?'

'Yes, I know Zack,' Harry conceded, 'but I'm not responsible for how he runs the bar. If he's infringed the licensing laws or-'

'Have you ever been there?' Arshad cut in. 'Have you been upstairs to the rooms above the bar?'

'Yes, I've been there,' Harry replied, continuing to smile graciously towards the inspector. 'But no, I haven't been upstairs. Those are private rooms where Zack and his wife live.'

'Would you be surprised to hear that, when we searched the premises yesterday we found fifteen young women living up there?' Jonah asked, still speaking in mild tones as if such a discovery were unremarkable.

'Absolutely!' Harry declared. 'But

then, as I said, what Zack gets up to there is nothing to do with me.'

'You say it's your father who owns the premises,' Jonah suddenly switched tack. 'Where can we find him?'

'I'm afraid he's out of the country at the moment,' Harry smiled back complacently, 'at his villa in Marbella.'

'I assume you have a contact number for him.' Jonah remained calm. 'Can we have it please? He ought to be informed about what's been going on in his property.'

'Sure. No problem.' Harry took out his mobile phone and brought up a number on the screen. He held it out towards Jonah. Bernie leaned over and took down the number on her own smartphone.

'Thank you,' Jonah smiled up at Harry. 'We'll be in touch with him just as soon as we've finished here. Meanwhile, are you quite sure you don't want to reconsider what you said about your movements the Wednesday before last? We have two witnesses who positively identified you as having been in Oxford that evening and up to a dozen more who saw you at Pimm's bar later that night.'

'It seems that I must have a doppelganger, doesn't it?' Harry grinned back, apparently unperturbed.

'Why don't you stop playing

games and admit that you and Pimm have been exploiting vulnerable young women for gain?' Arshad demanded. 'Mollie Burgess has told us all about it. You lured her here pretending to be in love with her and then passed her on to Pimm when you got bored with her. And now you're doing the same with Pandora Birch. You've got her here somewhere, haven't you?'

'I'm sorry,' Harry shook his head, continuing to smile, 'I really don't know what you're talking about.'

* * *

Peter and Bernie stood looking round. They were in the stable yard, a concreted area surrounded on three sides by loose boxes. Horses' heads looked out over the doors of two of them. The place appeared to be deserted, but Peter could hear a soft voice coming from somewhere nearby. He could not distinguish any words, but he recognised the tone that people use when trying to calm a child or an animal.

He walked round the yard peering into the loose boxes one by one. Bernie, following his lead, started searching the boxes along another side. It was not long before she came upon the owner of the voice.

'Hello there!' she called out quietly, leaning on the lower part of the stable door as she waited for her eyes to adjust to the relative darkness inside. 'You must be Pandora. Could you spare us a few minutes?'

The occupant of the loose box, a dapple-grey gelding, flinched at the sound of her voice, then turned its head and stared towards the newcomer. The girl whose voice Peter had heard responded more slowly. She paused in grooming the horse and stood for several seconds with her back to the opening and both hands resting on the animal's side. With her left hand, she patted its shoulder while the right still held the curry comb that she had been using to brush its sleek coat.

THE SECRET GARDENER

She turned to face the entrance of the loose box just as Peter came up behind Bernie to see what she had found.

'Yes,' she said at last, 'I'm Pandora. Who are you? What do you want?'

'Your parents are very worried about you,' Peter told her gently. 'We're with the police. They've been looking for you everywhere.'

'But – but Harry sorted it all out with them!' the girl dropped her hands to her sides and stared at Peter in disbelief. 'He said they were cool with me staying here for the Summer.'

'Have you spoken to them yourself recently?' Bernie asked.

'No. I've been busy and they've been away. Harry told me they had to go over to Canada to see my Auntie Simone, because she's ill. They forgot to leave us a number to ring them on.'

'I'm afraid Harry's told you rather a lot of things that aren't true,' Peter informed her kindly. 'He's not such a nice person as he's led you to believe.'

'I think we'd all better go up to the house now,' Bernie added, unbolting the stable door and pulling it open a short distance. 'We'll introduce you to the police officer who's been leading the hunt to find you, and he'll see you get back to your parents.'

'So they're not in Canada?'

Pandora asked, wide-eyed. 'Are you sure?'

'Yes,' Peter assured her quietly. 'I'm afraid Harry has been lying to you to keep you here and to prevent your parents taking you back.'

'He's done it before,' Bernie continued, closing the door behind Pandora, taking the curry comb from her hand and putting it down on a handy mounting block. 'We've been talking to a girl called Mollie who came to stay here with him three years ago. He passed her on to a man who kept her shut up in a room over a bar in Oxford.'

'I don't believe you!' Pandora suddenly rounded on Bernie. 'It can't be true what you're saying! Harry's not like that. He loves me!'

'That's what he told Mollie,' Bernie insisted gently. 'But you don't need to take my word for it. You'll be able to speak to Mollie yourself later.'

'But the first thing is to let the police know that we've found you and then for them to tell your parents,' Peter said firmly, holding out his arm to usher Pandora out of the stable yard.

As they rounded the corner of the barn and stepped out on to the track, a police van drew up and uniformed officers began to pile out, led by Anna Davenport with a search warrant in her hand.

'Anna!' Peter called to her. 'Let

me introduce you to Pandora Birch. Pandora: this is DCI Anna Davenport. She has a warrant to search Harry's house, because he's been mixed up in some very nasty crimes. Now, we're all going to go up to the house together and Harry's going to be arrested, but you mustn't worry. Nobody's going to hurt you and nobody's going to be cross with you about anything. We just want to get you back to your parents safe and sound. Do you understand?'

Pandora nodded tearfully, then sniffed and wiped her arm across her face. 'Couldn't I … ? Couldn't I just stay here, with the horses until … until after you've taken Harry away?'

Peter studied her bedraggled yellow curls, anxious blue eyes and tear-stained face. 'OK,' he said after a few moment's thought. 'Go on up to the house, Anna, and tell Arshad we've found his runaway. I'll ring for a car to come and pick Pandora up and take her back to Oxford. And we'll wait with her here until it comes.'

'Look, it's not my fault young girls keep throwing themselves at me and fantasising about me,' declared Harry, grinning across the table of the interview room at Arshad and Jonah, who were trying vainly to persuade him to admit to his crimes. 'That Pandora girl told me her family had all gone to Canada for the summer and left her behind on her own. I felt sorry for her! That's why I invited her to stay. I had no idea she'd run away from home.'

'That's not how she tells it,' Arshad said coldly. 'She says it was you who made up the story about them going to Canada.'

'I told you: she's a fantasist!' Harry insisted, still smiling. 'You can't believe a word she says.'

'And Mollie Burgess?' challenged Jonah. 'She also lived with you for several months before you passed her on to Zack and his wife. What happened? Did you get tired of her and want a newer model?'

'I don't know what you're talking about. Yes, I admit Mollie did come to my house a few times, but she never lived there and I didn't have anything to do with her ending up in that place over Zack's bar. I suppose she must've been here one time when he came to see me, and he persuaded her to go with him. All that stuff about me promising to marry her is all in her head! She's a nymphomaniac and for some reason she picked on me for her fantasies.'

'OK,' Jonah said calmly, but with a hint of menace in his voice, 'let's go back to that Wednesday night when Robin Hillier was killed. We have two witnesses who positively identify you as having been there in the Fellows' Garden of Lichfield College when it happened.'

'Hardly reliable witnesses,' Harry interjected, still smiling. 'I don't know who this Amanda is that you keep talking about, but I do know that you can't believe a word Mollie Burgess says. She was upset when I told her I wasn't interested in her, and she's making all this up to spite me.'

'We won't argue about that for the present,' Jonah replied quietly. 'I'd like to ask you about this knife that you had in your pocket when we arrested you.'

Arshad placed a plastic evidence bag containing a narrow-bladed knife in a leather sheath on the table in front of Harry.

'What about it?' Harry continued to smile, but now it looked forced and there was an underlying expression of anxiety on his face. 'It's just a knife I carry with me on the farm for cutting baler twine and that sort of thing.'

'A knife similar to this was used to stab Robin Hillier to death,' Arshad told him. 'We'll be sending it off for analysis and, if it *is* that one, there'll be traces on it of Hillier's DNA. It will be much better for you if you tell us now what happened than if we have to rely on that evidence to convict you.'

Harry's smile finally faltered and

he looked uncertainly towards his solicitor sitting silently next to him. The lawyer looked back and nodded slowly.

'OK,' Harry said after a long pause, 'I'll admit I was there. Zack rang me, all in a flap because two of his staff had gone missing and he was worried for their safety. When he told me one of them was Mollie, I agreed to come over and help him look for them. I felt a bit responsible, because I'd introduced them a couple of years before. We spotted the two of them in Goose Lane. There was this old guy in a boiler suit with them. He looked pretty vicious and they were obviously scared of him. He dragged them in through a gate in the wall. Zack said we had to get the girls away from him. I didn't like the idea of us going in after them. I said we ought to ring the police, but Zack wouldn't. That's when I started to wonder if he wasn't telling me the whole story about the work they were doing for him – know what I mean?'

His smile reappeared and he winked towards Arshad and Jonah.

'Go on,' Jonah said coldly. 'You still haven't explained how Robin Hillier ended up with a hole in his heart made by a knife like yours.'

'Like I said,' Harry resumed, still smiling, 'I didn't want to get involved in a fight with a dangerous thug, so I told Zack if he went in he was on his own. I tried to persuade him to let it go, but he wouldn't listen, and then …,' he paused dramatically and looked Jonah directly in the eye, 'I know it was the wrong thing to do, but I gave him my knife. I never meant him to hurt anyone with it! I thought he could use it to threaten the guy with, to make him let the girls go. I'm sorry if he killed the guy. I never knew. Zack just came out a bit later, with the girls, and he handed me back the knife and I thought that was it.'

'Now Mr Pimm,' Anna said grimly, putting down a pair of shoes, sealed in an evidence bag, in front of Zack, 'please have a look at these shoes, which we found in the wardrobe of your bedroom, and tell me if they belong to you.'

'I've got some like that,' Zack admitted sulkily. 'What about it?'

'The left shoe exactly matches a print in the flower bed next to the body of Robin Hillier,' Anna informed him.

'So what?' Zack blustered. 'I bet loads of people wear shoes like that.'

'But not all of them have the same wear pattern on the heel,' Anna replied coldly. 'I'm going to send these off to the lab for tests. If there are any traces of the soil from the Fellows' Garden at Lichfield on them, they'll be able to tell. And then we'll know for certain you were there – quite apart from the fact that we have two witnesses who say categorically that you were!'

Zack sat in silence, apparently thinking this over. Then he took a deep breath and looked round at Anna and Andy.

'OK, OK. Yeah, I was there. After the girls ran away, we went looking for them.'

'You and Harry Lockhart?' asked Andy.

'Yeah. You gotta understand – he was the boss. I just did what I was told. He said we gotta get them back or they might … Look, I know I'm going down for letting them girls work from them rooms over the bar, but whatever I done it don't include killing no-one!'

'Alright, Mr Pimm, why don't you just tell us what happened?' Anna suggested coldly.

'Like I said, we went out to look for the girls,' Zack resumed. His smile was gone now and he spoke in a defeated sort of voice. 'We caught sight of them on the corner of Goose Lane and Lichfield Street. I called out to them, friendly like, asking them to come home, but they ran off down Goose Lane. Harry ran after them and I followed on behind. There was a door in the wall on the left. They went in through that and I thought we'd lost them, but then

Harry, he goes in after them.'

'I see,' Anna nodded. 'Go on.'

'I looked in, careful like, not knowing what I was going to find, and there was this bloke lying on the floor and Harry was standing over him with a knife in his hand. I couldn't see the girls anywhere.'

'And then?' Anna prompted.

'Harry pulled me in through the door and slammed it shut behind me. Then he dragged me across the grass to another door. It was a sort of tool-shed thing. The girls were in there, hiding at the back. Harry yanked them outside and duffed them up a bit. They gave in then and came away with us, back to the bar. I'm not proud of what I done, but I never killed no-one and I never laid a finger on them girls neither!'

'We'll let the Jury be the judge of that,' Anna said impassively. 'OK. That'll do for now. We'll take you back to the cells for the night and you'll be formally charged tomorrow.'

'What with?' Zack asked anxiously.

'Human trafficking, false imprisonment, brothel-keeping, causing, inciting and controlling prostitution for gain – do you really want me to list it all?'

'But not murder?' Zack persisted. 'I never killed no-one, no way! You gotta believe me!'

'We'll have to see about that,'

THE SECRET GARDENER

Anna told him seriously. 'If you co-operate with us over the rest of the offences – and if your account agrees with what the other witnesses say, so we can believe you're telling the truth – then maybe the prosecutor will believe your story that it was Harry who stabbed Robin Hillier. On the other hand,' she added menacingly, 'if we find you've been lying to us, then why would we believe you about that? Think about it.'

16. LOOSE ENDS

There were more guests than usual at Saturday High Tea the next weekend. Charles and Amanda were due to fly home to Sri Lanka soon and this would be the last opportunity for the family to meet them again before they departed. Peter invited Father Damien, who was keen to hear the outcome of the investigation to which his sister's evidence had contributed – as were Martin and Paula.

The police force was well represented. Lucy, who was one of

baby Donna's godmothers, had asked Anna to bring her over to play for the afternoon. Bernie, who had a soft spot for young Andy Lepage and considered that he needed bringing out of himself, had included him in the party. Finally, and unexpectedly, at the last minute Jonah had insisted on inviting Arshad Khan and his wife Anita.

Fortunately, the weather, which had alternated that summer between heatwaves and heavy rain, was currently set fair and they were able to take their sandwiches, scones and blackcurrant pie outside for a picnic in the back garden.

'Can I show Donna the tree house?' Lucy asked Anna, pointing across the garden at a wooden ladder that led upwards and disappeared amongst the foliage of a large oak tree. 'I'll be careful with her. I won't let her fall out.'

Anna looked down at twenty-month-old Donna in Lucy's arms and then up at the tree.

'OK,' she agreed. 'You go up and I'll hand her to you.'

'Better let me,' Peter intervened. 'I'll be able to reach better.'

'That's a magnificent tree house!' Anita commented, watching as Peter carefully handed up the smiling infant into Lucy's waiting arms. 'Who made it?'

'Peter and Martin built it for Lucy's eighth birthday,' Bernie told her. 'It was Martin's idea. Apparently his father used to talk about one that he'd had in his garden in Germany before the war.'

'Your family were immigrants then, Dr Riess?' Anita asked, turning to Martin.

'My mother and I, yes,' he replied a little stiffly, unsure of the purpose of Anita's question. 'My father did not get the opportunity. He was refused permission to leave the Democratic Republic of Germany and died in the custody of the Stasi.'

'Oh! I'm sorry. I didn't realise!' Anita exclaimed in some confusion. 'So you and your mother were refugees from the communists?'

'Or perhaps we were merely

economic migrants,' Martin said drily. 'It's so hard to distinguish sometimes.'

'Some Polish friends of ours had graffiti sprayed across their house last night,' Paula explained, 'telling them to go back where they came from.'

'Let's all sit down in the shade,' urged Peter, hoping to head-off any political argument. 'Would you like tea, Mrs Khan? Or maybe a cold drink?'

'Peter's homemade lemonade is very good,' Bernie added. 'Just the thing for this hot weather.'

They all settled down in the shade, and Bernie and Peter handed round iced lemonade. Overhead,

THE SECRET GARDENER

Lucy's voice softly pointed out to baby Donna the many features of her "arboreal dwelling" (as Jonah was in the habit of describing it).

'Look here, Donna! This is the cupboard where I used to keep all my special things … and this is where I put my camp bed the time I stayed out here all night … and look at how these shutters on the window open and close!'

'Your little girl is very sedate,' Anita commented to Anna. 'At that age, our two were running around getting into everything.'

'I – I'm afraid Donna is unlikely to be doing any running around, or not for a while yet,' Anna said hesitantly, looking sideways at Peter for moral support.

'Donna was born with spina bifida,' Peter explained.

'The medics say that when she's older she may be able to walk with leg braces,' Lucy called down from above. 'And if not, she can always use a wheelchair, like Jonah.'

'Lucy's right,' Jonah agreed. 'These days, technology can solve a lot of the problems that disabled people have. It's just a matter of finding the right gadgets to suit each person.'

'And getting everyone else to recognise that just because your legs don't work it doesn't mean your brain doesn't either!' put in Bernie vehemently. She looked up into the tree. 'You'd better come down now, Lucy, love. We're ready to eat.'

'Hand Donna back down to me,' Peter instructed, getting up and standing at the foot of the ladder, 'carefully!'

'When will the trial take place?' Charles asked Anna earnestly, once they had all returned from filling their plates at the buffet that Peter and Bernie had set out on the large wooden table that stood on the patio behind the house. 'Will Amanda have to come back here to give evidence?'

'That's not up to me,' Anna told him. 'The Crown Prosecution Service is responsible for bringing the case before court. There's still quite a lot of work to do yet, tracking down other people who've been trafficked by the gang and are being kept in places all across the country. And we don't know whether Harry Lockhart's father, John Lockhart, was the head of the enterprise, or if Harry was doing it all behind his back. So I'm afraid it could be a good while before the case comes to court.'

'But what about the murder?' asked Paula. 'Surely that doesn't have to wait while you dot all the i's and cross all the t's of this trafficking business?'

'I don't know,' Anna repeated. 'As I say, it's out of my hands.'

'If I was the prosecutor, I'd want

to wait,' Jonah observed. 'I wouldn't want any uncertainty about exactly what was going on above Pimm's bar, and who was responsible for it, to cast doubt on the motives that Pimm and Lockhart both had for killing Robin Hillier. At the moment, they're both accusing the other of being the leading light in the trafficking business and the actual killer of Robin Hillier. We don't want them both to get off on the technicality that the jury can't make up its mind which one of them wielded the knife.'

'They'll both be kept in custody until the court case,' Arshad assured them. 'They've been refused bail in case they tried to intimidate any of the witnesses. Personally, I hope the trial can go ahead sooner rather than later. If it was up to me, I'd go for the offences that we're confident will stick now, and bring them back to court later for the rest.'

'I have to admit to still being confused,' Martin said through a mouthful of cucumber sandwich. 'How did Hillier and the two girls come to be in the Fellows' Garden in the first place? I know *he* was just sheltering there because he had nowhere else to go, but where did Mollie and Amanda come in?'

'He just saw us looking lost and tried to help,' Amanda explained nervously. 'He was nice. He said he was worried about us being out on the streets at night on our own.'

'He had two daughters of his own, remember,' Peter pointed out.

'Then why didn't he go to them for help when he lost his home after Augusta Peckforton died?' asked Martin.

'He hadn't seen or spoken to them for several years, by all accounts,' Andy explained. 'I think he felt guilty about not doing more for them and would have been embarrassed to go to them for help.'

'Although everyone seems to agree that Augusta didn't give him much choice about that,' Bernie added derisively. 'She seems to have been a perfect dragon of a woman – and devious and manipulative with it!'

'I'm glad it's not just me that she intimidated!' Martin laughed.

'But why didn't he just get out?' wondered Lucy. 'I mean, it's not like he was dependent on her for anything. He had a job –until he gave it up to look after her – and a home he could've gone back to. Why did he let her control his life the way he did?'

'I suppose he loved her and was afraid of losing her if he stood up to her,' Anna suggested. 'I've seen it often enough with *women* before, but never with a man.'

'But why?' persisted Lucy. 'Why would he fall in love with a woman fifteen years older than him, when he already had a wife and kids?'

'Flattered by the attention of a Fellow of the college?' Paula conjectured, grinning towards Martin.

'His younger daughter was only a baby when he shacked up with Augusta,' Jonah pointed out. 'Maybe he was finding family life a bit of a strain – not much sleep, his wife not having any time for him, that sort of thing – and Augusta comes along and makes him feel desired again.'

'I still think there must've been something wrong with him not to have got out when she started stealing his money and all that,' Lucy insisted.

'I don't know,' Amanda began

tentatively. 'I – I – it's not so easy. I mean, looking back, there must have been lots of times when I could have just walked away from Zack and Stacey and gone to the police, but somehow I never dared to try.'

'That's right,' Arshad agreed. 'That's how these people work. They undermine their victims' confidence so they really believe that there's nothing they can do to get out of the situation they're in. And they undermine their self-respect so that they think that they don't deserve anything better.'

'What will happen to all those other women?' asked Lucy. 'Will they all just be deported?'

'Not right away. They'll be looked

after and given a chance to say what they want to happen,' Anna told her. 'Some of them may want to apply to stay here, but I expect most of them will want to go home.'

'Provided their families will take them back,' Anita added. 'In some cultures they wouldn't be welcome any more.'

'I think we ought to be careful about assuming that the same wouldn't apply here too,' Father Damien cut in quickly. 'We may not go in for honour killings, but I've come across plenty of parents who aren't that keen on taking back daughters who've been prostitutes or drug addicts or who've been in trouble with the law.'

'What about Mollie?' asked Amanda anxiously, looking round at Anna and Arshad. 'Does anyone know how her mum and dad are taking it all? She was worried they wouldn't let her keep the baby.'

'At least it's too late for them to try to make her have it aborted,' Lucy observed with satisfaction. 'The poor baby can't help what happened to her. And, if she doesn't want to keep it, there are plenty of childless couples who'd love to adopt it.'

'It's a big commitment for Mollie though,' Anna pointed out gently, 'even if she goes for adoption – especially when you consider that she's already missed out on three years of her education. I could understand her parents wanting her to try to put it all behind her and concentrate on getting some GCSEs before it's too late.'

'But you don't really believe in abortion, do you?' demanded Lucy with a puzzled look on her face. 'You kept Donna, didn't you? Even though Philip wanted her aborted?'

'I'm not talking about what I'd do,' Anna explained patiently. 'I'm just saying there's more than one side to it all.'

'And psychologically, it's going to be difficult bringing up a baby without knowing who the father is,' Anita added, 'for Mollie and eventually for the baby too. I know it's illogical, but I think I'd always be worrying about how the child was going to turn out – especially if it was a boy. I'd be wondering if he'd end up being a sexual predator too.'

'It's really not as black-and-white as it seems at first,' Damien ventured tentatively. 'I believe in the rights of the unborn, but sometimes it's a really tough decision to make.'

'Why?' demanded Lucy. 'It seems simple enough to me. You wouldn't kill a baby *after* birth, so what's the difference?'

'What if the mother's life is in danger?' ventured Peter.

'I suppose, if you were really *sure* there was no other way, then maybe you'd have to consider it,' Lucy admitted reluctantly, 'but these days,

THE SECRET GARDENER

I bet the doctors could do things to reduce the risk, and … and in that case, how could you possibly decide?' she continued after a long pause for thought. 'I mean: why should the mother's life take precedence over the baby's?'

'Maybe because the mother has other responsibilities,' Damien suggested, 'other children in the family, for example, or an important job – maybe one that's going to save lots of other people's lives.'

'I suppose so,' Lucy said slowly, 'but even so, the baby's completely innocent. How can the mother justify killing an innocent child for the sake of her own safety?'

'Who's to say the mother isn't

innocent too?' demanded Amanda. 'Mollie didn't choose to get pregnant! She didn't want to have sex with ten or more men in a night! I admire her for wanting to keep the baby, but I wouldn't have thought any less of her if she'd gone through with the abortion.'

'According to the family liaison officer, her dad's decided to take early retirement so he can be there full-time for Mollie and then for the baby,' Andy told them unexpectedly in the uncomfortable silence that followed this outburst. 'She seemed to think that he's badly shaken up by all this and determined to make some changes.'

'This house-husbandry seems to

be becoming fashionable,' Bernie joked. 'What with Peter, and Anna's Philip, you could start a club!'

'I don't think Jessica would like the idea of Philip being described as a house-husband,' Anna said with a pensive smile. 'She's very clear in her mind that he's just a child-minder for the times when neither she nor I are available. I'm honestly not sure how things are going to work out between them.'

'Give it time,' Peter advised. 'Once she gets involved in university life, she'll most likely be glad of him relieving her of some of the responsibility for looking after Donna.'

'The other thing I don't

understand,' Lucy commented, 'is why Mollie and Pandora were taken in by that Harry Lockhart character. How could they have been so stupid as to believe that he was in love with them? Didn't they listen to any of the warnings at school about predatory men grooming girls?'

'Isn't most of that focussed on online grooming?' Paula suggested. 'Didn't these men approach the girls in person? Maybe they didn't realise it was the same thing.'

'I think it was mostly wishful-thinking,' Amanda said quietly. 'It was with me. I can see that now. I was so desperate to get a job, to justify the cost of my university course and to be able to send some money home to help Mum and Dad, that I didn't want to believe that it was a scam.'

'In Mollie's case, I think she was desperate to feel that someone cared about her,' Jonah agreed. 'She had lots of friends and her social life was a constant whirl of activity, but from speaking to them, I got the impression that none of them were really close.'

'And her parents hardly seemed to notice her,' Bernie added. 'Her mother was far more interested in her business than in her daughter! I'm glad her dad has decided to start taking some responsibility at last!'

'That's not the case with Pandora though,' Arshad observed.

'Her parents are devoted to their kids. They don't have a lot of money to spare for horse-riding lessons and ballet classes and all those things that Mollie had, because Mrs Birch stays at home to look after them all instead of going out to work, but they do all sorts of things together as a family. They showed me pictures of them all on walking expeditions and doing amateur dramatics in the garden. And they've got this big mural all over the back of their house, which they all painted together. It made me feel a bit guilty seeing it all. I started to wonder if I ought to make more effort to spend time with our two girls.'

'But maybe that was what the

problem was!' Lucy cried out. 'Maybe she was fed up with being organised by her mother all the time. Maybe she wanted to be on her own and do her own thing.'

'I've always maintained that there's a lot to be said for benevolent neglect,' Bernie agreed with a smile. 'Pandora's sixteen, isn't she? She might well have decided that she doesn't want to do everything with her family all the time. What age are her siblings?'

'Pandora's the oldest of five,' Arshad told her. 'She has two brothers and two sisters. The youngest is seven.'

'My guess is her mother was subconsciously starting to worry that the kids were getting too independent and she was soon going to be redundant as a home-maker,' Bernie declared. 'Where a lot of people would go back to work or find things outside the home to do, she probably expected the kids to keep on needing her to look after them and arrange activities for them to do together, and Pandora felt smothered by it and wanted to get away.'

'Or maybe she was just bowled over by having this handsome young man telling her he loved her,' suggested Anna. 'You have to admit Harry Lockhart *is* good looking and still young enough to be able to talk the same language as a sixteen-year-old.'

'Mollie told me he was very nice to her when they first met,' Amanda agreed. 'He told her he'd never met anyone like her before and said all sorts of things about how lucky he was to have found her at last. He's a very plausible liar. He took us both in.'

'And what will you do now?' asked Anita, turning to Amanda. 'Once you're back home, I mean?'

'Amanda will be staying at home with me for a while,' Charles told her at once.

'Yes,' Amanda nodded. 'It's going to be strange with Mum gone. That's the worst part of it all really – not being there when she was ill, when she and Dad needed me.'

'There are some jobs in the church that she can help with until she finds something that will use her degree,' Charles went on.

'And I'll be making sure Dad looks after himself,' Amanda added with a smile. 'I'm sure he's lost weight while I've been away. I'll see to it that he doesn't forget to eat properly.'

'And talking of eating,' said Bernie, getting to her feet. 'Has everyone had enough? There's plenty more if anyone would like seconds of black currant pie.'

As he and Anita helped to clear away the remains of the meal,

THE SECRET GARDENER

Arshad approached Peter.

'How are your grandchildren?' he asked casually.

'All growing up fast!' Peter replied. 'Even Abigail is hardly a baby anymore.'

'And your son and daughter-in-law?'

'Both well.'

'Good.' Arshad hesitated, unsure whether to go on or to leave well-enough alone. 'I've been wanting to say ...,' he paused again and looked away. 'I'm sorry about ... Look! I know I haven't handled things very well in the past, but ...'

'Forget it,' Peter cut in as Arshad faltered again. 'You were only doing your job.'

'I wanted you to know how much I admire you,' Arshad tried another approach. 'The way you've taken DCI Porter into your home, for example. Not many people would do that.'

'He's been a good friend to us,' Peter replied dismissively, 'especially to Lucy. She was the driving force behind inviting him to stay.'

'Still, I've seen all the things you've done to your house: automatic doors, his own bathroom downstairs, hoists, ramps and all sorts! Most people would think it was too much trouble. Not to mention the lack of privacy involved in having someone from outside the family moving in with you. Anita's dad died last year and we talked about having her mum to live with us, but we came to the conclusion we'd never manage to make it work.'

'Well it's not my house for a start,' Peter pointed out. 'It's Bernie's – or rather, it was Richard's. Look, I know what you're trying to do, but don't go making out that I'm some sort of saint. I just do my best, the same as everyone else.'

'OK. Sorry,' Arshad mumbled, busying himself with piling up the bowls that they had used for the pie. Then he looked up again and added, 'DCI Porter seems to think you are one, though.'

'You're joking!' Peter's jaw

dropped and he stared directly at Arshad for the first time. 'Or else he's having you on,' he resumed with a grin. 'I know what Jonah thinks of me: I'm old Peter the plodder – slow but sure. Don't forget, we go back a long way. I knew him when he was a young PC, out to impress my boss and to catch the eye of a pretty, young junior doctor he'd set his sights on. We know each other far too well to have any illusions of that sort.'

Arshad sighed and tried one more time. 'Look, all I'm trying to say is that I know what a dickhead I was back then – when your wife died, I mean. I was arrogant and opinionated and I just didn't think.'

THE SECRET GARDENER

'And now you want Peter to tell you it's all OK now and it doesn't matter, so you can feel better,' Bernie cut in from behind him. 'The thing is: it isn't as simple as that. You can't unsay all those things you said about Peter not understanding what it was like for his kids being mixed race or that he ought to have encouraged Angie to mix more with other West Indians. Do you have any appreciation of the damage you did? Can't you see how-?'

'OK Bernie,' Peter interrupted, putting his hand on her arm. 'Let's leave it at that, shall we?'

He picked up the pile of bowls and headed towards the kitchen with them. Arshad looked towards Bernie who returned his gaze with a hard stare. Then she relented and smiled at him. She held out her hand towards him.

'I'm sorry. I shouldn't have said all that. I know I was only twisting the knife in the wound. It's just …'

'I know,' Arshad smiled back, shaking her hand warmly. 'It's harder to forgive when it's someone else who's been hurt. I understand that.'

PETER'S SUMMER PUDDING

Ingredients

2lb mixed soft fruit (raspberries, redcurrants, blackcurrants, blackberries in any combination)

Strawberries to decorate

About 8 slices of bread

8 oz sugar

Method

1. Wash the fruit (apart from the strawberries) and put it in a pan with the sugar and a little water.

2. Stew until tender.

3. Drain the fruit through a sieve over a large bowl.

4. Line a 2-pint pudding basin with cling film.

5. Cut the crusts off the bread and soak the slices in the juice. Arrange them to cover the inside surface of the basin, trimming them as necessary.

6. Tip the fruit into the basin and cover with a layer of bread slices.

7. Pour the remaining liquid over the pudding.

8. Place a small plate (the right size to fit into the top of the basin) over the top of the pudding and weigh it down with a 2lb weight or some tins of food. Leave in the fridge

overnight.

9. Remove the plate and peel back the cling film. Put a larger plate over the top of the basin and turn out the pudding. Remove the cling film and add a garnish of strawberries.

10. Serve with cream.

THANK YOU

Thank you for taking the time to read "A Secret Gardener?". If you enjoyed it, please consider telling your friends or posting a short review. Word of mouth is an author's best friend and much appreciated. Thank you,

Judy

ACKNOWLEDGEMENTS

Many Facebook friends and LinkedIN contacts contributed ideas to this book. Special thanks go to Marion West, who helped me to hone the title, and to Robert Namushi who made suggestions that improved the cover picture.

I would like to thank Gillian Gilbert for reading the manuscript, giving helpful comments and pointing out typographical errors.

I am indebted to the authors of a wide range of internet resources, which have been invaluable for researching the background to this book. These include (among others):

- Google Maps (www.google.co.uk/maps)

- The university of Oxford (www.ox.ac.uk/)

- Cowley Road Carnival (www.cowleyroadcarnival.co.uk)

Every effort has been made to trace copyright holders. The publishers will be glad to rectify in future editions any errors or omissions brought to their attention.

DISCLAIMER

This book is a work of fiction. Any references to real people, events, establishments, organisations or locales are intended only to provide a sense of authenticity and are used fictitiously. All of the characters and events are entirely invented by the author. Any resemblances to persons living or dead are purely coincidental.

Many of the locations and institutions that feature in this book are real. Their inhabitants and employees, however, are purely fictional. Other organisations depicted here are pure invention. In particular:

- Lichfield College, St Luke's

College and Holy Cross College, while intended to be typical of many Oxford colleges, do not exist and they are not based on any specific one of them;

- While Cowley Road Methodist Church is real, Sally Pearson, who is depicted here as its minister, is not; nor is she based on any minister of religion from any denomination.

- None of the police officers featured here are representative of any members of the police service in Thames Valley or anywhere else.

MORE ON BERNIE AND HER FRIENDS

There are now thirteen **Bernie Fazakerley Mysteries**. The other twelve (in chronological order of the action) are:

1. **Two Little Dickie Birds**: a murder mystery for DI Peter Johns and his Sergeant, Paul Godwin.

2. **Murder of a Martian**: Peter and Jonah solve a double murder and Peter meets Martin Reiss for the first time.

3. **Grave Offence**: Peter investigates an assault and a suspicious death, while Jonah is in rehab in the spinal injuries centre.

4. **Awayday**: a traditional detective story set among the dons of Lichfield College.

5. **Death on the Algarve:** a mystery for Bernie and her friends to tackle while on holiday in Portugal.

6. **Mystery over the Mersey**: a murder mystery set in Liverpool.

7. **Sorrowful Mystery**: Jonah investigates a child abduction and Peter embarks on a new journey of faith.

8. **In my Liverpool Home**: Bernie and her friends return to Liverpool to investigate a suspicious death in Aunty Dot's Care Home.

9. **Organ Failure**: a body is discovered under the organ in St Cyprian's Church and Jonah is called in to investigate.

10. **Rainbow Warrior**: One of their friends is injured in a hit-and-run incident and Jonah is convinced that this is attempted murder.

11. **Admission of Innocence**: Father Damien calls Peter and Jonah out of retirement to solve a murder case and prevent a miscarriage of justice.

12. **Lethal Mix**: Three of Lucy's student friends are injured in an anti-Muslim hate crime in Liverpool. Jonah, Peter and Bernie assist Merseyside Police to bring their attacker to justice.

Bernie also appears in two other novels:

- **Changing Scenes of Life**: Jonah Porter's life story, told through the medium of his favourite hymns.
- **Despise not your Mother**: the story of Bernie's quest to learn about her dead husband's past.

There is also a book of short stories, in which Peter narrates his side of the story:

- **My Life of Crime**: the collected memoirs of DI Peter Johns. This includes some episodes that appear in other books, but told from a new perspective, as well as some completely new stories.

THE SECRET GARDENER

You can find them all on Judy
Ford's Amazon Author page:
www.amazon.co.uk/-/e/B0193I5B1M
Read more about Bernie
Fazakerley and her friends and
family at
sites.google.com/site/llanwrdafamily
Visit the Bernie Fazakerley
Publications Facebook page here:
facebook.com/Bernie.Fazakerley.P
ublications.
Follow Bernie on Twitter:
twitter.com/BernieFaz.

LIST OF POLICE AND FORENSICS PERSONNEL

The following officers and staff recur in many of the Bernie Fazakerley Mysteries. This alphabetical list is provided to give some background to them and for reference.

- **Rupert Andrews:** (Thames Valley) Detective Sergeant 2000, Detective Inspector 2012.

- **Malcolm Appleton:** (Thames Valley) Police Constable 2007, Sergeant 2018.

- **Penny Black:** (Thames Valley) Forensic Anthropologist

- **Alison Brown:** (Thames Valley) Detective Inspector 1989, DCI 2004, Chief Superintendent 2015.

THE SECRET GARDENER

- **Amanda Burgess:** (West Mercia) Detective Constable 2016.

- **Tracy Burton:** (Thames Valley) Police Constable 1999, Sergeant 2005.

- **Michael Carson:** (Thames Valley) Forensic Pathologist

- **Anna Davenport:** (Thames Valley) Detective Sergeant 2007, Detective Inspector 2015. Married in 2001 to Philip Davenport. Separated in 2017. Three children: Jessica (2001), Marcus (2002), Donna (2017). Archaeology and Anthropology graduate from Cambridge.

- **Karen Evans:** (West Mercia)

JUDY FORD

Police Constable 2010, Detective
Constable 2011 Detective
Sergeant 2013. Married Paul
Godwin in 2018.

- **Sarah Farrow:** (Merseyside)
  Police Constable 2003

- **Bryony Foster:** (Merseyside)
  Detective Constable 2016

- **Jordan Fox:** (Thames Valley)
  Police Constable 2001, Sergeant
  2006, Inspector 2018

- **John Gamble:** (Thames Valley)
  Police Constable 2017

- **Stella Gilbert:** (Thames Valley)
  Trainee Police Constable 2019

- **Paul Godwin:** (Thames Valley /
  West Mercia) Detective
  Constable 1993, Detective

THE SECRET GARDENER

Sergeant 2002, Detective Inspector 2008, Detective Chief Inspector 2017. Moved from Thames Valley to West Mercia Police 2008. Married Karen Evans in 2018.

- **Luke Gray:** (Thames Valley) Senior SOCO.

- **Pamela Gregson:** (Thames Valley) Custody Sergeant.

- **Gavin Hughes:** (Thames Valley) Police Constable 1988. Specialises in community policing and building bridges with rough-sleepers.

- **Peter Johns:** (Thames Valley) Police Constable 1969, Detective Constable 1973, Detective

JUDY FORD

Sergeant 1978, Detective
Inspector 1993, retired 2011.
Married to Angie in 1978 and to
Bernie in 2006. Father of Hannah
(1980) and Eddie (1982).
Stepfather to Lucy (2000).

- **Lee Jones:** (Merseyside) Police
  Constable 2015

- **Arshad Khan:** (Thames Valley)
  Detective Sergeant 2002,
  Detective Inspector 2006,
  Detective Chief Inspector 2014.
  Specialises in cases involving
  ethnic minority victims.

- **Aaron King:** (Thames Valley)
  Police Constable 2001, Sergeant
  2009.

- **Janet Kingman:** (Thames

THE SECRET GARDENER

Valley) Forensic photographer

- **Sandra Latham:** (Merseyside) Detective Chief Inspector 2014.

- **Christopher Lucas:** (Greater Manchester / Merseyside) Detective Inspector 2009.

- **Andrew Lepage:** (Thames Valley) Detective Constable 2007, Detective Sergeant 2015. Graduate in criminology (1st class) from Leicester University in 2005. Lives with his mother in Headington Quarry.

- **Ruby Mann:** (Thames Valley) Senior SOCO.

- **Jennifer Moorehouse:** (Thames Valley) Civilian staff.

- **Janet Morecambe:** (Merseyside)

JUDY FORD

Police Constable 2010

- **John O'Connor:** (Merseyside) Police Constable 2016

- **Monica Philipson:** (Thames Valley) Detective Constable 2002, Detective Sergeant 2008. An ambitious police officer, who studied at Keble College, Oxford.

- **Richard Paige:** (Thames Valley) Detective Constable 1960, Detective Sergeant 1967, Detective Inspector 1973, Detective Chief Inspector 1981, Detective Superintendent 1995, died 1999. Married to Bernie in 1997. Father of Lucy (2000).

- **Joshua Pitchfork:** (Thames Valley) Detective Constable 2015

THE SECRET GARDENER

- **Jonah Porter:** (Thames Valley) Police Constable 1977, Detective Constable 1979, Detective Sergeant 1983, Detective Inspector 1987, Detective Chief Inspector 1996. Retired 2018. Married to Margaret in 1982. Widowed in 2014.

- **Louise Otterbourne:** (Thames Valley) Police Constable 2017

- **Thomas Pullinger:** (Merseyside) Police Sergeant 2012

- **PD Q:** (Thames Valley) Police Dog 2014. General Purpose dog. German Shepherd Dog.

- **Oliver Ransom:** (Merseyside) Detective Constable 2015

- **Alice Ray:** (Thames Valley)

JUDY FORD

Police Constable 2015, Detective Constable 2016

- **Charlotte Simpson:** (Merseyside) Detective Sergeant 2015

- **Melanie Stanton:** (Thames Valley) Police Constable 2009 and Dog Handler 2014

- **Ben Timpson:** (Thames Valley) Police constable 2018

- **PD Wesley:** (Thames Valley) Police Dog 2015. Drug and firearms search dog. Spaniel.

- **Melanie Wharton:** (Merseyside) Police Sergeant 2010.

Scott Wilding: (West Mercia) Joined the police from the army in 2008. DI 2016.

ABOUT THE AUTHOR

Like her main character, Bernie Fazakerley, Judy Ford is an Oxford graduate and a mathematician. Unlike Bernie, Judy grew up in a middle-class family in the South London stockbroker belt. After moving to the North West and working in Liverpool, Judy fell in love with the Scouse people and created Bernie to reflect their unique qualities. She has worked in academia and in the NHS.

As a Methodist Local Preacher, Judy often tells her congregation, "I see my role as asking the questions and leaving you to think out your own answers." She carries this philosophy forward into her writing and she hopes that readers will find themselves challenged to think as well as being entertained.